Praise for Family Ties Family Lies

"Boulden's story presents small-scale but beguiling mysteries backgrounded by a vibrant portrait of a small town that's both warmly close-knit and slightly claustrophobic. It's also a meditation on family love, loss, and remembrance, conveyed in plangent prose grounded in rich, concrete detail . . ."
—KIRKUS REVIEWS

"A sweet slow burn—as past and present collide in this compelling tale of small-town drama, family ties, and life-changing surprises. When a determined journalist investigates the story of her own life—she unearths answers she never could have predicted. A novel full of loving details and devastating decisions—so curl up with a cup of tea and enjoy this emotional and relatable story."
—HANK PHILLIPPI RYAN, *USA Today* BESTSELLING AUTHOR

"Some things can never be undone, but they can be forgiven. With *Family Ties Family Lies*, IPPY Award-winning author Jacqueline Boulden has delivered a powerful and poignant tale about fateful choices and the transformative power of forgiveness. You won't want to miss this heart-wrenching but uplifting story about the strength and flexibility of family. Complex, captivating and compelling. Fans of small-town dramas will love *Family Ties Family Lies*."
—TINA deBELLEGARDE, AGATHA NOMINATED AUTHOR OF *WINTER WITNESS* AND *DEAD MAN'S LEAP*

"Jacqueline Boulden's vivid descriptions transport readers to a world of Lake Amelia that radiates natural beauty and small-town charm. At the same time, her deft handling of complex family dynamics and emotional trauma will keep you on the edge of your seat. This heartwarming tale of homecoming and healing is a must-read for anyone who has ever struggled to find their place in the world and make peace with their past."
—Suzie Housley, Midwest Book Review

"Boulden's contemporary drama closely explores unspoken familial inheritances and the hidden selves our loved ones will never know. . . . The journey to uncover the family secret is engaging; readers will eagerly follow Rose as she employs journalistic skills to solve the mystery."
—Blue Ink

"Author Jacqueline Boulden wraps a busy city girl with small-town leisure and a cast of characters that make you wish you could stop by and stay awhile. But the quiet comfort masks a storm of trouble and Rose can't help but get involved. *Family Ties Family Lies* will pull you in with wonderfully placed clues, but it's so much more than just a mystery. Beneath the bonds that hold family together and the lies that threaten to pull them apart are people who will touch your heart and leave you wanting more."
—Nanette Littlestone, award-winning author, Bella Toscana

Praise for Her Past Can't Wait

"An engrossing tale about sexual assault that skillfully covers a tough and timely topic."
—KIRKUS REVIEWS

"*Her Past Can't Wait* is a scathing commentary on how society treats women when they do something as simple as trying to set physical boundaries. Gut-wrenching, intriguing, and twisty, Boulden's thought-provoking story lays bare just how far we have to go as a society when it comes to believing and protecting women."
—LISA REGAN, *USA TODAY* & *WALL STREET JOURNAL* BESTSELLING AUTHOR

"The World Health Organization singles out Eye Movement Desensitization and Reprocessing (EMDR) as one of the top 'evidence-based treatments of choice' for PTSD. In her fast-paced and absorbing novel, *Her Past Can't Wait,* Jacqueline Boulden illuminates the courageous and timely story of a woman facing her traumatic past and how EMDR eased her suffering. A must-read for all trying to live like the past is in the past, when it's actually still buried in their subconscious."
—DONNA KNUDSEN, PSY.D., EMDR INSTITUTE FACILITATOR & CERTIFIED CONSULTANT

"Well-written and very believable."
—JACK RIGHTMYER, ALBANY *TIMES UNION*

"An accomplished news journalist, author Jacqueline Boulden has applied her keen observation and reporting skills to telling a powerful story too many women know well, and one woman in particular must remember in order to live in peace."
—Renée Bess, GCLS Goldie Award & Alice B Readers Award-winning author

"The building of the suspense is excellent. The tension building steadily until it peaks at the culmination of the climax—that was brilliant. It was exciting and terrifying. A real page turner!"
—*Judge, 31st Annual Writer's Digest Self-Published Book Awards*

"Beginning as a mystery and building into a nail-biter of a thriller, HER PAST CAN'T WAIT is a powerful, intense, and emotionally rich novel that hooks the reader from the first page. Author Jacqueline Boulden has explored sharply relevant and contemporary issues through a layered and twisting story driven by a tenacious main protagonist."
—*Indie Reader*

Also by Jacqueline Boulden

Her Past Can't Wait

Family Ties Family Lies

Jacqueline Boulden

To Helen

And to all of my other family, with love and gratitude

Chapter One

She should have said no. She should have stayed in her cozy Philadelphia-area condo, sipping coffee, and reading the newspaper. She could have let herself take it easy for a change instead of working because she was afraid to miss a big story. If only she'd made a different decision, she wouldn't be in such a hot mess.

"Rose. Rose. Where are you?" Her colleague called over the boisterous crowd.

Some guy's arm pushed against her mouth and most of one eye so she couldn't respond. She raised her right arm to break free of the protestor's grip, but he had a good hundred pounds on her. She was more concerned about her Nikon D6 and 200mm lens than she was about almost anything else.

Except for breathing.

The man's shirt, smelling of sweat and a bacon-and-eggs breakfast, inched more into her mouth, further impeding her breathing. His beefy arm squashed the right side of her nose. She pushed again. Nothing. Panic battled for space in her oxygen-deprived lungs. She sucked in a whistle of wind through her remaining open nostril, then shouted the way her self-defense coach had taught her. It was challenging with a mouthful of arm. She pushed with all her might. The protestor jerked away. Gravity pulled Rose toward the dark gray pavement between Philadelphia's City Hall and busy Market Street.

She threw out her right arm to break her fall. An elbow jabbed into her ribs. She moaned at the searing pain and loss of control. At that moment, two muscular hands reached under her arms and kept her from falling. Rose breathed a sigh of relief. It didn't last long. Those hands pulled away as another body spun her around so quickly all she saw was a blur of dark blue union T-shirts. Rose grabbed her camera tighter to her chest and felt the earth drop away again. Her shoulder screamed as her body twisted and her right shoulder swiveled in a way it wasn't made to.

Rose hit the pavement. Hard.

A loud crack preceded the pain in her right arm as it took the brunt of her one hundred thirty-five pounds. Something shattered. A piece of hard plastic—likely part of the lens cap or the camera body itself—pierced Rose's side as she collapsed.

Rose lay on the pavement, the front end of a dirty sneaker filling her vision. The last voice she heard as her eyes flickered closed was her colleague calling out again.

"Oh my god. Rose!"

Chapter Two

A beeping phone at six in the morning rarely brought good news.

"Ouch." Rose reached for her cell with her right arm, forgetting it was in a splint and couldn't stretch that far. She wiggled into a sitting position and fumbled for the phone with her left hand. Just a little farther. Her fingertips felt the glassy surface. She must have hit the connect button. Aunt Tess called out her name.

"Hang on, Aunt Tess. I'm getting up."

Rose winced at the pain in her ribs as she pulled herself into a sitting position on the edge of her bed. Her eyes squeezed shut. She struggled to think. Then it hit her. There could be only one reason for her mother's younger sister to call.

"What's wrong? Is it Mom?" she blurted.

"We're at Saratoga Hospital. Your mom fell. How soon can you get here?"

Rose looked at her useless arm. The raucous rally still gave her nightmares and flashbacks. She was on the mend, but slowly. "What happened?" She used her legs to lift herself out of bed and shuffled across the room to the closet. Using her foot, she slid the door open and saw her overnight bag back in the corner.

"I drove over to pick her up for dinner last evening and found her sprawled on the living room floor," Aunt Tess explained. "She had an egg-sized bulge on her forehead and dried blood on her lower lip. She was unconscious."

Rose stopped moving. "Does she have a concussion? Did she break any bones?"

"I don't think she broke anything, but they don't know why she fell, whether she passed out." Aunt Tess's voice shook, sending Rose's pulse racing and her mind imagining the worst. "Doctors ran blood tests and took X-rays, but we don't know the results yet. I didn't call you last night because I didn't want to worry you until we learned if it was serious. Your mother is pretty shaken up in addition to whatever is going on with her physically. How soon can you get here?" she asked again. Insistent.

"She's going to be okay, isn't she?" Rose leaned against the wall and tried to clear her head. Surgery on her right arm was three days ago and she'd struggled to find a comfortable position in bed to accommodate her wounded arm, which was wrapped in a splint and gauze from her fingers to halfway between her elbow and shoulder. She hadn't had a solid night's sleep since the rally.

"Let's hope for the best," Aunt Tess said.

"Have you called Kirk?"

"We spoke briefly. He was on his way out the door already. He's got a trial going on and is super busy."

"It's not like he'd drop everything to fly to Lake Amelia anyway," Rose said. 'I can't remember the last time he visited Mom."

"I promised to update him when we know more. Hopefully we'll have something new from the doctors by the time you get here. Don't drive too fast, but please hurry."

"I'll pack and get on the road as soon as I can." Rose disconnected the call and tucked her phone into a pocket. She dragged her suitcase out of the closet and put it on the bed.

Then she thought about Jeremy. Should she let him know? He was a morning person like her and might be awake, but they didn't have any plans scheduled over the next several days, not even over the next couple of weeks. They were going through another cool period in their relationship. Nothing had happened, and that was part of the problem. They simply weren't connecting. Again. Jeremy was reasonably handsome, nice—sometimes to a fault—and easygoing. Rose liked him well enough, but there weren't any sparks. Didn't everyone want sparks?

Jeremy had called her after the accident and stopped by the afternoon she was released from the hospital. He brought take-out from their favorite restaurant and a bottle of wine. She hadn't heard from him since. Contacting him wasn't urgent. She'd text him after she learned what was going on with her mom and knew how long she'd be away.

It took a few tugs to slide the zipper around three sides on her suitcase. Using her left hand was awkward and often ineffective. She'd do her best to pack quickly. It wouldn't be easy. She stepped across the hall and into the bathroom.

"I look like I went six rounds with Laila Ali," Rose said to her reflection in the mirror. "Make that one round. I never would have lasted six." Her hazel eyes were red and puffy; her pale white skin dotted with purple bruises on her face, legs, and places she couldn't see but hurt to touch. She stopped staring at her face, picked up the brush, and tried to run it through her hair. On the third attempt, the brush became tangled. She pulled it free and dropped it on the counter. "It doesn't matter how I look," she told her reflection. "I've got to find out what's going on with Mom."

Oops. She had another problem. She hadn't told her mother or Aunt Tess that she'd spent a night in the hospital after doctors repaired her broken arm. She'd been meaning to call but didn't want her mother to worry, because, of course, she would. No doubt her mom and Aunt Tess would chastise her for not calling right after it had happened.

Rose's career was on hold. Her best camera and lens were cracked and dented, damaged beyond repair. Years of paying dues to professional organizations for insurance on her equipment and her health proved their worth. She had other gear, but she couldn't hold the camera steady with one hand, and she didn't know of any company that made a camera you could shoot with your left hand. Even if she could take photos with her backup camera, her bruised ribs wouldn't let her carry her gear bag plus the tripod farther than ten feet.

She grabbed clean underwear from the top dresser drawer and tossed them into her suitcase. Two drawers down, she located jeans, T-shirts, and a couple of pairs of shorts. Back in the closet, she removed three cotton tops from their hangers. The small bag filled with travel-sized cosmetics was on the closet floor—the last item to go into her suitcase before she zipped it up.

Rose had coffee and breakfast while checking the weather on her phone. Radar showed a blanket of clouds over the east coast, but forecasters didn't predict rain. The trip to Lake Amelia took about four-and-a-half hours, unless traffic through North Jersey and on the New York State Thruway slowed to a crawl.

Out of habit, she picked up a notepad from the coffee table and slid it into the thin compartment on the front of her suitcase. She dragged the bag to her SUV, stifled a groan as she lifted it, and slid it in the back. Also out of habit, she packed her knapsack with her backup camera gear and set that on the floor of the front passenger side. She paused before climbing in. Was she forgetting anything? Rose struggled to think about what she needed. Her mind kept flashing to images of her mother in a hospital bed, head wrapped in bandages.

Stop thinking. Start driving.

Rose stepped on the gas before remembering she only had one functioning arm. Not only that, during her post-op visit to the surgeon yesterday, he'd told her not to drive for at least a week. Well, she had no other option. Still, she eased up on the gas.

She was anxious to find out what was going on with her mom, but trips to her hometown in upstate New York filled her with mixed emotions. The area was beautiful and people were friendly. But being in Lake Amelia sometimes felt like that scene in *Star Wars* where the sides of the garbage pit kept closing in on Han Solo and company. When Rose graduated from high school, she was so intent on exploring other places she'd practically run out of town wearing her graduation gown.

Small towns charmed outsiders with their red geranium planters on Main Street and flag-waving Fourth of July parades. Eyes misted as the high school band blasted out "You're a Grand Old Flag," with decorated veterans and civic boosters marching behind. But outsiders didn't know that the people gathered around Lake Amelia's Creamery snacking on ice cream cones and hot fudge sundaes were also there to chat with neighbors. About neighbors.

Sometimes people forgot that behind the small-town quaintness, people were living in a fishbowl where secrets were shared in quiet voices more often than they were kept.

Chapter Three

Rose's rumbling stomach reminded her she hadn't eaten since she gulped down a container of yogurt and a banana. The cafeteria was a short walk past the welcome desk on the first floor, but Rose needed to see her mother before she did anything else. She clipped the visitor's badge on the collar of her blouse, thanked the volunteer at the desk, and followed signs to the elevators.

The doors to the third floor slid open and Rose's sneakers squeaked with every step on the clean linoleum floor as she hurried toward the nurses' station.

"Good morning," she said to the first person who looked up. "I'm here to see Carly Webster."

"Charlie Webster?" the nurse asked.

"No, *Car-ly* Webster. An ambulance brought her in last evening from Lake Amelia. I'm her daughter, Rose."

The nurse glanced at Rose's badge while tapping on her keyboard, then looked at the monitor. "Room 317. Down the hall on your right."

A wave of laughter drifted into the hallway as she neared the door to her mom's room, and the familiar sound of her aunt's voice eased Rose's concerns. *How bad could it be if Aunt Tess is laughing?* Rose eased around the corner into the room.

The beds were against the right wall and the one closest to the door was empty. Her mom had the window and a view overlooking the courtyard gardens. Aunt Tess sat in a chair next to the bed. Rose couldn't see her mother's face until she took another step into the room. She looked like a child in that big hospital bed with fluffy pillows all around her. Rose had expected the IV stand but not the clear plastic hoses delivering oxygen through her mother's nose.

Rose was surprised at how her mother looked, but that didn't compare to how her mom and Aunt Tess reacted when they cast their eyes on her.

"Rose Caroline Webster, what on earth happened to you?" Her mother looked pale and weak, but the voice that called out was strong and commanding.

"Good heavens, girl. What happened?" Aunt Tess jumped up from her chair and reached out to Rose, who raised her left hand, palm out.

"No hugs," Rose said. "Not yet." She explained what had happened at the rally as she moved into the room and alongside her mother's bed. "My ribs are sore, and my arm required surgery. I'll fill you in more about what happened, but first, I want to know what's going on with you, Mom."

Rose grabbed her mother's outstretched hand, careful to avoid the tubes and clear tape that held them in place. She rubbed her thumb along the inside of her mother's wrist, feeling the paper-thin skin and wondering if the brown spots were darker than the last time she'd seen her.

"I guess I fainted and bumped my head," her mom said. "Tess found me when she stopped by to pick me up for dinner. Instead of eating on the deck at Dack's last night, we dined here. I'm afraid Tess ate breakfast here as well."

"I told you not to worry," Tess said. "Rose, how about if I

get you a cup of coffee, maybe a sandwich?"

"Sounds good, Aunt Tess. Thanks."

Rose smoothed the covers and found a spot on the bed. Her eyes took in her mother's pale face and swollen lip. But it was her weight that struck Rose the most.

"Have you been eating enough? You've lost a lot of weight since Christmas."

Her mother started speaking, but a deep cough consumed her. She grabbed the side railing on the bed with one hand and covered her nose and mouth with the other. Rose winced as her mother pushed out a raspy cough and struggled to take in air. Rose was about to call for a nurse, but her mother stopped coughing and leaned back into her pillows, exhausted.

"How long have you had the cough?" She stroked her mother's arm. "You sure didn't have it last winter because I would have noticed. Is that why they have you on oxygen? Does it hurt as much as it sounds?"

"Slow down with the questions, honey, I can only answer one at a time. I can only even recall one at a time." Her mother's voice was wheezy and softer than Rose remembered. "I started off the New Year with a severe cold and the cough has lingered. With allergies this spring, I haven't been able to shake it."

"Why are they keeping you in the hospital? Is it because you need oxygen?" Rose couldn't stop herself from voicing the questions popping into her head at a rapid speed. "When Aunt Tess called me, she said they ran blood tests and took X-rays. What were the X-rays? Are doctors concerned about a concussion?"

Her mother covered Rose's hand with hers and closed her eyes. "Rose, I don't have any answers. It'd be better if you talk with the doctors when they come around again."

Sleep took hold as her mother's voice drifted off and her eyelids fluttered. Rose stroked her mother's arm one more time, then stood, about to turn toward the door. But she couldn't look away from the once robust woman who'd hiked the Adirondacks with her as recently as a few years ago. The woman in the bed was so fragile, vulnerable. *How could Mom change so much in such a short time?*

Aunt Tess came down the hallway carrying the cardboard food holder with the confidence born from years of serving customers at her popular diner. She motioned Rose to follow her past several rooms where patient monitors beeped and families spoke in hushed voices. They turned at the end of the hallway and passed through the glass doors leading into the atrium. Windows on two sides welcomed the bright summer sun. A man in a wheelchair watched television with a young woman at the far end of the room, the TV in a large bookcase filled with paperbacks, some jigsaw puzzles, and games. A man and woman who looked to be in their late fifties ate lunch at a table near the windows, their conversation so intense they never glanced up as Aunt Tess led Rose to a spot where they could have privacy.

"Here we go. Two black coffees and chicken salad sandwiches on whole grain bread." Aunt Tess set the food on the table. "The woman behind the counter said they made the chicken salad this morning. Under her breath, she told me it was a better choice than the turkey, which I noted was gray around the edges. You know my rule: always take the advice of the person serving the food."

Rose pulled out the chair across from her aunt and sat. "So, tell me about Mom's condition."

Aunt Tess rested her elbows on the table and folded her

hands under her chin. "The doctors don't know yet, and they can't tell us until the bloodwork comes back. They took X-rays of her lungs because of that persistent cough, which, frankly, your mom's been downplaying for months. I only realized how bad it was after sitting in the room with her for hours."

"Did the doctors or nurses say when they would have more information?"

"Sometime today. That's all they'd say." Aunt Tess took a sip of coffee then picked up her sandwich.

"Mom and I talked for a bit until she drifted off to sleep. I studied her face and I've never seen her . . ." Rose's voice cracked, and she bit her lip to stop the tears gathering in her eyes. "She looks . . . so old."

Aunt Tess dropped her sandwich and reached across the table for Rose's hand. "I know. Something's going on. I hope we'll find out soon."

There were so many questions and not enough answers. Rose chewed her sandwich and glanced out the window at the Adirondack mountains rising behind the fields and valley forests in more shades of green than the local paint store had in stock. She took in the view with deep breaths and let it calm her down. She may not be a big fan of small towns, but she loved this part of New York.

An older woman with a walker shuffled into the room, a nurse at her side. The nurse helped the woman onto the couch, then sat beside her. Rose watched them as her thoughts raced off to scary places and dire medical findings. Her mother had had the cough since January? Why hadn't she mentioned she'd been feeling ill? And was yesterday's fainting incident, or whatever it was, the first or had there been others? Others her mother hadn't mentioned to Rose or Aunt Tess.

Rose's eyes dropped to the wounded arm resting on her lap. She hadn't called her mom when she'd been lying in a hospital bed with unknown damage to her arm or her shoulder, hadn't told her mother about the surgery, hadn't mentioned that she might not be able to work for months. How could she criticize her mother for withholding information when Rose was just as guilty?

Chapter Four

The pace of the hospital slowed as the day wore on. The evening staff spoke in lower voices and walked a little lighter in their Dansko clogs. Rose read an old magazine she'd found in the atrium while her mother napped. When the two of them did chat, they talked about the weather and the latest news about people in town. Rose's mind swirled with what Dr. Connor had said and what he didn't. The doctor scheduled more tests but didn't go into specifics. Years of looking at people through her camera's viewfinder had taught Rose how to read emotions. The doctor was holding back.

The nurse arrived with her mother's sleeping pill shortly after nine. When Rose walked out of the hospital's main door and climbed into her car, she could've sworn she'd been inside for twenty-four hours or more. Rose rubbed her tired eyes, took a sip of cold coffee from the Wawa cup in the holder, and drove the winding roads east to the family home in Lake Amelia.

Rose punched the button on the dashboard and turned off the engine. The drive from Philly, the long day at the hospital, the lack of answers from the doctors drained her. All she had to do now was drag her bags inside and collapse. Her mom always kept fresh sheets on the bed in Rose's old room, so that was one less chore.

The light next to the front door cast a soft glow over the half dozen steps up to the porch of the expanded Cape Cod-style home. The rest of the house was cloaked in darkness. Rose had forgotten how the night sky settled over everything this far north, like a heavy wool blanket on a cold winter night. She glanced at Mrs. Shaw's house. No lights on there either. Rose pulled out her overnight bag from the rear of the SUV. She considered leaving her camera bag until morning, but her city instincts warned her not to leave anything in the vehicle. She beeped the locks out of habit and trudged up the steps. It took two trips. Once inside, she flipped on the hallway light and locked the front door.

She sniffed. The house smelled a little like her mother's favorite peppermint tea, a little of furniture polish, and—she sniffed again—a little doggy. Hmm, Mom was usually a meticulous housekeeper. Rose walked through the living room and into the kitchen, which was the beginning of a large open space that led from the kitchen to the dining room and then to an overstuffed leather couch in front of the fireplace at the other end of the room. Rose turned on the light and grabbed a glass from the cupboard. The tap water ran clear and cool, and Rose watched her glass fill. Too many cups of coffee at the hospital had left her parched. The water rushed over her dry throat. She finished one glass and poured another while taking in the kitchen. The coffee pot sat on the counter next to a distinctive red plastic container of Folgers. Darn, she'd forgotten to bring her favorite coffee blend. Well, she'd manage. After all, she'd survived cafeteria food today.

The drop-leaf table where Rose had done homework so many years ago occupied the prime spot in front of the sliding glass doors. Rose sat at the table and recalled Dr. Connor's assessment of her mother's condition. The X-rays showed spots on her mother's lungs. That could explain the persistent cough. He'd consulted with an oncologist, who'd ordered a PET scan for the following morning to find out whether the spots were cancerous and if they had spread.

The bloodwork was a different and equally scary issue.

Dr. Connor explained that part of her mother's shortness of breath was likely from her low red blood cell count. She was anemic. He said further blood tests, also scheduled for the next morning, would shed more light on the issue and determine when she could come home. Rose thought the doctor had started to say whether she could come home. He'd corrected himself, but Rose had heard the pause. *Whether* Mom could come home. She downed her second glass of water, left the light on over the kitchen sink, and returned to the front room for her bags.

Despite all the unknowns about her mother's health, Rose's thoughts never strayed far from her own injuries. If she stayed in Lake Amelia for more than a couple of days, she'd need to find a physical therapy center to rehab her arm. She also needed to see the surgeon to determine when a cast could replace the splint and whether her arm had begun mending itself. Would her arm heal well enough so she could work again in the physically taxing environment of news photography?

The light switch at the base of the stairs bathed the staircase and second-floor landing in light. She lifted her overnight bag off the floor and took the steps one at a time, then walked down the hallway toward her childhood bedroom.

During her teenage years, Rose had persuaded her parents to let her paint her bedroom walls a deep blue. Several years ago, she and her mom agreed the blue was too intense, and they chose a lighter paint labeled Green Trance. Rose had also bought "sea foam" green sheets and a bedspread of soft greens and blues and an occasional splash of soft yellow. The room itself was calming and Rose needed all the help she could get.

Rose dropped her bag onto the chair in the corner, dug out her soft cotton T-shirt and terry shorts, put them on, and slid into bed. She wiggled into a comfortable position on her back, placing one pillow under her right elbow as instructed by the physical therapist she saw in Philadelphia. After another deep breath to settle into the mattress, she fell asleep.

It took a moment to remember she was in Lake Amelia. In her old bedroom, lying on her side, her sore right arm falling across her body. She winced as she rolled onto her back. Her shoulder screamed out in pain, and she bit her lip. Had she taken any ibuprofen at bedtime? Nope. She'd been too tired to remember and now every inch from her shoulder to her fingertips was shrieking. Breathe in and out, she told herself. *Slowly. In and out. Now think about sitting up. From my back? Sore ribs won't let me do that. I'll try rolling out of bed on my left side.* Rose rolled back over, carefully slid her left arm along the sheets, and pushed her body up. She was almost upright when her left hand slipped, and her face slammed into the pillow. "Mumpft," she shouted. A few deep breaths later, she tried again and succeeded.

A shower to wash off yesterday's sweat and hospital smells sounded like a good idea until Rose realized she had no one to help wrap her arm in plastic. A sponge bath would have to do. Brushing her teeth with her less coordinated left hand spread more toothpaste on her chin than her teeth. She grinned at herself in the mirror as she wiped off the toothpaste. Then she splashed cold water on her face and deemed herself clean enough.

Back in the bedroom, she pulled clothes out of her bag, dressed, and traipsed downstairs.

She stared at the container of Folgers, her lips pressed together. This morning called for something stronger. She didn't want to drive to Stewart's for coffee and bring it back home, even though she loved the taste of their dark roast. Where else? Her eyes lit up when the light bulb in her brain clicked on. The diner, of course. It was quarter to eight. The diner was a short walk, and the fresh air would do her good. Rose gathered up her handbag and cell phone. The keys were where she'd left them last night on the hallway table. She swept them up and walked out the front door.

Chapter Five

A few cars cruised the pine tree-lined streets. Rose enjoyed the quiet as she walked a couple of blocks, soaking in the beauty of Lake Amelia—the lake, not the town—sparkling blue up ahead. She turned left onto Main Street, picked up her pace, and a few blocks later, strode up the steps into the Main Street Diner.

Coffee. The aroma of hot, wonderful, tasty coffee filled her nostrils. A steady hum reverberated throughout the diner as people chatted and ate their breakfast. The booths in front of the windows were almost full and only a few seats remained at the counter. She took a seat at the counter, turned over the cup in front of her, and caught the eye of the server. Although she usually drank her coffee black, Rose added a splash of half-and-half to cool it down and took in a mouthful.

"Aaaah, thanks, Iris. It's nice to see you again, especially when you're holding a fresh pot of coffee." The first sip of the day was the best. Rose took a couple more gulps, the heat and caffeine winding their way through her tired body.

The door to the kitchen swung open. Aunt Tess came out carrying a tray of hot food balanced on her shoulder and hand.

She smiled at Rose, crossed the diner to a booth in front of the windows, and delivered the food to an appreciative trio of young men. Forks and knives clinking against the ceramic plates drowned out their conversation. After Aunt Tess topped off their coffee cups, she plopped onto the yellow vinyl stool next to Rose.

"Good morning!" she said, wrapping her arm around Rose's waist. "Have you heard from your mom or the hospital?"

"No, nothing from either of them yet."

They both turned their heads when Iris called out. "Tess, order up."

Aunt Tess acknowledged Iris, then kissed the side of Rose's head. "Back to work. What can I get you to eat?"

"I haven't thought about food yet." Rose picked up her coffee and took another sip.

"Leave it to me." Aunt Tess got up as quickly as she'd sat down, picked the tray up off the counter, and scurried back through the swinging door.

Rose spotted a newspaper and pulled it over in front of her. The *Lake Amelia Dispatch* published weekly, so the news often wasn't current. She scanned the headlines, read a story about efforts to clean up the trails around Felton Falls, which emptied into Lake Amelia, and another article about an ongoing investigation into bike thefts in the region. She was about to turn the page to check baseball scores when a steaming plate of food landed on the counter. Her aunt disappeared into the kitchen.

She picked up her fork and cut into the omelet, watching gooey cheese ooze out. A pile of crunchy home fries with sautéed onions sat alongside the omelet. Buttered toast had its own small plate. She devoured the food in minutes, asked Iris for a small glass of orange juice, and sighed as she drank the cool, tangy liquid. She should stop at the grocery store after surveying her mother's cupboards to make sure she had enough food in the house, but she could always get breakfast at Aunt Tess's. One less thing to worry about.

"Hi, Deputy Stover," called out a voice behind her. Rose looked toward the diner's front door as a county sheriff's deputy walked in and said hello to the person who'd greeted her. A minute later, the deputy claimed the stool where Aunt Tess had perched, removed her hat, and placed it on her knee. She ran her fingers through her short afro as if trying to rub out the ridges her hat had left behind.

Iris filled the deputy's cup with hot coffee. "Are you hungry? Want the usual?"

"I'd appreciate that, Iris. Thanks." The officer turned to Rose. "Deputy Maxi Stover," she said with a curt nod.

"Nice to meet you, Deputy Stover. I'm Rose Webster." She set down her glass of juice with her left hand.

The deputy eyed Rose's splint. "What happened?"

"I'm a photojournalist. I got caught in the middle of a protest with people much bigger and stronger and was on the losing end of a shoving match."

"I don't recall hearing about it."

"It was in Philadelphia."

"What brings you to Lake Amelia?" The deputy sipped her coffee and nodded at a man as he walked by. "Did you come here for some R&R?"

"No, I'm here to see my mom in the hospital. I grew up here."

They both turned toward the busy swinging door as it opened again, the sound and aroma of sizzling bacon drifting into the diner and demanding their attention.

Aunt Tess smiled and approached the counter. "Here's breakfast, Maxi. I see you've met my niece."

"I didn't know she's your niece, Tess." Her eyes darted back and forth between them, looking over their faces.

People often commented on how much Rose looked like her aunt. They had the same oval faces, full lips, upturned noses, and light brown hair, which Rose wore almost touching her shoulders. Aunt Tess pulled her hair into a ponytail whenever she was at the diner.

"Now that you mention it, I see the resemblance." Deputy Stover squirted a generous amount of ketchup on her hash browns, picked up her fork, and dug into her scrambled eggs.

"Rose is here to help her mother." Aunt Tess's eyes swept the room as she spoke, likely checking for customers waving for service.

"So she said. I hope your mom gets better soon, Rose." The deputy took another large forkful of eggs. "Eggs taste great as usual, Tess. Thanks."

"You bet. By the way, one of my customers asked if there's any word on the missing bikes. The article in the paper is a few days old and I haven't heard any updates."

"That's because there's nothing more to report yet." Deputy Stover wiped a spot of ketchup off her upper lip. "Tourist season is picking up and so is the number of missing bikes, from Fulton County to Warren County and around. Something'll break."

"I hope so. Rose, please call me as soon as you hear anything. I'll see you at the hospital after the lunchtime rush is over." Aunt Tess headed back into the kitchen.

Rose turned toward the deputy. "I read about the bike thefts. Thieves are stealing them and selling them in places like Lake George or over in Vermont. Do you know who's responsible?"

"We're working on it," Deputy Stover said, standing and reaching for her wallet. She slid a ten-dollar bill under her plate. "Does your mom live in Lake Amelia?"

"Yeah, on Cedar Street."

Deputy Stover looked thoughtful as if trying to place it.

"It's a nice area. You'll have to excuse me now. Time to get back on patrol." She put her hat on and tapped it once. "I'm at Tess's for breakfast or lunch a few times a week. I hope to see you around." She lingered for a moment, a smile on her face, then left the diner.

Chapter Six

The little bit of research Rose had had time to do about the possible causes of her mother's medical issues buzzed through her mind like the bees flitting around the bright yellow and red flowers bordering the sidewalk. She didn't know whether to focus on the fainting or the severe coughing, and so her list of questions grew longer, not shorter. Rose's eyes followed the flight of a butterfly as it flew up past the street sign. Wait. She was at Oak Street? She'd missed Pine, two blocks back where she usually turned toward home.

Then Rose realized she stood in front one of her favorite places in town: the Lake Amelia Public Library. Her haven when she was a young girl seeking adventures and escape. She'd spent hours combing the shelves for trips to faraway places with interesting people who spoke different languages, trying foods she didn't even know yet, and letting her imagination run free. She felt that familiar tug of longing for a book to disappear into for a few moments, and the desire to inhale the special smells of old and new books on the shelves. A brief detour wouldn't hurt, would it?

She unlatched the wrought iron gate and paused, appreciating the beauty of the restored Victorian home. The two women whose father had helped put Lake Amelia on the map had bequeathed it to the town. First, he'd developed a ski resort, then an eighteen-hole golf course, and finally, the Amelia Art Gallery, showcasing the talents of local artists who captured the beauty of the region in their paintings and photographs. When navigating the three-story home had become difficult for the sisters, they moved into a smaller one-floor house several blocks from the lake. The sisters' condition for donating the Victorian home to Lake Amelia village fifty years ago was that it be maintained as a library accessible to all, including summer visitors who could borrow books with special seven-day passes.

Dark green paint covered most of the flat wood surfaces of the old house, with wide swaths of magenta paint providing accents. The house sat on a three-foot base of large, rounded river stones. The six steps led her up to the front porch with its green and beige columns and matching three-foot-high railing. Rose closed her eyes and recalled running up the front steps some thirty years ago, racing to the children's section on the second floor.

Rose pulled the heavy walnut door open—it still had that slight squeak from the top hinge on the right—and her eyes rested on the familiar entryway with its wide pine floors and walls adorned with red-flowered wallpaper. A woman sat at the reception/checkout desk at the base of the stairs. Rose didn't recognize her, but then the librarians when she was a child were older, graying women who had to quiet Rose when she erupted in laughter or disbelief while paging through a book. Which had happened a lot.

At the sound of the door closing, the woman looked up from the computer screen. "Welcome to the Lake Amelia Public Library." She glanced at Rose's injured arm and seemed ready to ask the usual question, then stopped. "Can I help you with anything?"

"I was walking by, and my memories pulled me in. I grew up in town."

"Are you here visiting family, then?"

"Sort of."

The slender woman with short, dark hair walked around the desk. "I'm Brianna Martelli, assistant librarian, which covers a lot of tasks in a library this size."

Rose introduced herself. "I don't have a lot of time right now, but I'd like to browse."

"Of course. I don't know if things have changed much since you were last here. We like tradition. If I can help you find anything, please ask."

Rose thanked her, turned to the right, and walked into the front parlor. Its bay window let in the morning light and the green velvet covering the deep window seats looked too nice to be original. Adult fiction books filled the room and continued through the curved archway into the next. Nonfiction books —including regional books, history of the area, psychology, and self-help—were on the shelves on the opposite side of the house. A nook, perhaps once a closet, held cookbooks. Mindful of the time, Rose turned away from nonfiction and smiled at the back stairs leading to the second floor. She ran up the stairs like the child she once was.

The children's area was a big open space with floor pillows for storytelling time and books of varying heights packed on shelves. To one side of the area, six child-sized chairs were tucked under a small round table. She moved into the next section, seeing books for middle-grade kids, then tweens, and into young adults. The books tempted her to look for some of her old favorites, but she was mindful of the time and moved on.

Rose walked into the next room. A girl was nestled in one

of the oversized chairs. She took no notice of Rose, who guessed from the girl's size that she was too old for kindergarten, not yet into middle school. Rose wasn't around children often, so she had little to go on. She tilted her head and leaned down to read the title and author of the girl's book. *As Chimney Sweepers Come to Dust* by Alan Bradley.

The book lowered. The girl's face appeared: her lips pinched closed, eyes squinted into narrow slits, and her dark brown hair parted in the center with bangs falling halfway to her eyebrows.

"Adult fiction is on the first floor," the girl said, raising the book in front of her face.

"I know. I wanted to visit the children's section where I spent a lot of my afternoons and weekends when I was a kid."

"The children's section is back over there, where you first came up to the second floor." One hand let go of the book and pointed. The book remained in place, the girl's voice terse. "This is young adult."

Her attitude amused Rose, and she tried to think of something clever to say. The girl appeared too young for YA books, and she wasn't inviting conversation. Rose tried again.

"Do you spend a lot of time reading books in this section? You must be quite an advanced reader."

An enormous sigh must have come through the girl's lower lip because it lifted her bangs off her forehead. The book lowered again.

"Yes, I read. Whatever books I want."

"It's nice to meet another avid reader. By the way, my name is Rose Webster."

The girl studied Rose for a moment. "Webster? Like the dictionary? Do you know a lot of words?"

"Pretty many I think. What's your name."

"If I tell you my name, will you leave me alone?"

Rose nodded.

"It's Ellie." The book went back up.

"All right, Ellie. Nice to meet you. I'm on my way."

"Goodbye, Dictionary Lady."

Rose paused. No one had used the nickname in years. No family ties ever documented a connection to the famed dictionary founder, Noah Webster. Middle school classmates trying to come up with nicknames for their friends around the lunch table one day had first tagged her Dictionary Girl. The moniker continued through high school, where fellow English Class students used it as a sign of respect given Rose's love of words and writing.

Rose had more questions for Ellie, but the little girl made it clear she was not interested in talking. She worked her way through the rest of the second-floor rooms and down the front stairs.

Chapter Seven

Back at her mother's, Rose stuffed one of Gladys's favorite toys in her pocket, grabbed two cans of dog food, and held them in the crook of her left arm. She paused, stepped into the living room, and spotted Gladys's dog bed. Did Mrs. Shaw have a bed for her? Rose couldn't carry the bed or the canned food in her right hand. What about under her arm? She set the cans on the coffee table and wedged the bed under her right arm, hoping she had the strength to keep it there until she got to Mrs. Shaw's. Holding a can of food in her left hand, she walked down the front steps, straight out the brick walkway, and hurried next door. Judging by Gladys's familiar barks, she heard Rose coming.

"My goodness, Rose Webster, what happened to your arm?" Mrs. Shaw asked as she opened the door. "I thought your mother was the one who needed medical attention."

Rose stepped into the hallway as an excited Gladys circled her legs and punctuated her happiness with several sharp yips. The little Maltese mix was pure white except for some splotches of black, thanks to her Shih Tzu blood. She was quick to excite and just as quick to settle down.

"Hi, Mrs. Shaw. It's a long story. I broke my arm on assignment, but I'm on the mend." Rose handed Mrs. Shaw the dog food and dropped the toy on the floor. Gladys grabbed it with her front teeth and found the squeaker. She trotted off to the living room, squeaker noises trailing behind her.

"Come in. How about a cup of coffee?"

"I ate breakfast at Aunt Tess's diner, so I've had all the coffee I want for a while, thanks." The two women followed Gladys into the living room. After dropping the dog bed on the floor, Rose and Mrs. Shaw sat on the couch in front of the bay window. "I can't thank you enough for taking care of Gladys while Mom's in the hospital."

"How's she doing?"

She explained how doctors were running more tests that morning to find out.

"Give her my best and tell her not to worry about Gladys."

"We appreciate that. I'm hoping I can bring Mom home today, but she's weak and we need to wait for the test results." The dog toy squeaked in quick succession and they both looked over at the squirming dog, biting her toy with enthusiasm.

"Would you like me to take Gladys for a walk before I head for the hospital?"

"She did her business in the backyard right after we got up. We've already been around the block twice. She's fine."

They chatted for a few more minutes, then Rose glanced at the clock on the fireplace mantle. She stroked Gladys's silky back one last time and returned to her mother's house. Rose intended to stop by the grocery store later that afternoon, so she surveyed the refrigerator and pantry. Her mother had a good supply of staples but few of the basic items Rose included in her meals. After making a shopping list on her iPhone, she left for the hospital.

Disappointment was written on her mother's face.

"What's wrong?" Rose rushed into the room and clasped her mother's hand. "Should I call the nurse?"

"No need. The doctor stopped by and said I couldn't go home today, something about low red blood cells and wanting me on the IV another twenty-four hours."

"The doc's been in already? I was hoping to speak with him."

"He stopped in to deliver the news a while ago and said he'd return in about an hour with the oncologist."

Rose sighed. She scanned her mother's face and rubbed her hand. The IV drip held two bags this morning. The beeping confirmed monitors tracked her heart rate, blood pressure, and body temperature. Rose felt better knowing her mom was getting excellent care, but that barely eased her concerns.

"How'd you sleep, Mom? Did the nurses pester you last night?"

"I prefer my bed, so I wasn't that comfortable," she said. "The nurse gave me something to help me sleep."

They turned at the gentle tap on the door.

"Good morning, Mrs. Webster." Dr. Connor strolled into the room carrying his laptop. His neatly trimmed dark brown goatee was a stark contrast to his bald head. The doctor walked to the bed and smiled at Rose. "Nice to see you again."

Rose guessed the doctor was in his late forties, maybe early fifties, and it looked like he spent time on a treadmill or jogged. She could tell her mother liked him.

There was another tap on the door.

"Hello," said a tall slender person with such a deep voice

and close-cropped haircut that Rose wasn't sure if they were a man or a woman. That was cleared up when Dr. Connor made the introductions.

"This is Dr. Naomi Fisk, the oncologist I told you I'd been consulting. This is Mrs. Webster, and her daughter, Rose."

"It's nice to meet you," Rose said. "What new information do you have about my mother's condition?"

"Conditions," Dr. Connor said. "Plural. I'll address the anemia. Mrs. Webster, your red blood cell count remains low. One medicine we're giving you through the IV will help with that, along with the vitamin B12. When you go home, the nurse will give you a list of iron-rich foods to add to your diet." He paused. "We're concerned because the anemia could be caused by internal bleeding. If so, we want to identify the source."

Her mom squeezed Rose's hand. "That doesn't sound good."

"It's not, but the medication will help," Dr. Connor said. "And that's the main reason I don't want to send you home. I'd like to monitor you for another twenty-four hours and run a couple more tests. Dr. Fisk?"

She opened her laptop and looked at the screen. "The other news is about your cough, Mrs. Webster. It's the reason we took the PET scan this morning. There are quite a few spots on your lungs. Most nodules are not cancerous. They're often scars from a previous infection. However, we won't know unless we do a biopsy, and I'm recommending we do that tomorrow morning."

The monitor's beeps echoed in the room. The clock on the wall ticked off the seconds. Rose raised her eyebrows and tears welled in her eyes as she looked at her mother.

"Well, that's not encouraging news either, is it, Doctor?" her mother said.

"No, it's not," Dr. Fisk said, her eyes softening. She

glanced at her lap and tapped a few keys. "Given your age, seventy-four—"

"And feeling every day of those years right now," her mother whispered.

"We'd need to discuss treatment options. But let's not get ahead of ourselves. Let's do the biopsy and go from there." Dr. Fisk looked back and forth between mother and daughter. "I know this is a lot to take in. Dr. Connor, do you have anything else to add?"

"No, that's where we stand. We should know more tomorrow."

"Do you have questions for either of us?" Dr. Fisk asked.

"Not right now," Rose said. "But I'm sure I will." She turned toward the bed. "Mom?"

She shook her head. "Thank you both. I may be weak now, but I'm a strong woman and I don't want you sugar-coating anything. Will I see either of you later today?"

"Yes, I'll check in later." Dr. Connor smiled and closed the laptop. "I give you my word, I'll be candid with you and your daughter every step of the way."

Rose and her mom silently watched the doctors leave.

"That's a one-two punch, isn't it?" Rose said.

"That's a good way to put it. It's late, Rose and I'm very tired. Why don't you go home? I know this has been stressful for you as well."

"I can stretch my legs and come back in a bit."

"No, honey, go home. They'll give me dinner in a little while and then a sleeping pill. I'll be fine. It's been a long day."

Rose sniffed and bit her lip. "Okay, I'll head to Lake Amelia. I'll be here in the morning."

Her mother's eyelids closed.

"I'll be here," Rose said again, a catch in her voice, "for as long as you need me."

Chapter Eight

Rose stopped for groceries at The Fresh Market on her way out of Saratoga Springs. She pushed the small cart along with her right hand resting on the red plastic handle and passed through the produce section, picking up containers of organic blueberries and strawberries, a bunch of bananas, a bag of romaine lettuce, and broccoli. Next, she grabbed a loaf of whole grain bread, two kinds of sliced cheese from the deli, and a package of plain croissants. Rice and canned organic beans followed. From the coolers, she picked up a few containers of yogurt and a dozen eggs. She headed for the checkout when she remembered almond butter. Rose pushed the cart down two aisles before she found the jam and peanut butter section. She preferred almond butter if the store had a quality brand, and they did. A shot of pain tore through her ribs when she stretched to reach a jar on the top shelf. She winced and lowered her arm.

"Can I help you?" Rose turned around to find a young man wearing a green Fresh Market polo shirt smiling at her.

"You came along at the right time. Grocery shopping is a

bit of a struggle." Rose didn't like to ask for help, but she was getting better out of necessity.

He looked at her cart. "Looks like you're managing. Is this the one you want?" He pointed, picked up the container, and handed it to her.

"Perfect, thanks so much." Rose watched the checkout clerk scan and pack her groceries, a job Rose normally would have done, and returned to her car. A few minutes later, she crossed over the Northway and veered toward Lake Amelia. The two-lane roads wound around rich green farmland, through the valleys punctuated by flowing streams, and over the dense pine, maple, and oak mountaintops.

After dinner, Rose walked next door and rang the door-bell. Gladys barked as if alerting Mrs. Shaw an intruder was at the door. *I must have caught her sleeping.* It took a minute before the door opened. *Maybe they'd both been sleeping.*

"I hope I didn't come at a bad time. I'm here to take Gladys for a walk." Rose stepped into the hallway and knelt to pet the little dog. "I may need a walk more than she does," Rose admitted, "but I'd like her company for a while this evening." She updated Mrs. Shaw on her mother's health as she took the bright blue halter, put it over Gladys's head, then clicked it into place around her chest.

"Oh dear, I'm sorry to hear that. Can I do anything to help?"

"You're already doing it, Mrs. Shaw, taking care of Gladys so we have one less thing to worry about. Tomorrow morning I'll have a better idea of when I can bring Mom home. Tomorrow might even be the day. In the meantime, do you need more canned food or treats?"

Gladys barked as soon as Rose said treats and pranced around her feet.

"No, thank you. I have plenty of both."

"Okay. We'll be back soon."

The lingering edge of the sun dipped behind the hills. Hints of pink and orange peeked over the trees on the horizon. Gladys strutted along the sidewalk, sometimes pulling a lot more than her ten pounds suggested she could, and other times stopping to sniff an interesting spot in the grass. When they crossed over to the lake side of Main Street, they turned left and joined others enjoying the evening along Amelia's Lakeside Walk. A wide grassy area led up to the edge of the lake, where a three-foot-high black aluminum fence kept people and animals from venturing too far. Benches placed along the walkway gave people places to sit, a respite from their busy lives, and a view of some of nature's finest work.

The grass path ended at a cement walkway that continued along the waterfront. Stores and restaurants that fronted Main Street enjoyed prime lakefront space. People filled the restaurant patios, enjoying the postcard-perfect evening. Rose sucked in several deep breaths of a breeze coming off the lake mixed with the pine-scented mountain air. Her body released some of the day's tension, while Gladys sniffed for previous four-legged visitors. Eventually, they turned around and made their way back to a bench on the grassy area.

Rose pulled her phone out of her back pocket and glanced at the screen. She had a few text messages, including a couple from Kirk. They kept missing each other's texts. She was going to text him back, decided a conversation would be better if he was available, and tapped on the green connect button.

"Hey, Rose. Did you see my texts?"

"I spotted them just now." She filled him in on what the doctor said. "You should see her, Kirk. It's scary." She paused, waiting for her brother to say something. Instead, the sound of tapping keys came through the phone line. He was on his laptop, working. "Kirk?"

"Sorry. I'm busy getting ready for court tomorrow. Did you read my texts?" he asked again. "I'm in the middle of a big case. We've already had several delays. I can't ask the judge for a few days to come north right now. I don't think he'd let me unless, you know . . . " He paused. "Unless there's a death."

"Well, if you put it off long enough, there might be."

"Please don't exaggerate. My hands are tied."

"I'm not exaggerating. Mom's anemic. She might have lung cancer. And when she comes home," Rose refused to think if, "I've got to take care of her with one bum arm."

"Mom said you would get a home health aide."

"You spoke with her?"

Kirk sighed. "It would help if you read my texts. I called her about an hour ago and talked with her and Aunt Tess. It's easier to reach them than you."

"I might have missed your latest text while I was driving back from the hospital and walking the dog." She stretched her right arm slowly across her body and stroked Gladys on the bench beside her, the dog's little nose twitching with the aromas of fresh-cooked seafood and steaks from nearby restaurants.

"Give me some credit, will you? I also spoke with Aunt Tess earlier in the day. I'm doing the best I can under these circumstances."

"I was just hoping you could help us out here. Tourist season is beginning, and Aunt Tess is busy with the diner, not only the day-to-day operations, but getting ready for the increase in business. She's pitching in with Mom as much as she can, and there's so little I'm able to do."

"How's the arm?" His voice was sincere, but the tapping of keys started again and grew louder. He was focused more on work than on their conversation.

"Nothing new to report, but I have to follow up soon with doctors in Philly. I left home with an overnight bag, so I don't have many clothes. Plus I have to find someone to pick up my mail." Telling Kirk the tasks she needed to address—

and soon—added to her stress level. "I'm so much in limbo right now."

"I'm sorry things are difficult for you. I meant it when I said I would get there as soon as I could."

"Well, you almost never visit her. I figured you didn't want to make the trip."

"I don't like coming to Lake Amelia any more than you do."

The silence drifted between them. The unspoken words they'd been dancing around since their father died more than a decade ago. And Kirk had refused to attend his funeral. Until Rose told him to stop thinking about what he wanted, that he needed to be there for their mother, no matter what resentments Kirk held against their father. He'd acquiesced, came alone, and taken a late flight home that evening.

Chapter Nine

"Damn," Rose swore at the flashing red and blue lights coming up behind her. She'd gotten a late start and was trying to make up time, thinking so much about her mom that she'd lost focus and was driving well over the speed limit. Maybe she could sweet-talk the cop out of giving her a ticket by telling him she was in a hurry to get to the hospital. Looking for a little pity with her arm in a splint might also work.

The flashing colors grew brighter in her rearview mirror, and Rose winced as the sirens pierced her ears. The highway ahead was flat and straight, with no other cars in sight. Rose slowed down, turned on her blinker, and looked for a place to pull over. The dark blue sheriff's SUV swerved into the other lane and kept going, passing Rose in a blur. She took some deep breaths to slow her racing pulse and turned off her blinker. But she kept her speed at about fifty miles an hour until she stopped shaking. The cop didn't care the least how fast she was going? Where were they headed?

Her answer came about five minutes later when she rounded a curve. Two county sheriff's SUVs sat in the parking lot of a bar Rose and her friends had visited with their fake IDs while in high school. The vehicle that passed Rose had left two tire tracks in the loose stone when it skidded to a stop. Deputy Sheriff Maxi Stover stood alongside it, explaining something by waving her arms to the deputy who'd just arrived.

Rose needed to get to the hospital, but ignoring her journalistic instincts was impossible. The two cops watched her pull into the lot, looking at her with equal measures of curiosity and annoyance. Rose grabbed her press credentials out of the glove box, got out of the car, and approached them. Deputy Stover looked a little less annoyed when she saw Rose. The expression on the other deputy's face didn't change.

"Hi," Rose said, credentials dangling from her left hand. She had no camera, no notebook, and hoped the cops wouldn't notice. "The deputy's car sped past me at a high speed a few minutes ago, and when I saw both cars here, I figured something was going on. What's up?"

"It's none of your business," the other deputy said, hands on his hips and a sneer on his face. "Get in your vehicle and move on."

"Deputy Stover? Can you tell me why you're here? I am a credentialed member of the news media."

"Not in this state you aren't," Stover said, the hint of a smug smile on her face, her arms crossed across her chest.

"This is an Associated Press credential, which is a national organization, so actually I have credentials in every state." Rose tried to keep her voice light, but she'd gotten into journalism because of her endless curiosity, and she wasn't in the habit of taking no for an answer.

"Just because you got yourself a lanyard with a laminated piece of paper and a media logo doesn't mean you're entitled to information. Like I said before. Move on." He took a step toward Rose.

"Deputy Edwards, why don't you check around behind the building? I'll deal with Ms. Webster."

"You know her?"

"More or less. I'll handle this."

Deputy Edwards grunted and kicked up stones with his steel-toed boots as he shuffled away. He glanced back at the two of them, then disappeared between the building and pine trees. Rose and Stover didn't speak until he was out of view.

"So, what's up?" Rose asked again.

"I'll fill you in some, but you can't do anything with the info until I tell you. Agreed?"

Rose didn't like getting information off the record because she couldn't use it without official confirmation, but she nodded.

"We found bikes stashed behind the bar. They haven't been there long. This may be a rendezvous point for the thieves we've been investigating."

"How many bikes?"

Deputy Stover shook her head. "That's all I'm saying. I shouldn't even have told you that much, but I got the sense at the diner I could trust you. Even if you are with the media."

Rose pressed her lips together, and the corners of her mouth turned up. "Ouch. You could have stopped when you said you could trust me."

The cop returned the smile. "Where are you headed?"

"The hospital in Saratoga Springs. Mom had a biopsy this morning. Maybe it will tell doctors what's going on."

Deputy Stover seemed to take time thinking about her next question. "Will you be at the hospital all day? Do you want to grab a beer or dinner later?"

"I'll probably eat at the hospital. Besides, do you dare have a drink in a public bar with a member of the media?"

"I can handle it," she laughed. "Maybe another time then. Right now, you need to get out of here." Deputy Stover kept a smile on her face, but her voice was firm. Rose's grace period had expired. She got back into her car and half an hour later was at Saratoga Hospital.

Rose and her mother stared at each other, eyes moist, neither able to put into words the weight of the news from Dr. Fisk.

"I know it's a lot to take in," Dr. Fisk said. "Think about whether you want to consider the treatment options when you're stronger. The sooner you could begin the treatment, the more effective it should be on the cancerous cells. Call me or Dr. Connor with any questions." With that, Dr. Fisk left the room.

The TV filtered through the speaker lying on her mother's pillow. Rose cleared her throat, but the lump that began growing as the doctor gave them details about her mother's condition was too big to get past. Her mother wasn't doing much better with her eyes lowered and hands clutched together.

"Since doctors don't think you're healthy enough for chemo or radiation treatments, we need to build up your strength, Mom. Aunt Tess and I will come up with some meals rich in iron, like chicken, seafood, all kinds of beans, and spinach, lots of spinach." Rose looked at her mother and tried to determine if she'd fallen asleep. "Mom?" she asked softly.

"You know the treatment for cancer is often worse than the disease. I read a lot, especially about health issues as I've gotten older." She lifted her chin and looked at Rose. "Chemo and radiation do more than kill the cancerous cells, they kill healthy cells too. Even if the treatment is successful, the doctor said the survival rate for stage 3B lung cancer for someone of my age and with my general health is maybe a year. A year," she repeated. "I don't want to spend the rest of my days in the bathroom."

Rose stroked her mother's hand. "The decision is yours, Mom," her voice cracked. "I'll go along with whatever you want. Kirk and Aunt Tess will too."

Her mother smiled, a wistful smile that softened her face. "Kirk will likely agree it's my decision, but my strong-willed younger sister might have a different opinion. She's more of a fighter. So are you."

"Maybe so, but Aunt Tess will respect your wishes. And I'll be here to help."

"You can't sit at home waiting for me to die, Rose. You have a career and a life of your own."

"I can't work for several more weeks, Mom, and anyway, I'm not leaving you. You'll need someone to help you every day."

Some color was returning to her mother's face as she processed what needed to happen next. "We'll hire a nurse to check on me every day. Your father made a good living, invested well, and had a generous life insurance policy. We can afford to bring in people to help me. I don't want to spend it on treatments delaying the inevitable; I want you and Kirk to receive your father's money—"

"Kirk and I don't need Dad's money. It's for you. We'll make sure you have the best care possible."

The apparent surge in strength didn't last long. Her grasp of Rose's hand weakened. "There's plenty for all of us."

Her mother squeezed Rose's hand once more and then it slipped onto the bed.

Chapter Ten

Rose didn't know how long she'd sat at her mother's bedside and watched her sleep, but she needed to move. She left the hospital and walked the streets behind the small medical complex, away from traffic and skirting the edges of a golf course.

Lung cancer is bad. Stage 3 with any cancer is bad. Would it have helped if Mom had seen a doctor about her cough earlier? Could she have been cured of the cancer if they'd found it sooner? Could she have lived another ten years, maybe more?

Stop. Don't go there. I am not going to blame Mom for how she took care of herself. Or didn't. That won't do any good now.

She returned to the hospital and walked to the cafeteria in search of a cup of coffee. Without thinking, she asked for a turkey and cheese sandwich and nodded mindlessly as the woman asked if whole wheat bread was okay, whether to add lettuce or tomato. Rose sat at a table and took a bite. It tasted like moldy cardboard. Aunt Tess had warned her about the turkey lunchmeat the other day. She wrapped the sandwich up with the trash and sipped her coffee, trying to think positively about whatever time she had left with her mother. What could she do to help her during this last stage of her life? Well, that was the wrong way to think of it. Her eyes filled with tears, and she used her last napkin to wipe them away.

A woman stood at the side of her mother's bed, a clipboard in her hands with a stack of papers. Rose introduced herself as she walked into the room.

"Hi, Rose. My name is Nancie. I'm a social worker. Dr. Fisk asked me to visit your mother and explain the paperwork she needs to fill out, as well as options with palliative care and hospice if that becomes needed."

"Yes, they mentioned you would stop in." Rose looked at her mother. Her eyes were alert as she took a sip of water from the plastic cup on the tray alongside her bed. She hadn't napped long, but it seemed to have given her some energy.

Nancie eyed Rose's splint, then looked back at her mom. "Dr. Connor mentioned your daughter had injured her arm and that you're probably going to need help at home getting out of a chair, your bed, and climbing stairs."

"I only have a few steps up to the front porch. Everything else is on the first floor," her mom answered. "I can still get out of my recliner most of the time and that's mostly where I've been sleeping lately."

"You're technically not eligible for hospice care because you haven't declined treatment," Nancie said, "so I recommend you contact the Visiting Nurses Association to schedule a nurse visit at least a few times a week. There's information about the organization along with a contact number in these papers." She looked at Rose. "You can also look them up online before you reach out to them to review your options."

"Sounds good. I'll do that. And Aunt Tess could help in the evening," Rose said to her mother.

"Tess has a busy schedule with the diner. She's at work

before dawn and doesn't leave until late afternoon. I don't want to impose on her."

"Okay. We'll be careful when and how much we ask her."

Nancie nodded as she listened to them. "I also have flyers and pamphlets of information about Community Hospice. Again, I know you haven't scheduled or decided against treating your lung cancer with chemo or radiation, but you should look into hospice sooner rather than later. You'll likely need it in the next six months or a year if you decline treatment."

A year? Six months? Rose looked at her mom.

"Thank you, Nancie. We'll see what hospice has to offer and let you know if we have any questions."

"There are just a couple more things I want to go over with you," Nancie continued, "about legal documents." She shuffled through the papers and pulled out one. "Have you heard of a Living Will?"

"Yes, I have, but I've never completed one."

"New York State doesn't have an official Living Will document, but you can fill out this form, or make any revisions you want, to indicate what kind of treatments you would or wouldn't want. And this," she pulled out another sheet, "is the DNR, the Do Not Resuscitate document. This document tells doctors or ambulance paramedics what procedures or treatments you've elected to not have if you become unresponsive and can't answer for yourself, like whether you want to receive CPR or a tube feeding or other life support measures."

Rose and her mother stared at Nancie and nodded.

Nancie glanced at her notes. "Your doctor says your son has Power of Attorney. Is that correct?"

"Yes, we signed that several years ago."

"You could also consider filling out this Health Care Proxy form. It allows you to appoint someone, say your daughter to make health decisions for you. If you haven't expressed your wishes to your daughter or son about your choices of medical treatment, you should do it soon so no one has to guess what you want if you become incapacitated."

Rose blinked several times.

"I'm sorry. I feel like I'm overwhelming you," Nancie said softly.

"Borderline," Rose said. "It's not that I don't understand." She took her mother's hand. "It's just the weight of what all these documents mean."

"Of course," Nancie said. "You don't need to rush into filling these out, but given the seriousness of your diagnoses, Mrs. Webster, you should have these conversations with your daughter soon."

"I understand. We've had some discussions, and we'll have more." Her mother's weary eyes looked up at Rose.

"Okay. One last word about hospice and then I'll leave you two. When it becomes necessary, hospice will deliver medicine like morphine to help you deal with any pain. A hospice nurse will check on you, Mrs. Webster, not every day but a few times a week." She looked at Rose. "You can call hospice whenever you have questions. And when the time comes, hospice will set up a hospital bed in your home in your living room, bedroom, wherever you want it."

"Maybe we should set it up in Dad's old office so you can look out the sliding glass doors into the yard."

"No." Her mother spoke so sharply Rose jerked her hand away.

"Mom?"

Her mother's eyes cast down and her voice still had an edge to it. "I am not spending my final moments in his old office."

. . .

Rose thought about her mother's words on the drive back to Lake Amelia. She and the social worker had been stunned into silence by her mother's abrupt and stern rebuke. Nancie had handed the stack of papers to Rose and left the room. Her mother told Rose to take the papers home with her. They'd fill them out after she was released from the hospital the next day. Rose had kissed her mother goodbye. The tension between them followed Rose all the way home and into the house.

A year? Six months?

Rose put the papers on the table next to her mother's recliner. She ran her fingers along the arm of the chair, thinking about how her mother often rubbed her hand back and forth when she was thinking or watching a gripping documentary. She raised her left hand and touched the lap robe draped over the back of the recliner, a gift from one of her mother's friends. A half-empty mug of tea still sat on the table. Rose had looked at it many times over the last three days, thought about taking it into the kitchen. Thought about dumping the rest of the tea into the sink. And stopped. There was something too final about emptying her mother's last mug of tea. Her LAST mug of tea? Shit. Rose pushed away the tears welling in her eyes.

She needed a drink. More than one. She'd finished the pain pills a couple of days ago and now took an occasional ibuprofen, so she was allowed alcohol. She didn't want to drink alone in her mother's house. But she also didn't want to include Aunt Tess because she wasn't up to much conversation. She headed out the front door.

Chapter Eleven

Gladys wouldn't get a walk this evening and Rose felt guilty, but she didn't dwell on it. She walked the two and a half blocks to Thom's Brew Pub. Rose waved to the bartender—a high school boyfriend—who pointed her toward the two-seat tables on the left side of the room.

People dressed for a day of walking around town or hiking the falls sat at the bar drinking beer and munching on sandwiches. Streaming music from the overhead speakers was a pleasant mix of the latest hits and not too loud. The section where Rose sat had a comfortable feel to it, and she relaxed. Rose gave the approaching server a smile, accepted the plastic-coated menu, and ordered a pint of Amber Ale. The server was back in less than a minute, slapped a paper coaster on the table, and set the ale down.

"What can I get you to eat?"

"I'd like to sip my beer for a few minutes."

"You bet. I'll check back. If you're ready sooner, give me a wave."

Rose raised the cold beer mug to her lips. She took a long

pull and swallowed, letting the ale linger in her mouth to savor the citrus and pine. The change of scenery and cold beer helped ease her constant worries. She took another sip and recalled that Thom brewed his craft beers with as many local ingredients as he could grow and find. It's possible the pine she tasted came from the woods around Lake Amelia. That'd be pretty neat. Crisp Adirondack air and clear Adirondack lakes. They weren't in the Adirondacks but close enough to see them rising in the distance. The beauty of the area, and maybe the ale, drew visitors and people who lived in the region to Lake Amelia.

Rose studied the menu and considered the shepherd's pie because she wanted comfort food. That would fit the bill, but it came with ground beef. A burger was also ruled out because the last time she ate beef her body objected in ways she didn't want to repeat. She'd avoided meat for so long now she couldn't digest it anymore, which was better for her health. That left a grilled chicken sandwich on a brioche roll with bacon. Okay, there's a little meat there. And the special house sauce. She set the menu down and glanced at the front of the bar.

Deputy Sheriff Stover had just walked in. Her eyes swept the room, and when she saw Rose, she stopped. Her eyebrows rose and her eyes opened wide, shooting Rose a look that was less than friendly. Rose motioned Stover over. The deputy paused, then moved toward her table.

"I thought you were going to be at the hospital until this evening." She sounded annoyed.

"Yeah, well," Rose sputtered, but the server arrived before she finished her sentence.

"Hi, Maxi. What can I get you?"

Maxi? thought Rose.

"Hi, Judy. I'll have an ale, please."

Judy eyed Rose's glass. "Looks like you're about ready for another one."

"Yep, the first one's going down easy. When you come back with the beers, I'll be ready to order dinner."

The two stared at each other across the table. Rose looked at her glass, picked it up, and took another sip. As she swallowed, she looked up.

"Maxi, huh?"

"Yep. You can call me that when I'm not on the job. All other times it's Deputy Stover."

"Understood." Rose took a breath and slowly let it out. "I don't want to get into a big discussion about my mom's health because it's depressing. The biopsy shows she has lung cancer. Stage 3." Rose emptied her beer glass and set it on the table. "Mom was exhausted. I left the hospital about three o'clock and came here because I needed to eat, wanted a couple of beers, and I didn't want to sit home alone."

Maxi's face softened. "I'm so sorry."

"Yep, me too." She stopped as Judy returned with their beers and set them on the table.

"Okay, what can I get you?"

"I'll have the grilled chicken with bacon sandwich," Rose said.

"Lettuce, tomato, onion?"

"No onion."

"Cheese? Cheddar, Swiss, American, Provolone?"

"Cheddar, please."

"Same for me," Maxi said, "but hold the bacon and give me a side salad, no dressing."

"Wow, healthy," Rose said as Judy picked up the menus and walked away. "Is the sandwich as good without the bacon?"

"Of course not, but my abs are better that way. My arteries too."

Rose nodded. "You've got to stay in shape. Anything new on the stolen bikes? Off the record, of course."

"Nothing you need to know," Maxi said, sipping her beer.

Rose struggled to find something to talk about. After another moment, she said, "You must come here often for Judy to call you by your first name."

"Thom's got some of the best beer in the area," Maxi said, looking around the bar, "and the food's not bad."

"You live near here?"

"North of here. I've got a few acres and a ranch house outside of Cambridge. Me and a couple of retrievers. It cost a small fortune to fence the place, but it's worth it to let the dogs roam and I don't have to worry about what time I get off work."

"I imagine you have irregular hours."

"Today's a great example. I caught an early shift because another deputy needed a personal day. When you saw me checking out the bikes behind the bar, I was less than an hour from going off duty. Instead, I wound up back at the station writing reports and fielding phone calls for a few hours. When I finish dinner, I'll go home, romp in the backyard with the pups, then crash."

"Do you like being a cop?"

"A deputy sheriff," Maxi corrected. "I enjoy helping people, and that's what my job entails most of the time. Why do you like being a photojournalist?"

"Taking a photo is another way of telling a story. I can write and I used to do more reporting. But when I take photos, I don't have to get dragged into who's telling the truth and who's lying. I point my camera and take the pictures, capture the moment. Let the reporter figure out who's telling the truth."

Maxi motioned toward Rose's wounded arm. "Is this the first time you've been injured on assignment?"

"Pretty much. I've gotten plenty of bruises working in tight situations with a couple dozen photographers and TV videographers jockeying for position, but nothing this bad before." Rose flexed her fingers. "Have you been injured in the line of duty?"

"Nothing serious. Knock on wood." Maxi tapped the table, then picked up her beer glass. "Have you broken a bone before?"

Rose's left hand stroked her splint, and her eyes drifted to the floor. "I broke my ankle once. Riding my bike. I got hit by a car." She dropped her voice as the memory carried her into the past.

"Be careful and remember to stay on the sidewalk," her mom said. "And do not ride on the Falls Street sidewalk. It's too busy."

"Yes, Mommy." Rose ran out the back door and rolled her bike out of the garage, pausing to lift her helmet off the handlebars and strap it on. She hopped onto the two-wheeler, pedaled down the driveway, and veered onto the sidewalk. Her parents didn't allow her to cross any streets, but she could ride three-quarters around the block going back and forth, and that satisfied the five-year-old. She used a neighbor's driveway to swing around at the end of the block and retraced her route, past her house, to the end of the block, then onto Elm. This was the first year Rose could ride her bike alone, after her brother and father made sure she could handle it. She'd fallen a few times and suffered some scrapes, but nothing shook her confidence.

On her second loop, at the corner of Elm Street, she circled her bike back around the way she had come, then spotted a woman with a wide baby stroller walking toward her. The woman was a few houses away, but she was taking up most of the sidewalk. Rose wasn't sure what to do. Should she stop her bike and wait for the woman to pass? Her tires hit a bump and unsettled her. At the next driveway, she veered left to turn around and steered down the driveway. The bike picked up speed and her little legs tried to find the brakes, but she wasn't fast enough. She hit another, bigger bump. Her bike rolled onto the edge of Elm Street. A horn blared. A woman screamed. Rose was thrown from her bike. Everything went dark.

Rose woke up hearing noises she didn't understand and opened her eyes to a room she'd never been in before. She turned her head toward the window where someone was talking on the phone.

"I've been trying to reach you for hours." It was her mom, and she sounded upset. "I'm at the hospital. Rose was hit by a car. Doctors have ruled out a concussion, but she broke her ankle. She also has a lot of bumps and bruises. When are you coming home?"

Rose looked around the room. She was in the hospital? Where sick people went? She struggled to remember what had happened. Her head hurt.

"Kirk's home with the flu. Tess, bless her heart, is there with him. He's been throwing up for two days and is running a fever." Her mother laughed, at least it sounded like a laugh to Rose, but she still seemed angry. "There's always another court case. You're never home when there's trouble."

Rose tried to swallow, but her throat hurt, and she coughed. Her mother turned.

"I've got to go. Rose is awake. Call me later and please get home as soon as you can. I never intended to raise two children by myself."

Chapter Twelve

The nurses helped her mom out of the wheelchair and into the front seat of the car. They put a plastic bag with her belongings and discharge papers on the back seat.

"Thank you for taking care of me," her mom told the nurses, reaching out to shake their hands. "You made a difficult situation bearable."

Rose wanted to talk on the drive home, but she got the impression her mom didn't, so she respected her silence until they pulled into the driveway.

"I know you want to see Gladys," Rose said, "but I think we should get you settled in first. That little pooch will be excited. I'm afraid she'll trip you. That's why I didn't pick her up last night from Mrs. Shaw."

"That's fine, honey. It's good to be home even without my little Gladys." Her mom sounded wistful as she stared out the window.

"I understand." Rose came around to her mother's side of the car. "Now I'm going to grip under your elbow with my left hand, and I want you to push up against the door. Can you do that?"

"Yes, I can. I'm glad you picked me up in my sedan instead of your SUV. It's easier to get out of the car."

"Okay. One. Two. Three."

Her mom raised, then steadied herself. She smiled at Rose. "We did it!"

"Do you want me to get the cane out of the back seat? The nurse said—"

"No, I don't need a cane. I'm fine."

The two trudged to the front door as if in slow motion. They passed several azaleas full of blossoms beginning to fade and Lenten roses with their pink and white flowers pushing above the hearty, dark green leaves. The scent carried on the breeze was sweet from the other flowering plants, whose names Rose never remembered. She might have been named after a flower, but gardening was not her strength.

She settled her mom into the recliner after a visit to the bathroom, returned to the car to collect the bags from the hospital, and set them on the coffee table.

"I'll leave these here so we can go through them later. Then I'll organize them and put them on the table near the front window for when we need them. Or for when the visiting nurse needs to check your history and the instructions."

"Whatever you think. Can you reach behind me and give me the lap robe draped over my chair?"

"Sure." Rose draped it over her mother's lap and legs. "How about a cup of tea?"

"That would be lovely."

Rose went into the kitchen. She returned with two mugs of tea, put one on the table next to her mom and the other on the table next to the other recliner. Floor lamps stood behind the side tables. The large TV was on the opposite wall. Her mother let the tea cool and stared out the window.

"Kirk and I were reminiscing last evening." Her mother looked more sad than happy at the memories.

"It wasn't easy, was it, bringing up Kirk and me?"

"I don't think raising children is ever easy. Some people might have it easier, but children are challenging. Luckily, Kirk was already in school when you came along because you were an unstoppable bundle of energy."

"Sort of like Gladys, huh?"

Her mom laughed. "Yeah, some days you could be like Gladys. But I loved you very much. Love you. Both of you."

There was something unspoken hanging in the air, something she and Kirk talked about only a few times, and she'd never mentioned to her mother. She didn't know whether it was the wrong time to bring it up, but she wouldn't find out unless she asked.

"What is it?" her mother said.

Rose cleared her throat. Took a deep breath in through her nose and pushed it back out between tight lips. "I don't know whether it was about us kids, but I know you and Dad had some difficult times. I asked Kirk, and he said you two didn't get along for a while."

"Every couple goes through ups and downs in their marriage, some more difficult than others." Her mother waved her hand back and forth through the air as if to dismiss Rose's comment. "I know you've had some boyfriends and lived with one or two of them, but it's different when you've committed to a marriage and raising children. Ask your brother. He has a greater appreciation of what your father and I went through now that he's got two of his own. Kirk's antics were especially challenging during his bad-boy period."

"When was that?"

"Oh, from when he was ten until eighteen." Rose and her

mother laughed. "He was always up to something, coming home with frogs and playing with them in the downstairs bathtub, occasionally losing them. I remember the time we were eating dinner and a frog jumped out from under the dining room table." She laughed again and Rose's mood lifted.

Her mother's laughter suddenly faded, and she sounded wistful. "I'd always wondered what a little girl of yours would look like. I guess I'll never know now."

They'd had this conversation many times. Years ago, Rose would bristle and say she'd get married and have children when she was ready. These last few years, she let the question roll off her shoulders, often not bothering to answer it. She didn't want to ignore it this time.

"I don't have the strong maternal instinct you have to be a mother," Rose admitted. "And to be honest, I never found a man as interesting as my career. If I had met someone special, I probably would've figured out how to have both. Maybe I still will. But I have no regrets."

Rose once met a man unlike any other she'd encountered before. She knew he was special the minute they began talking. They finished each other's sentences and laughed at the absurdity of knowing someone so well when they'd just met. He was everything she wanted in a life partner. Almost. Getting involved with him would have complicated her life in ways she could not accept. She sighed at the memory of him, then returned her attention to her mother.

"No regrets, even now, when it's possible your injury might cost you your career? Have you thought about that?"

Rose gave a half-hearted laugh. "Until Aunt Tess called and told me you were in the hospital, all I could think about was my broken arm, my torn shoulder muscles, my cracked ribs, and what they meant for my career. Could I chase after a newsmaker with a camera bag slung over my left shoulder, banging against my side, while trying to hold the camera steady and take a photo with my right hand? Those situations were challenging before my injury." Rose massaged the fingers on her right hand. "So yes, I've worried the best days of my photojournalism career may be behind me, and if I take photos again, it might be at the mall with Santa." Rose picked up her tea and took too big of a gulp, grateful it had cooled off enough not to scald her throat. Voicing the fears that had been eating away at her for the past several days made them more real. She turned to her mom, who stared at her with glistening eyes.

"You never told me you were worried about the long-term effects of your accident."

"We've had more important things to discuss, Mom. I don't deny I'm concerned about my situation, but it can wait. I'm more worried about you."

"How did we get on this subject?"

"Marriage. Children. Relationships."

"Hmm, well, whatever issues your father and I may have had during our marriage, we moved beyond them and were happy to have raised two beautiful children. Successful children." Her mom took a quick sip of tea. "We took a lot of photos of you kids growing up, of us as a family. Can you get the photo albums from the attic later? I haven't gone through them in a while, and I think we might enjoy looking at them together."

"Sure, Mom. Why are they stashed in the attic? I thought you kept them on the bookshelves in here."

"I've been buying so many used books at the library sales —do you know they have a used book sale every summer, and other libraries have their book sales too? I ran out of space and moved the photo albums to the attic."

The attic was a poor location for storing photos. The temperature shot up to a hundred degrees in the summer with no air circulation. It was also musty and dusty. She glanced at the bookshelves on the other wall, debating whether her mother ran out of space, or maybe Kirk's hint about their parents' troubled marriage was the real reason. If her mom grew tired of seeing the reminders of difficult times and put those old and painful memories out of sight.

Chapter Thirteen

ose sneezed. Damn. That hurt. She bent over at the waist and sneezed again, questioning her decision to traipse into the attic. When was someone last up here? She straightened up and flipped the switch on the wall. Light filled the front half of the attic, where she'd accessed it through the opening in the ceiling of the master bedroom closet. Rose couldn't imagine her mother climbing the stepladder with two bulky family photo albums in her arms. Tracks in the dust suggested maybe her mother hadn't come into the attic at all. She could have climbed, slid the board over, and pushed the albums into the room.

Rose picked up the top album and opened its padded cover to the first page of images. This must be the earlier album, judging by the photos. Her mom holding Kirk in the hospital. Her father holding Kirk. Kirk at home. Kirk playing on the living room floor. She thumbed through more pages of Kirk photos, put the album down, and picked up the other one. Finally, a photo of Rose. Newborn Rose in the hospital. Rose at home. Both parents holding Rose. Rose on the couch between them.

The albums were thick with photos, but almost never two images from the same gathering. Her mother must have sorted through the photos years ago and gotten rid of some or stored them somewhere else.

She stretched her back, brushed the hair out of her eyes, and surveyed the space. Packing boxes from U-Haul were stashed on both sides. Rose knew some boxes contained her stuff, mementos her mother had saved from Rose's life up to her college graduation. Rose walked over to those boxes and stooped where the trusses slanted lower. Her mother's tight cursive handwriting in a black Sharpie read, "Rose." The brown tape on the top had shriveled; lifting the flaps was easy. Her senior yearbook rested on top, other high school year-books underneath. She flipped through the pages, the images, and comments reminding her of her friends and accomplishments. She was a B-student in high school, president of the photo club, and co-editor of the yearbooks in her junior and senior years. As she thumbed through more pages, she remembered taking candid photos of her fellow students and assisting the woman from Lifetime Images when she shot the formal class photos. Rose had learned a lot from the photographer about lighting and composition.

Rose lifted other yearbooks, saw a couple of stuffed toys, her old Barbie doll, and a cell phone that must be twenty years old. It was cumbersome to go through the items with one hand, so she put everything back in and closed the box.

What about the boxes on the other side? She crossed the narrow attic, straightening for a moment at the roof's apex. The tape holding the flaps of the box closed was secure; no name written on top. Rose stared at it. Should she open it? She could ask her mom, but her nose twitched. Was that a sign of something special in these boxes? Her nose twitched again. She sneezed. Nope. More dust. Either today, or some day in the future, she'd have to go through the entire house and determine what to do with everything.

She used her thumbnail to split the tape, then peeled it back. More books. At first glance, she was pretty sure these books didn't belong to Rose or Kirk. Rose and Aunt Tess must have boxed up these books when they cleared out her father's den. Rose lowered herself to the floor and opened the flap. Two Grisham novels nested side by side. Underneath them, two more. Now she remembered. Her father was a fan of novels starring lawyers or written by lawyers. Kirk and Rose had enjoyed reading them as well, which is why she saved the books.

Rose pulled out books and read the titles. One box, then another. Toward the bottom of the second box, Rose found books by authors she'd never heard of. She opened one book and read the inscription on the title page.

"For Randall, with much appreciation for your help at the most important time in my life. KNT"

Hmm. Why did the other lawyer use initials instead of his name? She picked up the next book. Another book title and author unfamiliar to Rose. Another inscription as well.

"To RW, Many heartfelt thanks. KNT"

Why weren't they using first names? Rose leafed through the pages of the book. Something popped out and dropped to the floor. A piece of paper. No, a photograph. Of her father with a woman Rose didn't recognize. Did the woman give him the books? Was she a former client or a fellow lawyer?

Rose studied the image. Her father had been a reserved man, quick to offer a firm handshake to a colleague, but slow to show his affections, sometimes even with his wife and children. The man in this photo expressed more emotion. Her father and the woman wore wide smiles. Their bodies almost touched. Rose pulled the photo closer. Her father had his arm wrapped around the woman's waist. And his face held more than a smile. His head tilted toward her with a warm gaze that softened his face and traveled to the corners of his eyes. Rose, the expert at studying people's body language through her camera lens, stared at the two of them until she forced herself to look away.

Chapter Fourteen

Rose couldn't stand still. She paced from the kitchen stove to the fireplace at the other end of the room, waiting for the water to boil and for her mother to wake up. She'd wiped down the two photo albums with a damp towel and put them on the kitchen table next to the three books inscribed to her father by KNT. The photo of her father with the woman rested on top of the books.

Her mother had spoken about difficult times during their marriage. Did that include infidelity? Did her father have an affair? If he did, did her mother know? And what about Kirk? Did he know something about the woman? She grabbed her phone off the counter and texted her brother.

Do you have time to chat?

She stared at her phone. Finally, a ping.

On a quick break. In court, remember? Urgent?

No, Mom's okay. Something else. Talk later?

The teakettle whistled, and she jumped up to silence it, then stopped. Maybe the kettle whistle would wake her mother and she could ask her about the woman. But no, Mom needed rest. Rose turned off the burner, poured water into a mug, and dropped in a tea bag. Rose recalled more of her mother's phone conversation with her dad the night of her bike accident. Her mother had grilled him: Why did he have so many cases out of town? All lawyers didn't travel that much, did they? Why was he in court so much, almost too busy to talk with her mother?

Rose picked up her tea, settled at the kitchen table, and looked at the photo. She'd never seen the woman before. She probably didn't work in her father's law office because Rose knew the people who'd worked for him. Plus, the woman's golden-brown face was a sharp contrast to her father's pale white one. Upstate New York, especially near the Vermont border, didn't have a large population of Black and Brown people. Was the woman from the area? Maybe from downstate?

"Rose," her mother called out. "I think Gladys needs to go."

"I'll be right there," she hollered, sliding the photo between the books and picking up the albums. The dog had remained by her mother's side, or in her lap, ever since Rose had popped over to Mrs. Shaw's that morning and retrieved her. Rose walked into the living room, set the albums on the coffee table, and went to her mother's recliner.

"Come here, girlfriend." Rose scooped the dog from her mother's lap, carried her to the sliding glass door, and set her down on the patio. The dog scampered away to find her favorite spot of grass while Rose surveyed the space and admired the slate patio. The interlocking tiles were different size squares and rectangles, and colors varied from light gray with swirls of pink to a darker gray shaded with streaks of black. Her parents had added the patio a couple of years after they'd renovated the kitchen and dining room area. Her mother persuaded her father to replace the windows with a sliding glass door. It looked better and increased the value of their property.

Gladys ran back to Rose, circling her several times before running out of breath and plopping down. Rose knelt and rubbed the dog's back, then under her chin, and finally behind her ears. The last move prompted a soft moan from the pooch, which brought a smile to Rose's face. She stood, slid the door open, and they both slipped inside. Rose followed Gladys into the living room and watched the little dog jump on the footstool alongside the recliner, then onto her mother's lap.

"I see you found the albums," her mom said. "I haven't been in the attic since I put them there, and it was probably dusty."

"Oh, it was. I wiped the albums down as best I could. This is the oldest one because it begins with Kirk as an infant."

"You both were beautiful babies." Her mom's eyes lit up with a smile on her face as she took the album from Rose and opened it, setting it on the arm of the recliner so she wouldn't disturb Gladys. "Kirk was finicky until the doctor and I determined I was eating too much cheese, drinking too much milk. Kirk was sensitive to dairy products. Once I eliminated them from my diet, he ate better and didn't cry as much." She thumbed through the photos while Rose sipped her tea. Then Rose traded albums with her.

"You look so happy in these photos," Rose said. "Proud parents, for sure."

"Do you remember us telling you that your father and I tried to have another baby a few years after Kirk, but we had difficulties? I had a couple of miscarriages, and even though we continued to try, I couldn't get pregnant. When Kirk went into kindergarten, I resumed part-time hours in your father's law office. We accepted that we wouldn't have another child. His practice was growing, and I enjoyed working again." Her mom flipped through a couple more pages of the album, touching the protective plastic.

"One month I missed my period. I was thrilled, but I didn't tell your father right away. I wanted to be sure I didn't lose another baby. He was so busy and out of town almost once a month, I don't think he noticed my weight. I was about four months along when I told him I was pregnant. He was more subdued than I thought he'd be. He said he was happy about it, but it didn't show on his face. Maybe he was afraid of losing another baby."

Or maybe he was interested in something—someone—else.

Her mom pointed out photos of Rose playing with friends in the backyard, riding her bike in the driveway, of her and Kirk wading in the ocean while waves splashed their backs. Kirk had a tight grip on Rose's hand.

"I found other items in the attic." Rose pushed herself up from the recliner, walked into the kitchen, and returned with the books. She held the photo under the bottom of the books and showed them to her mother. "I found these in a box Aunt Tess and I had set aside when we cleared out Dad's office. I forgot we'd saved them. The novels were mostly about lawyers, but these at the bottom were different."

Her mother stared at her.

"Do you recognize them?"

"No. Should I?"

"I don't know," Rose said. "Someone with the initials KNT inscribed them to Dad. I didn't think it was someone in his office. Maybe another attorney he'd worked with?"

"Your father worked with many attorneys, and he had hundreds of clients," her mother said, petting Gladys and glancing out the window.

"I opened one of the books, and this photograph fell out. I thought perhaps it's a clue who gave him the books." She handed the photo to her mother. "Do you know who the woman is?"

Her mother took the photo with a shaking hand. With her other hand, she reached down to stop Gladys from licking her paw and then stroked the dog's silky ears. She pushed the photo back toward Rose. "I don't know the woman."

"It looks like Dad knew her pretty well."

"What are you suggesting?" Her mother's voice, which had so much energy while they were looking at old family photos, was weak and flat.

"I remembered you telling me you and Dad had some problems in your marriage, and I wondered if this woman was one of them."

Her mother squeezed out a soft sigh. "Rose, let it go. It doesn't matter now."

"Did it matter then? Did it affect our family?" Rose pushed her mother harder than she should have, not as hard as she would a reluctant politician, but too much for an ailing woman. Rose couldn't suppress her urge to learn the truth, to understand her father better. To better understand herself.

"Please drop it." Her mother's voice grew louder, firmer. "Nothing good can come out of dragging this up. Your father's relationship with this woman, whatever it was, doesn't involve you."

"But—"

"Stop." Her mother's body lifted off the chair as if the word propelled her. A tear fell onto her cheek. "I'm going to ask you one more time to please stop asking these questions. I wish you'd never found that photograph."

"Or at least that I hadn't found it until after you were gone. That would have been easier for you."

Her mother froze and Rose gulped, hearing the harsh words come out of her mouth. She wished she could take them back.

"Mom," Rose got up and knelt next to her mother's chair, "I'm sorry. I didn't mean that. It came out the wrong way."

"Yes, you did mean it, and you're right. But it would have been best if you hadn't found the photo at all."

"So you know who the woman is?"

"No, I don't. But understand this, please," she practically whispered. "Whoever she is, or was, it's not your business. It wasn't then. It isn't now."

Chapter Fifteen

Her mother slept. Rose fidgeted. The ringing doorbell was a welcome interruption. Aunt Tess lumbered in carrying multiple bags that filled the house with savory aromas of chicken and something sweet and fruity. Rose rushed to the door, hoping her aunt had made her famous strawberry rhubarb pie.

"Aunt Tess, let me help you with those bags."

"Thanks. I'm afraid I'm losing my grip on the chicken. Better use both hands." She looked at Rose and paused. "Maybe I should keep the chicken—"

"It's okay, Aunt Tess. I've got it." Rose grabbed the bag and walked into the kitchen, setting it on the counter. "Do I need to put this in the oven?"

"No. It's been roasting since about ten this morning. I'll warm it up later." Aunt Tess followed Rose and put the rest of her bags on the woodblock island. She put her handbag on the kitchen table and turned to Rose.

"Give me a hug! How are you holding up?"

"I'm hanging in there," Rose said, feeling the warmth of her aunt's arms as they wrapped around her.

"I woke up this morning thinking you and your mom may need a good, hot meal." Aunt Tess stepped back. "You look a little thin. I hadn't noticed before. How much cooking have you done since you broke your arm?"

"I make a mean yogurt, granola, and banana breakfast, although my banana slices are pretty erratic. And I'm good at holding a sandwich in one hand as long as I don't want a sip of my drink at the same time."

"Yeah, that's what I figured." Aunt Tess nodded. "I'll sort these and put them where they need to go. First, I want to say hello to your mom."

Rose opened the sweetest smelling bag first. She was right. Pie. She lifted the top off the tan cardboard box and sniffed the sweet strawberry and tangy rhubarb aroma, the juices so gooey they'd bubbled up over the lattice crust. Yum. Another bag held a loaf of sourdough bread, its signature sweet smell, yeasty, with a hint of sourness. Almost like spoiled milk, but not. A gallon zip lock baggie filled with fresh, cleaned spinach was in with the bread, along with three baked potatoes. And in the last bag, a bottle of wine, which Rose put in the refrigerator.

The level of tension increased when Rose walked into the living room.

"What's up?" Aunt Tess asked, looking back and forth between Rose and her mom. Neither spoke. After a couple of minutes, Aunt Tess jumped up from the footstool where she'd been sitting.

"Rose, why don't you take Gladys for a walk?"

"Gladys is fine right where she is," her mother said, her voice uncompromising. "She did her business before I went to sleep, and I didn't nap long."

"Oh-kay." Aunt Tess drew out the word. "Rose, why don't you pick up some muffins from the bakery for breakfast?

We're not eating for a couple of hours. I'll put the food away while you're gone and pop the potatoes into the oven."

Aunt Tess gave Rose a look that made it clear it wasn't a request.

"I'll get my wallet." Rose picked up the three books with the photo tucked between them and put them on the crowded dining room table. She was out the front door in less than a minute.

Rose and her aunt had always been close, and she knew Aunt Tess loved Rose like the daughter she never had. Aunt Tess had remained single long after her husband had left her. As with Rose, the working life suited her. She'd taught history at the high school and every summer worked as a server and backup cook at the best diner in Lake Amelia. One summer, the elderly gentleman said he'd planned to sell the diner within a year. He couldn't handle the hours or the stress anymore. He convinced Aunt Tess she was a good enough cook and had the smarts and energy to run the diner. They agreed to a one-year transition and very generous terms of sale in Aunt Tess's favor.

Rose power-walked toward Main Street as best she could with sore ribs, eager to burn off some of the tension Aunt Tess had noticed. She hadn't walked at this quick a pace in a week and it felt good, but she couldn't keep it up for long. She slowed as she neared the bakery. Closing time was in less than an hour, and not many loaves of bread remained in the baskets behind the counter. The display case, however, still contained muffins and scones. Rose walked toward the counter and stopped.

"Bill, is that you?"

The man ahead of her turned and a smile crossed his face, then disappeared when he saw her arm. "Rose, what the hell happened to you?" He reached out to hug her, backed up a little, then gave her a one-arm hug around her waist.

"Injured in the line of duty," Rose said. "It's not that bad."

"Can you hold a camera?" This from the man who'd trained her how to take news photos on the run.

She shook her head.

"Then it's as bad as it looks." He glanced toward the front of the bakery. Half a dozen tables occupied the space in front of the windows looking onto Main Street. "Do you have time for a cup of coffee, or are you in a hurry?"

"No, I've got a minute. I'd love to catch up. Let me grab some muffins for my mom so I don't forget."

Bill picked up a bag off the counter with a loaf of French bread sticking out. "I'll take my coffee with a splash of cream," he said to the woman, handing him his change. "It's her turn to buy." He smiled as he nodded toward Rose and went to claim a table.

"Two medium coffees," Rose said, "one decaf black. I've never known Bill to drink decaf—"

"Me neither," the young woman behind the counter laughed. "Can I get you anything else?"

"Absolutely." Rose glanced into the display case. "Two lemon poppy seed muffins and two strawberry scones." She watched the woman put them into the bag. "What are those bars made of?"

"Strawberries, of course, the freshest berry around at this time of year, with an oatmeal crumble and a drizzle of lemon glaze. These are the last two."

"They look delicious. Could you put them on a small plate? Bill and I will have them with our coffees." Bill returned to the counter and carried the coffees and plate of strawberry bars while Rose paid and took her bag of pastries to the table.

"What happened?" Bill asked as soon as Rose sat.

She briefly explained. "I'm not allowed to pick up a camera for a few weeks."

"How long will you have to wear the splint?"

"It's coming off in a week or so, replaced with a fiberglass cast. The cast'll be on up to eight weeks. It's a mess under here," she admitted. She rubbed her right arm from her wrist to her shoulder. "Police told me they're looking through video and photos from the protest to see if they can determine who shoved me. I imagine it'll take time, maybe even require subpoenas for news organizations and freelance photographers to comply with the police requests."

"Yeah. They won't want to set a precedent by giving up their video or photos without a fight." Bill took a quick sip of coffee with one hand and a bite of the strawberry oat bar with the other. "I heard your mom's been in the hospital. How's she doing?"

"Not good." She gave him the short version.

"I'm sorry to hear that. That sounds like a brutal one-two punch. What can you do for your mom with that injury?"

"I'm limited, that's for sure. My left arm's getting stronger since it's working harder, but my right hand is weak." She explained how the visiting nurses would help her mother and Rose. "Hell, I can't even shower right now."

"I thought I smelled something a little off."

"Very funny." She reached out with her left arm to punch him in the arm, almost knocking over her coffee.

"Does that mean you'll be here a while?"

"Yes, but I need a quick trip back to Philly to pick up more clothes and see the surgeon who fixed my arm."

"Will you have time to stop by the newspaper? I'd love to show you the changes we've gone through, from all print to microfiche files, to everything digital stored on the cloud." He waved his arms over his head. "Or in some big servers up there. I'm not sure where it all goes. I'm not part of the technical team, but I've seen it evolve."

"That's because you've been around Lake Amelia, like, forever," she laughed, draining her coffee cup and wiping some oat crumbs off the table in front of her.

"Thanks for that."

"Since you've seen a lot of comings and goings around here," Rose said, "I wonder if you can help me. I've got an old photo of my father with someone I think he and my mother worked with. I'm trying to locate some of their old connections, people she might want to see."

Bill tipped his cup, slurping the last drops of coffee. "Sure, bring the photo to the paper anytime. I'll see what I can do. Now, I gotta run. I'm making dinner tonight. A family favorite. Spaghetti and meatballs."

"Sounds yummy," Rose said as she and Bill stood and left the bakery together.

Bill knew everyone. He might know the woman in the photo. And if he didn't, he'd know how to find out.

Chapter Sixteen

R ose opened the door and stepped inside. She walked past her sleeping mother and found Aunt Tess in the kitchen making dinner.

"Mom sleeps a lot," Rose said, putting the bag from the bakery on the counter.

"She's had one problem after another thrown at her, not all of them necessary." Aunt Tess pursed her lips and gave Rose a look. "The more rest she gets, the less agitated she is, the faster she'll heal, or at least feel better." Aunt Tess glanced at the dining room table. "Why don't you set the kitchen table? It'll be tight with the three of us, but the dining room table's a mess."

"I know. One of my goals is to go through all of that with Mom and toss out the old magazines and papers." Rose walked to the kitchen cabinet, took out three plates for the meal, set them on the counter, and took out three smaller plates for bread. She opened the drop leaf on the oak table and set a dining room chair facing the sliding glass doors. Then she tucked Gladys's bed under the dining room table, picked up another dining room chair and slid that in place at the table for three. Glasses of water, napkins, and silverware completed the settings.

"Looks like you're getting better handling items with one bum arm," Aunt Tess said as she opened the oven door and checked the baked potatoes. The chicken warmed on a shelf below the potatoes, sending out mouth-watering aromas of rosemary and garlic. Aunt Tess closed the oven door, opened the fridge, and pulled out the wine.

"I'll never be ambidextrous, but I'm getting stronger." Rose flexed the fingers of her left hand.

Aunt Tess laughed. "Grab a couple of wine glasses, would you, Miss Strong Hands? We've got about ten minutes before the potatoes are done. Let's chat."

Rose retrieved the glasses from a cupboard, and Aunt Tess poured the wine. Then they sat on the big leather couch in front of the fireplace. Aunt Tess turned to face Rose.

"What's going on with your father's stuff, the books and photo you found in the attic?"

Rose collected the books from the dining room table. "I found these three books inscribed to Dad from someone with the initials KNT."

Aunt Tess set her glass on the coffee table and took the books. She opened them one at a time, flipping through the first pages and reading the inscriptions. Her face was a blank canvas as she closed the last book. She looked at Rose and raised her eyebrows.

"This photo fell out of one book." Rose had been holding the photo, face down, on her leg.

Aunt Tess took the photo without a word and glanced at it.

Is that a flinch? "Do you know who the woman is?" Rose held her breath and watched her aunt's face for any sign of recognition.

"No, I don't. I'm sure I've never seen her. How old is the

photo?" She turned it over, but there was no printed date or written info on the back.

"I have no idea," Rose said, leaning over and picking up her wineglass. She tilted the glass and took a bigger drink than she'd intended. Aunt Tess wouldn't lie to her. She might not tell her everything, but Rose was sure she wouldn't lie.

"And your mother said she didn't recognize her either, right?"

Rose nodded. "But she winced when I showed it to her. Maybe she doesn't know this woman, but she knows something. And look how physically close they are. This isn't a casual photo with two acquaintances."

"You can't be sure." Aunt Tess's voice was sharp, and Rose leaned back. She didn't want to alienate her aunt or her mother.

"I know what I see in the photograph," she said with the soft determination of someone who knows they are right. "I take photos for a living. Their body language suggests a close relationship."

Aunt Tess put the photo on top of the books. "Rose, if I had an inkling of who this woman is, I would tell you, but I don't. And I don't think it's any of your business."

"But Aunt Tess—"

She put her hand up to silence her, then reached over and touched Rose's cheek with the back of her fingers. "Hear me out, Rose. Your parents loved you and Kirk. They were so grateful they had the two of you after the struggles with fertility. If there were issues in their marriage, it was between them. It wasn't about you and Kirk. It didn't involve you and Kirk. Do you understand?"

The timer on the stove beeped, and the women jerked their heads toward the kitchen.

"Rose, your mother is dying." Aunt Tess's voice caught. Tears welled in her eyes. "We don't know how much longer she'll be with us. Let's make her last days, months, whatever, as happy as they can be, okay? Please drop this. For her sake, and mine."

Rose looked at her aunt through her own teary eyes. She gulped and tried to find her voice. "I don't want to hurt either of you. I'll let this go as best I can."

"I'd rather hear you say you'll let this go. Period."

Rose nodded. She wouldn't lie to Aunt Tess any more than her aunt would lie to her. Rose pursed her lips, picked up her glass, and took a sip of wine. She wouldn't lie, but she couldn't make an empty promise.

During dinner, Rose mentioned how she'd run into Bill Poole from the *Lake Amelia Dispatch*. He told her what happened with a new high school intern a couple years ago. He'd overheard a police call over the scanner about an officer in trouble a block away. The teen had grabbed a camera and run out the door, but he forgot to check the camera for a SIM card. It didn't have one, so the camera wouldn't record images. The kid's phone battery was dead, so he borrowed someone else's phone, took a few photos, and emailed them to the editor. The drama was over by the time one of the newspaper's photographers got to the scene. They'd used the intern's photo in the online story, beating even the larger daily newspapers.

"You never did anything like that, did you, Rose?" Aunt Tess asked.

Rose and her mother looked at each other. "Well, one time I went on a story and forgot to take a reporter's notebook or a tape recorder. I didn't have any paper, and I couldn't get close enough to the cops doing the interview. When the police answered reporters' questions, I tried to memorize what he said, then jumped in my car and wrote down everything I could before I forgot it. Wrote some on my arm and some on the tail of my blouse. A beautiful white blouse I had borrowed that morning. From mom.”

“Did the ink come out?”

“It was black ballpoint ink, not as bad as a Sharpie, but no, it didn’t.”

“That may have been the last time I loaned you one of my blouses.” Her mother smiled at the memory.

Rose took her mother’s hand and squeezed it. “I love you, Mom. I’m sorry if I hurt you by asking questions.”

Her mother reached over and held Rose’s hand in both of hers. “I understand, honey, but I don’t want to hear any more about that photo or the books. Okay?”

“Yes, I won’t mention them again.”

Later that evening, after Aunt Tess left and her mother had gone to bed, Rose picked up the books and photo and carried them upstairs. She would keep her promise not to mention them again, but pursuing information and asking pointed questions was in her DNA. She couldn’t let a story go if there was a way to dig up more information.

But this wasn’t some news story. She was on a personal quest for the truth because she couldn’t believe her father would risk his family and his reputation by getting involved with another woman. Rose couldn’t have done what he did. In fact, she didn’t, even when her heart had begged her. The only way Rose could understand why her father had taken such a chance was to keep searching for answers.

And now she had to do it without involving her mother or Aunt Tess.

Chapter Seventeen

Rose and her mother were still in their pajamas. They'd eaten breakfast and were talking about hospice care when the woman from Visiting Nurses arrived. Rose let her in, took her into the living room, and offered her coffee.

"Which one of you is my patient?" The nurse smiled, introducing herself as Lettie Short. "My instructions say I'm to care for a seventy-four-year-old woman with cancer." She looked at Rose's mom. "That's you I presume."

The nurse's smile was warm and inviting. Rose liked her immediately.

"Yes, I'm Carly Webster," her mother said. Nurse Lettie set her handbag and tote bag on the footstool and held her mother's hands.

"It's nice to meet you. May I call you Carly, or would you rather Mrs. Webster?"

"Oh, Carly, please. Mrs. Webster is too formal."

"And I'm her daughter, Rose. Thanks for coming. It's nice to meet you."

Nurse Lettie turned to Rose and shook her left hand. "What happened to you?"

"I'm a photojournalist, injured on assignment."

Nurse Lettie nodded. "May I sit?" She picked up her bags, put them alongside the other recliner, and eased herself into the chair. Rose slid the footstool out and plopped down.

"Let me give you an overview, then we can get down to the specifics of your care." Nurse Lettie explained how Visiting Nurses provided home care at all levels, from post-surgery follow-up to hospice care. "Have you decided whether to continue treatment or are you interested in hospice care?"

"Rose and I, along with my son in Florida, are still discussing it," her mom said. "I'm leaning toward hospice care. I don't want to go through painful treatments to prolong my life if I can't enjoy time with my family."

"I understand. Cancer treatments have improved dramatically in recent years. Many cancers go into remission after chemo or radiation, or with advanced immunotherapy options." The nurse glanced at her papers. "Your doctors' notes show you have other medical issues that complicate how to treat your cancer, should you decide to do that. When you're ready, you can get hospice care through the state public health department, also county agencies, and Medicare covers that, mostly if you are in the hospital or an approved hospice facility. Are you aware of that?"

Rose and her mom nodded.

"Sorry for all that business, but I'm required to make sure you understand your options. Let's talk about how I can help you."

The three of them took several minutes reviewing what her mom needed, what Rose could help with, and how often the nurse should visit.

"I'll come every morning about this time," Nurse Lettie said. "And try to stop in once or twice a week in the afternoon.

We can be more flexible with the afternoon visits until you decide about hospice care." She made some notes. "How does that sound? I live in Hoosick Falls, a short drive away."

"Sounds good, don't you think, Mom?"

She nodded, then her brow furrowed. "I'm afraid I'll need you to handle the paperwork, honey. My head is spinning with all this information."

"Don't worry. I'll take care of it with Nurse Lettie." She reached over and took her mother's hand. "And I'll deal with Medicare and your gap insurance company. I can't remember who that is, but I'll handle those things." Her mother looked better, but she was very ill. Rose swallowed the lump in her throat.

"Now that we've gone over those matters," Nurse Lettie said, "how about a shower, Carly?"

"I'd like that."

"While you two use the downstairs bath, I'm going to head upstairs for my latest sponge bath," Rose said, rising to her feet. "Then I'm off to the outlets in Lake George because I only packed clothes for a few days, and I need some things. If I have time after I'm done shopping, I'd like to take a walk."

"That's fine. I'll be here for a few hours." Nurse Lettie looked at her arm. "How long has your arm been in the splint?"

"More than a week now," Rose said, flexing the fingers on her injured hand.

"And when was the last time you stepped into the shower?"

"Um, more than a week."

"Would you like me to help you wrap your arm in plastic and give you tips on how to keep it dry in the shower?"

"That's a wonderful offer, but you're here to take care of my mom, not me."

"I'm here to provide care. Period." Nurse Lettie delivered

her empathy in a firm voice that told Rose she wouldn't take no for an answer. "I've never known anyone wearing a splint or a cast who didn't appreciate the opportunity for help."

"You can use the downstairs shower," her mom said. "We removed the tub years ago when we renovated the back of the house. It may be easier than the upstairs bathroom."

Half an hour later, her hair washed and dried and her body smelling of lavender soap, Rose pulled on jeans and a T-shirt. She called out to her mom and Nurse Lettie that she was on her way out the door. It seemed odd leaving the house with someone else taking care of her mother, but she'd try to get used to the idea. It was going to happen more often. She climbed into her SUV and headed northwest out of town toward the outlets in Lake George.

Five days ago, in a near panic after Aunt Tess's call, Rose had tossed an assortment of clothes into her suitcase, thinking about summer in Philly, forgetting how much the temperature dropped in the evenings in the mountains. She needed a sweatshirt, yoga pants, a couple tops with long sleeves, and maybe a raincoat. When could she drive back to Philly, even overnight, to pick up more clothes and maybe check in with her doctor? She could buy clothes anywhere. She wasn't sure about a surgeon or physical therapy, and she was due for both.

Traffic slowed as she neared the stores. She went past the first two plazas, remembering that Eddie Bauer and L.L. Bean were a little farther on the right. Inside the Eddie Bauer store, she chose some sweats, a pair of yoga pants, and a couple of long-sleeved casual tops. Next door was L.L. Bean, where she found a pair of chinos, a couple more tops, and a lightweight raincoat. J. Crew was right across the street, and she loved shopping there but not on this trip. One more stop for underwear and an extra set of pjs and she was set. She pointed the SUV back the way she'd come.

The morning shower had been refreshing and lifted her

spirits, but the reality of her mother's health issues never drifted far from her thoughts. She'd need to handle paperwork, bum right hand and all, but she didn't have to do it alone. She'd call Kirk tonight and update him. And press him to visit as soon as his court case would allow.

Chapter Eighteen

T owering white pines lined the mountains or west side of Falls Street, one of Lake Amelia's busiest roads because it led to popular Felton Falls. At slightly over eighty feet, Felton wasn't one of the highest falls in the state, not by a long shot. It wasn't one of the widest either, but its layers of rock and shale jutting out in different places made it stunning year-round. Water trickled through the woods in the mountaintops, tumbling over cascades and rapids, forming Felton Creek as it journeyed toward Lake Amelia. Trails disappeared into the woods on both sides of the creek, some designed for beginning hikers and others more challenging, all of them dangerous and off-limits in the winter.

Felton Creek narrowed into a pool at the base of the falls, churned under the Main Street bridge, and flowed into Lake Amelia. Workers cleaned the picnic tables and benches every day, giving people ample places to sit and enjoy the beauty of the area. Although the nearby mountains drew skiers and snowboarders all winter, summer was Lake Amelia's most popular season. People had already claimed their tables or benches for a day of rest or activities.

When Rose wasn't worrying about her mother's health and what the coming weeks would bring, she wondered about her father's past and why he acted the way he did. Her brain needed a break. She found a semi-secluded bench under a red maple tree where she sat in silence, closed her eyes to center herself, and listened to the beat of flowing water. Rose moderated her breaths, counting to four when she inhaled through her nose, and to four again when she let her breath out through her mouth. The healing breaths calmed her body and slowed the thoughts from running rampant through her mind. She allowed the thoughts to return, and they didn't overwhelm her.

During the conversation with Nurse Lettie earlier that morning, Rose realized she'd been handling her mother's illnesses like a trained photojournalist, with a measure of emotional distance. But this wasn't a news photoshoot where she needed to check her emotions at the door. This was her mother, the woman who'd given her life, wiped her tears when she cried over a disagreement with her best friend, and hugged her tight when they'd had to put their old pup to sleep. Now their roles were changing. Or had already changed. Rose was the caregiver. Her mother required her love and help in ways she'd never needed before.

Rose blew out a deep breath. Well, that's intimidating. It's not like she'd had any experience taking care of other people or even a pet. She'd been on her own, accountable to no one or for anyone for the last twenty-plus years. She and her mom had taken some vacations together after her father died, visiting Kirk in Florida a few times so Mom could see her grandchildren. Rose had made all the arrangements—the flights, the rental car, all of it. This wasn't anything like getting the best seats on a flight from Albany to Fort Lauderdale. This was helping her mother in the final stages of her life.

Her phone vibrated. "Kirk, what a surprise to hear from you at this time of day."

"I know. The judge had an emergency dental appointment this morning, so court doesn't get underway until after lunch," he explained. "How're you? How's Mom?"

Rose tried to speak, but the words got stuck in her throat. She swallowed hard, sniffed back the tears. "She's dying, Kirk. I'm sitting on a bench at the falls, and it hit me hard that we're going to lose her, maybe soon."

Kirk seemed at a loss for words, and she waited while he seemed to collect his thoughts. "I know. Maria and I told the boys last night. And in telling them, I felt more pain about Mom's situation than I had before. I guess sharing the news makes it more real."

"That's definitely part of it." Rose held her cell to her ear with her left hand and leaned on her knees as best she could. "The nurse we hired for daily visits came this morning. Her name's Lettie, and she's nice. She helped me shower and then I was told to take a walk and do something with myself while she helped Mom shower and dress. I didn't know a nurse would make meals, but Nurse Lettie said she'd see to Mom's lunch."

"The nurse is right. You need to take care of yourself. You won't be much good to Mom if you don't."

Rose nodded out of habit. Talking with Kirk about their mother's health was helpful, even though the seriousness of the conversation weighed on Rose. Time to switch topics. "How's the trial going?"

"I think the jury's on our side. Our presentation in the civil case is going well, and the other side is on the defensive. I'm hoping we can wrap up in a few more days."

"I hope the jury decides for your client. It's always surprised me you followed Dad's path into law. You often sound angry when we talk about him."

"I didn't follow him into law. I made my own way." The edge in Kirk's voice reinforced what she'd said. Then he softened. "Dad and I had our differences, and, for a while, I resisted going to law school because I didn't want to follow in his footsteps. But it was too late because I'd already fallen in love with the law and knew I wanted to spend my career protecting people's rights."

"Well, it sounds like you're pretty good at it."

Voices in the background seeped into the gaps in their conversation. Kirk acknowledged someone in the room with him. "Rose, I've got to go. We've got a few loose ends to tie up before court goes back into session."

"There was something else I wanted to ask you about," she spoke quickly, realizing she may have waited too long to bring up the woman in the photo.

"If it's not urgent, it's going to have to wait. Bye." He hung up.

Darn, she should have mentioned the photo sooner. She knew her brother wasn't a bad person, but there were times he talked about their father with such anger, she couldn't help but wonder what he knew. Rose shook her head to rid her mind of the conversation and turned back the way she'd come. But instead of going home, she walked toward the pub for an early lunch.

"Hey, Rose. I didn't get to say hello the other day," Thom said when she walked into the brewpub. "Grab a table and I'll be right over."

She sat at the same table she had the other day and smiled as Thom approached with the menu.

"It's good to see you. Let me take your order, then maybe I can come back and chat."

"Good to see you as well. I'll have an iced tea and a Caesar salad with grilled chicken. Go easy on the dressing, please."

He slid the menu off the table. "Okay. Back in a minute."

Rose watched him walk away and smiled. Thom still had the best bum in town. She and Thom had dated their last two years in high school, and Rose thought he was her forever love. But she was going to college and moving to a big city where photojournalists were in demand. He was a local guy through and through. They had a teary but friendly goodbye the day she left town.

He returned with her tea and five minutes later was back again with her salad. Thom put the large bowl on the table in front of her, along with silverware wrapped in a cloth napkin. Then he took his cell phone out of his back pocket and plopped down in the chair closest to her.

"How's your mom?"

Rose gave him a status report and explained that she'd be hanging around Lake Amelia for a while to take care of her mother. She also told him what happened with her arm because he glanced at it several times but seemed hesitant to ask.

"Your life's been pretty full, hasn't it?"

She agreed. "How's your family? Got any photos?"

"Do I have any photos?" He smiled. "How long have you got?"

"More time than you," she laughed. "Come on, let me see."

He picked up his cell, swiped his fingers a few times, and put it on the table where she could see it. "Here are the five of us at Lake George last winter." He swiped the screen a few times. "And here's one of my favorite shots of the three kids."

"Look at those smiles. What a beautiful group." She pulled his phone closer to her and pinched the photo to enlarge it, to get a better look at their faces. "They're getting so big."

"Yeah, tell me about it. The tallest one there, Ned, is fifteen and needs new sneakers every six months. The twins don't need shoes as often, at least not yet, but they're thirteen and it's all about clothes. As it is for most girls their age."

Both turned their heads when a man called out hello to Deputy Stover, who walked straight toward their table.

"Hi, Thom. Got a minute? I need to talk. In your office, please."

"Uh, sure, Maxi, I mean Deputy Stover. Give me a minute to make sure Bob's got the bar covered." He picked up his phone and walked away.

"I'll be right there," Maxi said. She turned to Rose and said hello.

Rose smiled. "We've got to stop meeting like this."

"Why? Is that a problem?"

Rose stammered, unsure how to interpret the comment. She didn't know Deputy Stover well enough to know when she made a joke. Was that a twinkle in her eyes?

"I've got to talk to Thom," Maxi said. "Nice to see you again."

Rose thought about their exchange as Maxi walked away, trying to understand why she felt uncomfortable. Was Maxi being friendly in her own quirky way? The uniform was intimidating enough. When Maxi put on her tough deputy sheriff airs, even with a hint of a smile, Rose lost her ability to form a complete sentence. It threw her, because of all the characteristics people used to describe Rose Webster, timid wasn't on the list.

She finished her salad and drink, then realized she should get home. Rose paid the check and left, not catching sight of Thom or Deputy Stover again. They must still be talking in his office. What were they talking about, and why did they have to do it privately?

Chapter Nineteen

Rose knew every turn between Lake Amelia and the Saratoga Springs Hospital without consulting the map app. It'd been a week since her mother collapsed and the hematologist wanted to follow up on her bloodwork. After lunch, her mom had a consultation with the oncologist. Rose sat in the waiting room at the hematologist's office, flipping through the spring edition of *Adirondack Life*, with stories about the melting snowfall and breath-taking photos from the mountaintops of the six-million-acre park.

"Anything new?" Rose asked when her mom returned to the waiting room.

"Not really. The nurse said they'd call when the results are in from today's blood tests, perhaps about this time tomorrow."

"How about an early lunch in the cafeteria?"

Her mom nodded and walked toward the door. Rose put the magazine back down on the table and followed.

Rose got her mom settled at a table, then joined the line at the buffet. She grabbed a green plastic tray from the stack and dropped some silverware and napkins on it. The chicken soup smelled good. She got two cups. Rose eyed an egg salad sandwich. Her mom would only eat half, if that much. Rose would finish whatever her mother didn't eat. She added an oatmeal cookie, a cup of coffee for herself, and a cup of green tea for her mom. After she paid the woman sitting at the register, she looked at the tray. It weighed too much for her to carry. The man in scrubs behind her noticed.

"May I take that to your table for you?" he asked as he paid for his sandwich and drink with a swipe of his card in front of the electronic pad.

"I'd appreciate that," Rose said. "I have moments when I forget I can't do something as simple as carry a tray of food."

He made room for his sandwich and drink on her tray, picked it up, and followed her.

"How'd you hurt your arm?"

"On assignment in Philadelphia, near where I live."

"You're here having it checked out?"

"Actually, no." She explained about her mom.

"There's an excellent physical therapy department at the hospital if you need to rehab that arm while you're here. It's on the first floor, in the east wing. Any hospital staff can direct you."

"Thanks for the advice, Dr. . . . ."

"Dr. Levinson. I'm a surgeon. If you need any follow-up while you're in the area taking care of your mother, contact my office. Tell them you're the woman with her arm in a splint who needed help carrying a tray of food. I'll remember."

The doctor greeted her mother as he set the tray down and picked up his sandwich and drink. He wished them both the best. Rose thanked him and repeated his name to help her remember.

The soup container was so hot she put it on the table in front of her mother as fast as she could. Half of the egg salad sandwich followed, along with a napkin. She was right, her mom only took a few small bites of the sandwich while waiting for the soup to cool. In between bites and sips, her mom updated Rose about her old friends in Lake Amelia.

"Did I tell you I saw Thom yesterday at the pub?" Rose asked. "He showed me photos of his family. That son of his is big. And the girls are teens. I can't believe he has kids that old."

"His wife is lovely. I think she's a nurse here. Pediatrics maybe." Her mom sipped her tea.

Rose thought her mom would be too distracted to carry on a normal conversation with all the medical issues she faced, but she asked what Rose had been doing with her time, especially when her mom had been napping.

"Have you been anywhere else around town besides the pub and the diner?"

"You know me. The library was one of my first stops," Rose said. "I wandered through the different rooms on both floors, remembering how much time I used to spend among the books. On the second floor, in the young adult section, I met a girl named Ellie who reminded me of myself as a kid, immersed in a fictional world. I tried to talk with her, but she wasn't interested in chatting."

"Oh, Ellie. Her father is the library director. Her mother died several months ago. It was very sudden. A car crash." Her mother's eyes looked over Rose's shoulder as she recalled the accident. "I understand Ellie's struggling. Maybe you could try to talk with her again, find a connection around books. Tell her how you used to spend hours reading in that same space. I'll bet she's a voracious reader, given that her father oversees the library and her mother was a teacher."

Rose gave the idea some thought as she drained her cup of tea. "I'm not sure how to talk with a child. I don't have close friends with children her age and I wasn't around Kirk's kids much, especially when they were younger. Some people find talking to kids easy. Not me."

"It's not that difficult," her mother said. "Think back. You were a child once."

"Yes, but it's not like I took notes." Rose gathered up the trash and piled it on the tray.

"You're a photojournalist, used to asking people questions," her mother persisted as they both stood. "Talk to her about books. Find out what she's reading. I'm sure she could use some company." She paused. "Maybe you could as well."

The appointment with the oncologist followed lunch. Rose went into Dr. Fisk's office with her mom. After Dr. Fisk listened to her mom's lungs, the three of them discussed treatment options.

"I haven't made a final decision yet, Dr. Fisk, but I'm not inclined to have chemo, radiation, or any other invasive treatment."

"You understand if there's any chance of slowing this down—and it is remote, I acknowledge—it needs to be done now. Also, our scheduling calendar for chemo fills quickly."

"I understand, Doctor."

"I know you met with the social worker at the hospital and your visiting nurse can also talk to you about hospice care," Dr. Fisk said with a smile on her lips but a trace of sadness in her eyes. The doctor stood, walked around her desk, and took her mother's hand in both of hers. "Once you make a decision to refuse treatment and go into palliative care, you'll need to sign some forms, releasing the hospital of any legal responsibility for not treating you. Your visiting nurse or the hospice staff can explain those requirements."

"I understand the ramifications of my decision should I decline further treatment."

"I've enjoyed meeting you. You're a strong woman. I admire your courage."

Her mom held her head high as she walked out of Dr. Fisk's office, as if proving her determination, then fell asleep almost immediately after returning home and sitting in the recliner. Rose fed Gladys, took her for a quick walk around the block, and placed the dog on her mother's lap, on top of the multi-colored, crocheted lap robe. Her mom stirred long enough to rub Gladys behind the ear, then drifted back to sleep.

Rose respected her mother's decision, but she wished she'd talk more about what was going on. Her mother had a frustrating habit—frustrating to Rose, that is—of not telling her about a medical issue until after the fact. When her mother had gallbladder surgery several years ago, Rose didn't learn about it for weeks. She'd said it was a minor procedure, nothing to worry Rose about. Rose had asked her friend why she couldn't get her mother to confide in her more and whether Danica had the same experience with her mother or father.

"That's the way it is in our family as well," Danica had said. "My parents don't tell me if there's an issue with their health, especially my mom. That whole mother-daughter-as-best-friend thing is true about two percent of the time, I think. Mothers talk with their friends, their husbands, their hairdressers. It's fine for children, even adult children, to be vulnerable with their parents; it's not okay for parents to be vulnerable with their children. I think it's because parents always need to be strong for their children. That's the way it is."

Rose thought about Danica's comments as she poured a glass of wine and sat on the couch in front of the fireplace, stretching out lengthwise on the sofa. She fluffed up a pillow to find a better position for her arm, then leaned back and stared out at the patio. Her arm and ribs ached less, but pain still ripped through her shoulder whenever she tried to stretch those muscles.

She should follow up on the surgeon's comment about doing physical therapy. At some point, she needed to return to Philadelphia and see the doctor who'd operated on her arm. But she had no idea how long she was staying in Lake Amelia. The surgeon had told her the splint needed to be replaced with a cast in about a week. It was time. Perhaps she should look into available options at Saratoga Hospital.

What about work if she stayed here for more than a few weeks? How long could she stay here was a better question. Freelance work in upstate New York wouldn't be as lucrative as it was in the Philadelphia area. New York City was a short train ride from Philly, and she'd often had last-minute assignments there. But the city was too far from upstate for those kinds of short-notice photo assignments now.

Photos. Her mind took a detour. She thought of the photo tucked into the book in the box in the attic. Had she gone through everything in the attic? No. She'd left many boxes untouched. Rose picked up her wine, tiptoed through the living room, took the stairs to the second floor, and gingerly climbed back into the attic.

She went through one more box of books, opening their spines until some of them split, to ensure nothing was hidden between the pages. After shoving the last box aside, she spotted a travel bag tucked under the eaves. She tugged the bag, sneezed at the dust, then yanked it and fell hard on her butt, her right arm thumping against the floor. She swallowed a scream, squeezed the tears from her eyes, then sat still, catching her breath.

Finally, she looked at the brown leather bag. Her dad's travel bag. She lifted it again. It was too heavy to be empty. Why didn't Kirk take it after their father died? Right, he wouldn't want another reminder of Dad. Why didn't her mother clean it out and toss it? Maybe she wanted nothing to do with it.

Rose wiped off a thick layer of dust and slid the zipper back, revealing a light blue shirt and a couple of pairs of socks. Her father's clothes, maybe some of the last ones he'd worn. She swiveled around, found her glass of wine, and took a gulp. Looking through her father's books had been easy; poking through his overnight bag, his personal items like his clothes? That was unsettling. Maybe she should stop.

Who was she kidding?

She set her glass to the side and pulled out the shirt. Then she went through the bag, finding more clothes, including a T-shirt and pair of sneakers. His shaving kit rested at the bottom of the bag. Rose's hand paused as she reached for it. Her eyes filled with tears. Whatever had been going on, between her parents, he was still her father. Seeing his clothes and shaving kit, smelling a hint of his aftershave, touched the sore spot in her heart that still grieved for him.

Rose opened the shaving kit and lifted out his razor, shaving cream, after-shave lotion, toothbrush, toothpaste, and a travel-size bottle of shampoo. The leather kit was dry; nothing had leaked. She reached back inside. Her fingers found plastic. What else was in here? She pulled out the plastic and immediately dropped it. Her eyes shot open so fast and so wide, a pain tore through her forehead. She looked at the colorful package, took a breath, and reached back into the shaving kit, where she found several more. Condoms.

Condoms, Dad? What the . . . ?

Chapter Twenty

Aunt Tess had brought enough food the day before to feed a dozen people, and she'd promised to stop in regularly with more. Rose was grateful because it was too cumbersome to cook. More than that, she was too distracted.

Condoms! What would Mom think of that, huh? Dad didn't need those condoms for trips he'd made with Mom.

The visits to the doctors' offices exhausted her mother, so she ate on a tray table in the living room. That was fine with Rose, who sat on the love seat and caught up with the news on her laptop. Her mother glanced at the newspaper but wasn't interested. Just after six, she asked Rose to help her into bed and bring her a glass of water. When Rose checked on her half an hour later, she was sound asleep, with Gladys wiggling her legs and whimpering a doggie dream by her side. Rose picked up the book her mom had been reading, placed it on the bedside table, and turned out the light.

Rose tried to eat dinner, but she couldn't swallow a morsel, unable to get the sight or feel of the condom wrapper out of her mind. Cleaning the kitchen helped, including washing her hands repeatedly, but Rose also went to bed early. However, sleep was erratic. She climbed out of bed before the sun was up and was on her third cup of coffee when Nurse Lettie arrived.

"Morning, Rose. Is your mom still sleeping?"

"She was when I last checked about fifteen minutes ago. Is it okay if I dress and leave for a while now that you're here? I have some errands to run."

"Of course," Nurse Lettie said, putting her bag on the kitchen table. "I'll be here for a couple of hours. Take your time."

"Coffee's fresh." Rose put her cup in the sink and went upstairs. She was growing accustomed to her new morning routine. Getting ready was so much faster when she couldn't shower or fuss with her hair. She'd perfected the technique of putting on blouses by sliding her right arm into the sleeve first and moving her shoulder as little as possible. Putting her left arm in and buttoning up the blouse was still challenging, so she wouldn't be posting tips on YouTube.

The library wasn't open yet, and neither was the newspaper front office. She stepped into the bakery and ordered a strawberry scone and a bottled water. Sitting at a table by the window, she checked her email and texts. Jeremy texted a few times to see how she was doing and to tell her what was in her mail. He stopped by about every other day to make sure she didn't receive anything urgent, such as materials from the surgeon, the PT office, or the insurance company. She should call him. Later.

Some of her colleagues had also reached out, and she spotted a couple of calls she should return, but she wasn't up to talking. If anyone asked how she was doing, as they certainly would, what would she say? The condoms occupied her thoughts. She might not be capable of talking with anyone without blurting out, "Condoms!" Meeting with Bill, though, showing him the photo without mentioning the condoms, that she could do.

Rose tossed her napkin in the bin by the front door and left the bakery. She walked a few blocks along Main Street, then turned right at the gift shop, passing a real estate office and an insurance company. The business district continued less than a full block off Main Street. Homes replaced businesses, Cape Cod style homes like Rose's, ranch houses, Arts and Crafts homes, even center hall Colonials here and there.

Three blocks off Main Street, she crossed Falls Road. Half a block later, she stopped in front of the *Lake Amelia Dispatch*, its signature newsstand boxes looking a little tired, perched on either side of the entrance. The two-story brick building had been putting out newspapers since the 1880s on newsprint processed by paper mills from the spruce and pine trees so plentiful in the Adirondacks. The staff was much smaller now than when Rose worked at the paper during college. And the *Dispatch* printed fewer copies because more people read the news online. But many people, especially in small towns like Lake Amelia, preferred to hold the newspaper in their hands, pouring over articles about their neighbors, the police report (hopefully, not about their neighbors), the weather report, and rereading the ads until the ink was darker on their fingers than on the newspaper.

Five minutes after walking through the glass double doors, a dejected Rose clomped down the front steps and took a seat on a nearby bench. The woman at the front counter said Bill wouldn't be in for a couple more hours. Rose would have to circle back later. She pulled out her phone and checked the time. Too early for lunch, and besides, she wasn't hungry. The sun had barely cleared the mountains of pine trees in the distance, but it was high enough to warm her body.

Rose jumped when a big, dark blue SUV sped by spewing smoke that burned her nose, its loose muffler rattling so loud she felt it in her teeth. The SUV drove toward Main Street. Seconds later, a county sheriff's vehicle flew past her, lights flashing but, thankfully, no sirens blaring. Rose was curious. It didn't make sense to wait for Bill. She hurried toward Main Street.

At the intersection with Main Street, Rose stopped and looked in both directions. To her right, she spotted the flashing lights. Rose picked up her pace and found Deputy Sheriff Stover leaning in the driver's open window, taking some papers from him, and getting back into her vehicle. Rose joined the people who'd gathered on the sidewalk to watch.

Deputy Stover noticed the crowd the minute she stepped back out of her car.

"Move on, people." Stover motioned with a wave of her hand. "There's nothing to see here." She paused and waited for people to heed her request. Rose walked past the SUV and sat on a bench. A breeze carried cigarette smoke out of the open passenger window of the stopped vehicle. Rose couldn't see the driver, but she could hear his conversation with Stover.

"I told you to get that muffler fixed a couple of weeks ago, didn't I, Paul?"

"Haven't had time," he answered. "I've been working so much, I haven't gotten around to it. I promise I'll take care of it tomorrow morning."

"That's what you said last time when I gave you a warning." Stover tore a ticket off her pad and handed it to him, along with his papers. "Now I'm giving you a ticket, Paul, and if you don't have it fixed in two days, you and I are going to have a problem. Do you understand?"

He mumbled something Rose couldn't hear, took the papers from the deputy, and dropped them onto the passenger seat. His face pointed in Rose's direction and this time she heard him. Loud and clear.

"Power-hungry dyke." He put the car in gear and pulled

out. Stover stood in the road, staring after him. As Stover turned toward her patrol car, she saw Rose looking at her.

"Did you hear what he said?" Rose asked as the deputy walked over.

Stover looked at Rose with curiosity. "Of course, I heard him. It's not like he whispered. It's also not our first encounter or the first time he's called me a name."

"But you didn't call him out for using that language."

"We're not in liberal Philadelphia, Rose. We're not even in artist-friendly-but-still-a-little-snobbish Saratoga Springs. This is rural New York where almost everybody is white and straight. Guys like Paul come with the territory."

"Did you try to get a county sheriff's job someplace more diverse?" Rose quizzed Deputy Stover like a reporter following a lead.

She smiled. "In a perfect world, I would have landed a position in Albany County or Rensselaer County where I'd be working with and protecting a community with more people who looked like me. But that wasn't an option. They weren't hiring. So I tried to get a law enforcement job anywhere I could because I have a degree in criminal science and it's the career I chose. I didn't care where the job was. Matter of fact, still don't."

Stover watched Rose and waited.

"Is he right that you're gay? You're a lesbian?"

"Yep. Does it matter to you?"

"What do you mean?"

"Do you still want to go out for a drink or dinner?"

It suddenly dawned on Rose. "As a friend or as a date?"

"You tell me."

"I'm not gay," Rose said.

"Then as friends." Deputy Stover touched the tip of her hat. "I have to get back to work. See you around, friend."

Chapter Twenty-One

A man about six feet tall with a slender build and light brown hair stood at the library's information/checkout desk in the wide hallway a few steps beyond the staircase. Rose didn't have to wonder long if he was the library's director and Ellie's father.

"I'm Carter Paxton," he said, coming around the desk to greet her. His blue-and-yellow-striped shirt had a button-down collar and no tie. His shirt was tucked into neatly pressed khaki slacks, and he wore loafers, no socks. "I'm pretty sure I spotted you wandering the stacks a couple of days ago, didn't I?"

Rose introduced herself and mentioned that she grew up in Lake Amelia.

"Your mom is Carly Webster, right?" He continued after Rose nodded. "How is she?"

"Not a promising diagnosis." Rose explained what the doctors had said. "You might see me around here pretty often. I'm going to get away most mornings while a nurse stops by and takes care of Mom." Rose's eyes drifted toward the second floor. "How's your daughter doing? I heard about her mother. I'm sorry for your loss."

"Thank you. My wife was the child-rearing expert. I'm learning as I go. I've homeschooled Ellie pretty much since February. She's having trouble focusing. It's been six months since Brenda died, and Ellie seemed okay for a while . . ." He swallowed several times. "Teaching isn't difficult. It's her emotional state I'm worried about. I'm afraid she's depressed, and I don't know what to do about that." He stopped and ran his fingers through his hair. "Listen to me unloading on you like you don't have enough going on in your life."

"It's fine," Rose said. "It helps to hear someone else's story rather than keep talking about mine."

He nodded. "Was there something specific you needed today? I can set you up with a library card if you want to take out books while you're in town."

"I might take you up on that, but right now I'm trying to track down some information. Do you have any directories in your reference section?"

"Like phone directories?"

"Hmm, I didn't think of phone directories. They still print them?" Rose pursed her lips as she thought. "Anyway, no, I'm looking for a professional directory. The American Bar Association Directory for licensed attorneys in New York State."

"We carry some professional directories although they're expensive, so we don't update them every year. I'll show you where they are."

Rose followed Carter toward the back room of the library, which displayed books in categories like Society and Culture, American History, World History, Memoirs, and Biographies. To the left of those was the reference section.

Carter scanned the shelves. He snapped his fingers, an oddly noisy characteristic for a librarian. "Here it is." Carter pulled the large tome off the shelf with both hands. "This thing's heavy." He dropped the book onto an oak footstool whose once polished surface was scuffed by thousands of shoes. "There's a table in the room on the other side of the hall where you can look at this. Give me a minute to clean it off. I'll meet you there." He picked up the book, disappeared down a short hallway, and was back a moment later.

"This New York State ABA directory is five years old," he said, putting the book down on the table in front of her. "But unless you're looking for a relatively new member of the bar, you should find what you want. Some of these directories list deceased members as well, with active and death dates."

Heels clicked on the hallway floor and came closer.

"Here you are, Carter. The computer system is on the fritz again." Brianna said hello to Rose, then looked at Carter. "I can't fix it. Can you see what you can do?"

"Sure. Rose, let us know if you need more help." Carter's and Brianna's voices faded as they headed for the reception desk.

Rose ran her hand over the book's cover, feeling the soft material beneath her fingertips. Was it leather? Lawyers had enough money for leather, but it was most likely a similar, less expensive material. After another moment appreciating the book's exterior, she opened it, paged through the table of contents and the beginning pages. The book listed names alphabetically. She flipped the pages to the Ws and found her father's name.

"Webster, Randall Wallace," she read out loud, running her fingers over the text. Under his name were the dates when he passed the bar, when he began practicing in Saratoga County, and when he died. They listed no specialties under his name. "Small-town lawyer" probably didn't count, and that's what Rose had always considered him even though his office was just outside of Saratoga Springs, a city of almost thirty thousand people. But she knew he'd appeared in court throughout the region, in Saratoga Springs, Schenectady, Albany, sometimes traveling to New York City for cases. Isn't that what she remembered her mother complaining about? He traveled too much? But New York City was the only place where he'd need to stay overnight, wasn't it? Maybe Buffalo?

She looked at her father's information a little longer, then thought about KNT. Was she listed under N or T? Rose spent the next half hour flipping pages, finding so many possibilities her brain was ready to explode. Thousands of lawyers last names began with T. Maybe six thousand. And listings that included a middle name of N or two last names with N and T totaled two thousand. Nope, she didn't want to say it, but the words kept running through her mind: needle in a haystack, needle in a haystack.

She let the cover of the book fall, and the sound echoed in the room. Footsteps hurried down the hallway.

"Everything okay?" Carter asked.

"Yes, sort of. The directory contains so many names that I just searched Google for how many attorneys are licensed in New York State. Do you know the answer?" She didn't wait for a response. "Like three hundred thousand. Sheesh."

"You don't have the full name of the person you're looking for?"

"No, only the initials."

"That would complicate it for sure. I'm sorry you couldn't find what you're looking for. Can I help? Is it someone local?"

"Thanks, I may let it be. It's not that important." She looked at Carter. His hair wasn't as neatly combed as it had been when she'd first walked into the library. "Did you find the problem with the computer system?"

"No," he said, running his fingers through his hair, making an even worse mess of it. "Do you know anything about computers?"

"I can turn them on with no problem." Rose laughed, happy to see her comment brought a smile to Carter's face. "I know how to upload photos to my clients, to post photos on social media, and I've worked with WordPress on my website. That's pretty much it."

"Sounds like a lot of skills to me. And forgive me. I forgot you're a photographer."

"It's easy to forget looking at me now."

"I've been meaning to have new pictures taken of the library and update our website. Is that something you could help with? I mean, maybe not tomorrow, and I know you've got to care for your mom. But I'd like to hire you when you have time."

It hadn't even been two weeks since she'd broken her arm, and even though she was focused on her mom's medical issues, she missed work—a lot. Missed the creativity of her work and the challenges. Maybe she could help the library.

"I can't promise how soon, but I would love to work with you." She smiled at Carter. "So that's a 'yes' as soon as I'm able."

"I look forward to working with you as well. And if I can help you track down someone, please let me know. I've lived in the area for more than twenty years, although I've only worked in the library for the last eight years. I know many people and I'd be happy to help if I can."

Rose thought of the photo in her handbag but decided not to show it to Carter. She'd try Bill first. If Bill didn't know who the woman was or how to track her down, she'd take Carter up on his offer.

Rose thanked Carter for his help and took the stairs to the second floor. She'd planned to check in with Ellie but couldn't find her. Frustrated with her lack of progress about the mystery of KNT, she left the library no further along in her search than when she'd begun.

Chapter Twenty-Two

Rose hadn't taken a leisurely stroll along Lake Amelia's Main Street in years. She was eager to peer into storefront windows and see how much the town had changed. Her stomach growled and reminded her it was time for lunch, but she wasn't interested in conversation. That ruled out the diner and Thom's pub. The sun had worked its way higher into the bright blue sky, sending birds singing and soaring upward. The beautiful weather called for lunch outside at a picnic table at the base of the falls or on a waterfront bench overlooking the lake.

She paused in front of the bakery, salivating at the display of muffins, small cakes, oatmeal cookies, and croissants filled with fruit or savory flavors like ham and cheese. The ham and cheese croissant tempted her, as did the egg salad with gouda cheese, but she wanted to try one of the newer places in town. She continued sauntering on the lake side of Main Street, then crossed over to the falls side, past Aunt Tess's diner and two blocks later opened the door to Cuppa Jo coffee shop, which promised egg sandwiches all day long.

The aroma of fresh-ground coffee beans and an espresso

machine shooting out dark brown liquid enticed her farther inside. She surveyed the menu board hanging from the ceiling, wrapped in bright green ivy from the pots behind the banister on the second floor. Voices drifted down from the upper level, where many people stared at their laptop screens. She glanced at the menu again and thought about a fried egg sandwich, but that would be cold by the time she walked to the park. She liked egg salad and deviled eggs cold, but she couldn't tolerate a fried egg sandwich that wasn't hot. She settled on a chicken salad sandwich, picked up a bottle of Saratoga Springs Water, paid the bill, and was on her way a few minutes later, her lunch in a small, brown paper bag.

Most schools this far north didn't end classes until the third week of June, which meant maybe another week without crowds. People visiting the park included older couples and parents with young children. Rose brushed some twigs and leaves off the top of a picnic table and sat. The shop had tucked in a dill pickle spear when they wrapped her sandwich in white paper. She pulled it out and spread the bag on the table like a placemat. As she took her first bite, she glanced around. The park was beautiful, but even this lovely setting couldn't push aside her thoughts about the photo in her handbag and whether Bill could identify the woman.

She shook her head to get rid of those thoughts, that image. It would be nice to linger outside, but like a beagle with its nose to the ground, tracking a scent and unable to focus on anything else, she was determined to find Bill. She tossed her trash into the large metal can on her way out of the park and dropped the water bottle into the green-topped recycling container.

Bill welcomed her with a big smile the moment she walked into the newsroom. "Want a quick tour to see how things have changed?"

She wanted to say no because she was eager to show him

the photo, but she said yes because it was the polite thing to do. Many desks in the newsroom lacked a computer monitor or telephone or someone sitting at them. Fewer storage boxes lined the walls. Didn't anyone use notepads or print rough drafts of their copy anymore? Once there were stacks upon stacks of boxes with old newspapers and copy, waiting to be moved to the basement storage area. Fewer storage boxes and empty desks indicated the ascendency of the digital age and the reduced staff at the *Dispatch*.

The last door on the right led to the photography room and the office of another one of her former mentors. Earl Jackson was no youngster when she learned the news photography trade from him some twenty years ago. He must be nearing retirement. He sat in the back of the room, the ever-present baseball cap in the Mets' signature blue and orange sitting atop whatever hair he had left.

"Hey, Rose. Bill told me you'd be stopping by. Come here, girl!"

He was one of the few people who could get away with calling her girl, although she still cringed at the word. Earl was a good ole guy from the country and had raised three girls with his wife, who headed up the newspapers advertising department and the personnel department. The newspaper was too small to call it HR. Earl and Evelyn might hold the record for the longest tenure of any employee, but they were more than long timers at the *Dispatch*: their ancestors were among the earliest settlers in Eastern New York and neighboring Vermont. If something was going on around town, or a hundred miles in any direction, chances were Earl and Evelyn knew about it. Usually before anyone else.

"You can tell me about that splint on your arm in a minute," Earl said, "but first, how's your mom doing? We were concerned when we heard about her fall."

Rose filled him in on her mother's health, then told him

about the assignment that led to her fractured arm.

"That's a tough break, no pun intended," he said. "How long you in town for?"

"I'm going to take it one day at a time with my mom."

Earl gave her arm a long look. "Can ya work?"

"Not right now. Hopefully, I can pick up a camera again in a few weeks."

"Let me know. We're always looking for help. I know it wouldn't be as exciting as you're used to, but it's a lot less dangerous."

"I'm all for less dangerous." Rose smiled and grasped Earl's hand. "It's nice to see you. I'll keep you and Bill updated."

On their way across the newsroom, Bill and Rose stopped for an introduction of a reporter sitting at his desk. Then the two of them walked into Bill's office, which had a view of the parking lot on one side and the newsroom on the other. Bill closed the door and took the rolling chair behind the desk. Rose plopped onto the chair opposite, as close to his desk as she could, and sat. She pulled the photo out of her handbag and slid it across the desk.

"Why don't you start at the beginning," Bill said, glancing at the photo, then returning his eyes to Rose. "Tell me how you came across this." He lowered his eyes to the photo again and seemed to be studying it.

She explained how she discovered the photo in a book. "There were three books inscribed to my father from KNT. I want to know if this woman," she pointed at the photo, "is KNT and what she meant to my father."

"Why?"

"Excuse me?" Rose raised her eyebrows and stared at Bill.

"It's a simple question. Why do you want to know who she is?"

Rose hadn't expected to explain her motivation. She'd started asking questions because she wanted to know if her father had had an affair. She wanted to know if he'd struggled in his commitment to his marriage. She *needed* to know if having relationship issues was in her DNA, if she was like her father in a way she could not have helped.

"How long has it been since your father passed? About ten years?"

"Twelve."

"It's long past, Rose. What good can come out of pursuing this now?"

She leaned back in her chair and looked down. He wasn't just asking her to explain her motivation, and he didn't seem to buy the argument that she was driven by her journalistic instincts. Defend your actions—that's what he was saying. But she didn't want to tell him everything she'd been thinking, why she'd been digging into her father's past. Maybe asking Bill for help wasn't such a good idea. But he said he would. Did he change his mind?

"The other day, you said you would help me figure out who was in the photo with my dad."

"I said yes without thinking it through. People could get hurt by what you're doing." He glanced out the window into the newsroom. "Did you talk with your mom about this?"

"When I showed her the photo—"

"You showed it to her?" His voice popped higher and louder.

"I asked her if she knew the woman."

Bill rubbed his chin, pursed his lips, and pulled at his lower lip. "That took some guts, I guess. And your mom said what?"

Rose ran her hands over the tops of her thighs to calm herself. "She said she didn't know who the woman is, and she doesn't care. That if something happened with my dad and another woman, it was long ago and none of my business."

"But that doesn't work for you, huh?"

"I might have been able to drop it if I hadn't found the condoms." Rose stopped. Oops. She hadn't planned to mention the condoms.

The color drained from Bill's face. "Condoms? In the books?"

"In Dad's overnight bag. In his shaving kit."

They stared at each other across the desk, across the photo of her father and the woman. Neither one said the condoms proved her father was having an affair, but Rose imagined Bill had the same thought. It was time to move this conversation along back to the original question.

"Do you recognize the woman?" Rose asked.

He picked up the photo again and held it first at arm's length, then brought it closer to his face, dropping his reading glasses from his forehead to his nose, studying the photo so long Rose squirmed in her chair. "I'm not sure. As I recall, your father was quite active in the legal community, in the region, and with the state bar as well. She could be anyone. A lawyer. A client."

"Could you check with Earl? Or Evelyn? They might know."

"And then what do you intend to do with that information?" Bill looked at the photo one more time and set it on his desk.

"What?" Rose asked.

"What will you do with the information?" He repeated the words slowly for emphasis, or like repeating instructions to a new intern who didn't understand an assignment. "What will you do when you find out her name?"

Yep, that would be a logical next step. But Rose was so laser-focused on learning the woman's identity, she hadn't considered what she'd do after she'd found out. Bill stared at her, waiting for an answer.

She let out a long breath. "I'm not sure."

Chapter Twenty-Three

The western sky behind the mountains radiated bright red and gold with bands of purple trying to push the other colors aside. Gladys tugged on the leash and pulled Rose toward Felton Falls Park. The dog stopped to piddle as they walked on the grassy area past the small parking lot on the left. About twenty feet from the falls, Rose dropped onto a bench. She watched Gladys sniff the ground for pieces of food while Bill's voice bounced around inside her head.

"Why do you want to know who she is?" he'd asked her. "What will you do when you find out her name?"

Wasn't it normal to want to know? Maybe? Wouldn't her mother want to know? Perhaps Mom already did and didn't want to admit it. Fine, but why couldn't Bill—and Aunt Tess —understand Rose's desire for information?

We learn to understand ourselves when we understand our parents.

Where did she hear that? Did someone famous say it or was it a line that kept getting shared on social media because somebody liked it? And then a thousand people liked it. And then a million more. We share our parents' DNA, so we can't help acquiring some of their traits and characteristics. Morals too, maybe? Was she trying to understand why her father had an affair to recognize what happened—or didn't—in her own relationships?

As her mind wandered, she came back to how much Kirk knew, and when. He was seven years older. His bedroom was across the hall from their father's home office. He might have heard something, seen something. She'd meant to ask him the last time they'd spoken, but he'd had to drop off the call. It was after eight o'clock. Court must be over for the day. She tapped Kirk's cell number in her phone's Favorites, right below her mom's home and cell numbers.

"Hey, Rose, what's up?"

"Mom's about the same. The home health nurse is terrific handling things I can't help Mom with, and the list is long. Having her there a few hours a day helps me get out of the house, and I realize I need that time for myself."

"Good. What do you and Mom do together? Does she mostly sleep? I know I've woken her when I called."

Rose wished his trial would end soon so he could fly to Lake Amelia, and they could talk in person. She had so many questions and he had some of the answers. Despite wanting to ask Kirk about the photo right away, it would be better to ease into it.

"We also looked at some old family photo albums the other night," Rose said. "I found something else in the attic I want to ask you about."

"I haven't been in the attic in years. I took all my stuff when I moved to Florida."

"Do you recall how Aunt Tess and I packed up Dad's office, donated most of his books to the library, but kept the Grisham novels and other legal thrillers and mysteries?"

"You may have told me. I don't remember."

Kirk sounded disinterested, as he often did when they talked about their father, but Rose pushed ahead. "I found some books I'd never heard of. Three of them were inscribed to Dad from KNT. Do you know who that is?"

"Haven't a clue."

He was flipping through papers, most likely reviewing something connected to the trial. She was losing him.

"There was something else besides the inscriptions. A photo fell out of one of the books. Of Dad with his arm wrapped around the waist of a woman. I can text you the picture."

The silence was so pervasive she thought the call had dropped, which wasn't unusual around Lake Amelia. Cell coverage could be spotty.

"Kirk?"

"Yeah, I'm here."

"You know something, don't you? I always wondered why you and Dad grew apart." Rose's thoughts wandered back to her childhood. She visualized her father and Kirk and recalled a time they barely spoke to each other.

"Dad's dead. It doesn't matter now."

"It matters to me. How old were you?"

"Rose—"

"I'm serious, Kirk, and I'm not taking no for an answer. I deserve to know. How old were you when you and Dad were estranged?"

He sighed but didn't hang up. "I was twelve, maybe thirteen," he said after a few moments. "I used the first-floor bathroom one evening before bedtime. Crossing the hall to my room, I heard Dad talking. His office door was open a crack. He said, 'I can't talk to you now. You shouldn't have called at this hour.' I waited, standing as still as I could. I mean, he was always talking to a client, another lawyer, an investigator, about a case or an issue. Why would he suddenly not be willing to talk to someone? I heard him say, 'No, I can't get away then,' or something like that." Kirk paused like he was digging into his memories for more of the conversation.

"Then Dad's voice dropped. I almost couldn't hear him anymore. He said, 'I miss you too. I'll make it happen as soon as I can. I promise.'

"I wasn't paying enough attention and didn't hear him disconnect the call. Dad's door swung open. He looked at me. 'What're you doing hanging around my office, listening to my calls?' I told him I was on my way back to my bedroom. Dad stared at me as I walked past him. He never said another word about it."

"Do you think he was talking to the woman in the photo?"

"He was upset I'd overheard the conversation, and he didn't know how much I'd heard. That was clear. I didn't know who he was talking with, and I think it's a stretch to connect the two."

"Yeah, I get it," Rose said. "I mean, it's a little suspicious, but—"

Kirk cleared his throat. "There's more."

Rose gulped and pulled the leash tighter. She reached down and picked up Gladys, put her on her lap.

"You know how we'd take field trips to Albany and the state capitol building when we were in middle school or early in high school, maybe both?"

"Yep, I remember."

"I was on a school bus trip about a month after that phone conversation," Kirk continued. "After our tour and on the way out of downtown, our bus detoured down a narrow side street to get around construction. I looked out the window and saw Dad. I raised my hand to wave, but there was a woman with him. He was leaning into her, and she was smiling at him.

They were so close, I thought they were going to kiss. I ducked down before he could see me."

"Did you say anything to him that night at home?"

"He didn't come home that night. I remember because the next night he and Mom had a fight. Then I heard him go into his office, and he didn't come out again until morning. Things were tense with Mom and Dad for a while. I didn't tell him about seeing him with the woman. I mean, what would I say?"

They were both silent. Rose imagined what had been going on between their parents. And the other woman.

"Do you think you'd recognize her if you looked at the photo?"

"Rose, it was a long time ago."

"But you're remembering so much now."

"Yeah, I'm sitting here with my eyes closed and trying to bring it back because my pushy sister asked me to, but I can't recall the woman's face." His voice softened when he spoke again. "I guess it stuck in my mind. Mom and Dad's relationship improved over time, but I never felt close to him again. He betrayed Mom. I was sure of it. He betrayed us. I never forgave him."

Chapter Twenty-Four

Rose thought confirming her father had had an affair would make her happy—she would have learned the truth. But there was no satisfaction. Except maybe it explained the condoms. If he was screwing around— Rose thought the words, then revised—if he was having an affair with another woman, at least the condoms proved he was doing it safely. *Yay, Dad, there's one in your favor.* She shook her head, trying to clear her mind of any more images of her father and the other woman.

She stroked Gladys's back, enjoying the softness of the dog's silky hair while her brain and her heart fought each other over what Kirk said. Her brain wanted to understand what had happened, wanted to know who the other woman was, maybe wanted to find her so she could ask her why she had an affair with her father. Like that was a good idea. Rose realized it was her father, not the woman, she wanted to interrogate: Why had he risked damaging his reputation? Had he stopped loving her mother? Had he stopped loving his family? Her? Had he ever thought about leaving them? If her father were alive today, Rose would hit him with a barrage of questions. Maybe with her fist to his chest.

Her brain hurt so much she wanted to scream. Her heart ached with such pain she wanted to cry. Kirk knew there had been tension between her parents because he saw it firsthand. Rose was too young to know what was going on, but sometimes she could tell her mother was upset, like the time Rose was in the hospital and her mother complained to her father about traveling too much. Was Rose's home life more unsettled than she recalled? Was the tension Rose carried in her body now planted there during childhood? Had she blocked out painful memories?

Rose leaned over and dropped her head into Gladys' neck, smelling the combination of sweet grass and lemon shampoo. She closed her eyes, nuzzled the dog, and was rewarded with a quick lick on her hand. Then another. She kept loving the dog and letting the night settle over her.

When she straightened up and opened her eyes, the beautiful clouds were giving way to darkness. Streetlights cast a glow around the parking lot and floodlights bounced off the falls. Other parts of the park where tall, leafy trees and thick pines nestled close together, were almost pitch black, including where she and Gladys sat on a bench with a large maple tree maybe ten feet behind them. No one else was in the park. Lake Amelia was about as safe a place as you could find, but the "city girl" in her, the single woman who lived near Philadelphia, was on alert.

A vehicle illuminated the small parking lot at the end of Falls Road. The lot was popular with cyclists, who could choose from three different bike racks to lock their bikes. The approaching vehicle—it looked like an SUV—cruised the lot, likely unaware of Rose and Gladys in the shadows.

The driver stopped and turned off the headlights. Gladys gave a little bark that was too soft to be heard by anyone except

Rose, who quieted the dog with kisses. Someone's sneakers crunched on the gravel between the lot and the bike racks. A beep sounded. She squinted to see better. A splash of light caught a piece of red metal. Was it a bike? The item dropped into the back of the vehicle with a loud clunk. The driver closed the cargo door. Rose's news nose twitched. Were they picking up their own bike, or stealing it?

She turned her body to face the lot better and wrapped her arms around Gladys. "Hey," she called out as she stood. "What are you doing?"

The driver hopped into the front seat, closed the door, and sped off. They waited until they were farther down the road before turning on the vehicle's headlights. Rose pulled out her phone, thought of the conversation with Deputy Stover about the investigation into bike thefts, and found her number. Three rings in, her call went to voicemail. Rose left a brief message, explaining that she thought she'd seen a bike stolen from the Felton Falls Park. She thought she should dial 9-1-1 next when her phone vibrated.

"Deputy Stover returning your call. Tell me what's going on."

Rose filled her in.

"Did you get a license plate number?"

"No, it was too dark."

"Did you get the make and color of the vehicle?" Police chatter and sirens filled the background while Rose thought about what she'd seen.

"Uh, no," Rose stammered, realizing how little information she had. Some journalist. "You know how quickly the evening sky can fade away and the streetlights haven't come up to full strength. The park is in the shadows. It was a dark SUV; I could tell that much. And it looked like they put the bike in the cargo area."

"Male or female?"

"I'm not sure, but the way they lifted the bike and dropped it into the back of the SUV, it seemed like a guy." Rose paused and heard more police chatter on the phone line. "Where are you?"

"I can't say, Rose, and I can't do much about a possible stolen bike at the moment."

"But isn't it more likely you can nail the guy the sooner you go after him?"

"Yes, and I could put out a BOLO for a dark SUV, even though that's vague without a plate number. But there's a situation going down and almost every available law enforcement unit around Washington County is involved. No one's going after a stolen bike tonight."

Rose had gone online and investigated the stolen bike issue after her conversation with Stover. She'd read only five percent of stolen bikes were returned to their owners. Thieves resold the bikes as fast as they stole them, often for spare parts. Dealing in stolen bikes was a profitable venture, as long as the thieves didn't get caught. Mountain or trail bikes were popular in the Adirondacks, the Green Mountains in Vermont, and the Berkshires in Massachusetts, all within a stone's throw of Lake Amelia. A trail bike costs a couple thousand dollars. Top-of-the-line trail bikes could run six thousand.

"Do I drop it? It seems wrong to let it go without filing a report or something."

"It's not like I don't care, Rose. I'll connect with you tomorrow and see what I can do. Unless what's happening here ties me up for a second day."

"And what's happening there?" Rose pushed.

Deputy Stover laughed. "You're persistent, I'll give you that. Check out the local news—radio or TV tonight. Newspapers tomorrow. That should satisfy your curiosity."

"I'm a journalist, remember? Why can't you tell me?"

"Because it's not my show. See you tomorrow." The deputy's voice and background chatter ended.

Rose stared at her phone. What good was asking questions if you couldn't get the information? Her thoughts returned to her father's affair and put her back in a foul mood as she and Gladys shuffled home.

Chapter Twenty-Five

The June mornings were coming earlier and brighter. Rose couldn't wait to get outside. Nurse Lettie had phoned that she'd be coming later than usual. Not good timing. Rose needed to burn off some energy. She was stressed about her mom's health and worried about her wounded arm. She couldn't stand not working because she needed to get absorbed in a creative outlet, and her conversation with Kirk replayed over and over. One more straw on her burdened back and she would break.

If she'd been like her brother, she would have grabbed golf clubs and headed for the driving range, whacking golf balls one right after another. If she'd been like Aunt Tess, she would have cooked food for about a hundred people before eight a.m. If she'd been able-bodied like her friend and colleague Christine, she would have been up at five to shoot photos of sunrise at the shore and jog on the beach. But she was Rose. Stuck in Lake Amelia with her mother dying and her father's past exploding around her.

She was Daddy's Little Girl and always tried to catch his attention with her antics to bring a smile to his face, or sought a hug so she could bury her nose in his earthy scent and musky aftershave. From an early age, she strived to earn his approval because she wanted him to be proud of her. It's fortunate she didn't know all this before her mother asked to look at the family photo albums. If Mom were to ask now, Rose would find an excuse. There was no way she could look at photos of her father without bile churning in her stomach.

Rose needed to wash away the sour taste in her mouth. The doorbell rang while she was gulping down a glass of water. Rose greeted Nurse Lettie, told her that her mom was still asleep and that she was heading out.

Rose had no destination in mind, but she turned left at the sidewalk, then took the next street toward the mountains. She'd only be able to walk a couple more blocks before the tall pines, red and green maple trees, hearty oaks, and rhododendrons blocked her way up the hillside. In addition to the trails around Felton Falls, there were a couple of small parking areas on Falls Road with marked trailheads leading into the woods. Falls Road curved around to Main Street. Rose's feet hit the sidewalk with determination, her stress, anger, and sadness dissipating with each step. She reached Church Street and turned left, then passed a couple of chain hotels whose parking lots were about half full, until she got to Main Street.

At the corner of Main and Church, Rose paused, contemplating which direction to take. She saved herself the trouble of deciding by taking a seat on the closest bench. She scratched the inside of her wrist where the splint agitated her skin and stared out into the deep blue waters of Lake Amelia. A few fishing boats bobbed on the surface off in the distance. People ambled about on the sidewalk, others jogged or walked with purpose, and a few ventured onto the pier to get closer to the water.

Kirk had confirmed their father's infidelity, but that wasn't enough. Rose wanted to learn the woman's identity.

And what came after that? Bill had asked Rose what she would do with the information. She didn't know the next steps. Not yet.

Rose had planned to call Bill last night about the possible bike theft she'd witnessed at Felton Falls, but she was so distracted when she got home, she'd forgotten. It was too early for him to be in the office, but she pulled out her phone and tapped on his number before she forgot again. She left a message, explained what she'd witnessed, and suggested he contact the Lake Amelia police or Deputy Sheriff Stover. Would Stover call Rose today? According to the news, law enforcement officials had descended on a major drug operation last night in Washington and Fulton counties and arrested several people. Stover could be busy with the drug bust again today.

It was after nine. The library was open. Maybe she could see how Ellie was doing. Anything to focus on something else.

The library was a short walk away. She pulled the door open and stepped inside, letting the quiet of the room and the smell of printed paper embrace her. Brianna was on the phone. Rose gave her a quick wave and headed for the new releases. Reading before bedtime always helped her unwind, and she'd finished the books she'd brought from home. Her mom had a variety of paperbacks on the shelves in the living room, but Rose wanted to check out more recent releases. She picked up a few books and put them back and finally found two mysteries she thought she'd enjoy. Then she climbed the stairs to the second floor in search of Ellie.

At the top of the stairs, a young mother sat on the floor with a toddler, who pulled out one picture book after another and dropped them on the carpet. The pudgy hands tugged another book off the shelves and the child squealed. Her mom mouthed, "Sorry," but Rose waved her hand and shook her head. She ventured into the room with Young Adult books and found Ellie sitting in an overstuffed chair, using one of the chair's sides as back support, her legs draped over the other side.

"Hi, it's Rose Webster," she said, walking over to Ellie.

A quick glance up. "I remember."

"Do you mind if I sit there?" Rose pointed at the matching chair on the other side of the round pine table.

"Are you going to read or ask questions?"

"I don't know yet. What would you prefer?"

"To read, of course." Ellie looked back down at the book in her hands and made an exaggerated motion of turning the page.

Rose settled into the chair and opened one of her books. She leafed through the book for a few minutes, then turned to Ellie.

"Do you mind if I ask you a question?"

"We're supposed to be reading."

"I know, but I thought maybe you would talk with me. My mom is sick and sometimes it helps to talk about it with someone else." Rose's voice cracked and she took a deep breath. Her emotions caught her off guard.

"What's wrong?" Ellie asked, looking up from her book.

"She's very ill, and there's not much I can do about it."

Ellie looked at Rose, then dropped her chin. The girl was silent for so long Rose thought she wouldn't respond. Barely above a whisper, Ellie said, "My mom died a while ago."

Rose waited, but Ellie didn't say anything else.

"I heard, and I'm sorry. You see, that's why I wanted to talk. I know it's not the same thing, but, well, it's hard, isn't it, when your mom is sick or gone?"

Ellie sniffed and wiped her eyes with the hem of her sleeve. "I'm sorry about your mom, too." Her head remained lowered, but her little shoulders shook.

Rose fought the urge to hug Ellie, pretty sure the girl

wouldn't welcome her touch and unsure if it was appropriate. She wasn't as defensive as Rose had thought, but Ellie's pain was close to the surface.

"I thought maybe, if you didn't mind, we could talk once in a while," Rose said softly. "Not everyone can relate to what we're going through. What you've already gone through. Moms are special."

Ellie swiped her eyes once more and turned to Rose. "Maybe we could. I'll think about it. But if you don't mind, right now I want to read."

"Okay." Rose opened her book to the first chapter and started reading. After about half an hour, Rose closed her book and stood. "I've got to go, but I'll stop in again. We can chat or read, whatever you feel like."

"I guess that would be okay," Ellie said. "I'm here most days." She paused. "Mornings are best."

"I'll remember that." Rose felt Ellie's eyes on her as she left the room.

Chapter Twenty-Six

"Can you meet me in the parking lot at the end of Falls Road in half an hour?"

"Sure, Deputy Stover." Rose was about to ask whether she was still working the drug bust, but Stover had already disconnected the call. It was close to ten o'clock. Not too late for another cup of coffee and maybe a pastry. She covered the two blocks to the bakery in record time. Stover had been drinking coffee at the diner when they'd first met, but Rose couldn't remember if she used cream and sugar. She grabbed a couple of packets of sugar just in case and asked the woman behind the counter for two strawberry rhubarb muffins. Blueberry bushes in the area were bursting with fruit and blueberry pastries would soon replace the strawberry ones. Rose hated to see the strawberry pastries disappear, but she also loved blueberries. She loved any fruit tucked inside a pastry.

Stover's sheriff 's department SUV was in the lot. She stood near the bike rack. Rose wandered over, holding out a cup of coffee as she got closer.

"For me?" Stover nodded toward the outstretched cup.

"Yep. Sounds like you worked late last night. I don't know how you take your coffee, though."

"Black, like me," she laughed.

"I have some packets of sugar if you want them."

"No sugar, thanks, although my fellow deputies would say I could use a little sugar. But I don't pay attention to them." Stover took the cup, removed the lid, and took a sip. "You have no idea how much I need another coffee this morning. Thanks."

"And a strawberry rhubarb muffin if you're hungry." She held out the bag. "Don't get greedy. There's one in there for me."

Stover's head tilted. "Are you calling me greedy?"

"Kidding," Rose said quickly. "I didn't want you to think they're both for you. I'm a little possessive about my muffins."

Stover almost spit out her coffee. "Not saying a word," she said, shaking her head and laughing. She pulled a muffin out of the bag and bit into the small pastry. "Tell me what you saw last night." Stover listened as she ate her muffin, then pulled out a pen from a chest pocket and a small notebook from her back pants pocket. A few crumbs clung to Stover's upper lip, and she brushed them away with her notepad.

Rose pointed to the bench where she and Gladys had been sitting. Stover walked over with her. A Lake Amelia police cruiser pulled into the lot while Rose was telling Deputy Stover what she'd seen. A young man in a blue uniform got out and put on his hat as he marched over to them.

"Officer Coyne, glad you could join us." Stover asked if Rose and the officer knew each other. When they shook their heads, Stover introduced them and asked Rose to tell her story one more time. The three of them walked over to the bike rack, the two law enforcement officials eyeing the rack and talking about the latest bike theft. Rose sipped her coffee and watched.

"Thanks for calling the department last night and leaving a message," Officer Coyne said to Rose. "As you may know, we're a part-time force except in the summer, but we still rely on the county sheriff's department especially at night because we're shorthanded. And because these bike thefts have been occurring in several area counties, the county sheriffs' departments are in charge. Deputy Stover's one of the lead investigators. But if you see anything else in town, call 9-1-1." He touched the tip of his hat and left.

"What's next?" Rose asked.

"I'm going to write this up and we'll see if we can track down this dark SUV. Chances are slim we'll catch the person, but we'll try. Thanks for letting us know." Stover smiled. "And for the coffee and muffin."

Rose sauntered home, where she offered to split the muffin with her mom because she'd been so distracted thinking about meeting with Deputy Stover that she didn't think to buy a pastry for her mother. Or for Nurse Lettie, who brushed her apology aside, saying she didn't need any more calories taking up residence on her hips. And then Lettie went home, leaving Rose and her mother in the living room in their recliners.

"Did Lettie make lunch?" Rose asked.

"Yes. We had tuna sandwiches. I don't like tuna as much as I used to. I don't think it tastes as good, but I ate it anyway. There's some left if you haven't eaten."

Rose said she hadn't and went into the kitchen. She tried to stay in the moment, eating her sandwich and looking out the sliding glass doors onto the patio, but it was a struggle. She knew more about her father's past, more than she wanted to know, but the puzzle was coming together with answers to her questions. Answers she would not share with her mother to keep peace in the family. But she needed to talk with her mother about some things Nurse Lettie had mentioned. Rose wasn't sure how that would go, but she needed to try. She put her plate in the dishwasher and returned to the living room.

"Mom, Lettie asked me to talk with you about a few things. It would be best if we went over them now."

"Before I become too ill to have the conversation?"

Rose shifted in her chair. "If you want to put it that way."

"I'm a realist. I know what's needed," her mother said. "Right after your father died, Kirk suggested I update my will right away so that if I died suddenly like your father did, you two wouldn't have to deal with estate lawyers. He helped me draft a will, making sure you two are co-executors. I signed the paperwork in the presence of a notary. That's one piece of business we don't need to worry about."

"You've given Kirk your power of attorney, right?"

Her mother nodded.

"But you haven't decided whether to sign the DNR, have you?"

Her mother squinted her eyes.

"DNR," Rose said again. "Do Not Resuscitate. The form that—"

"Oh, yes, I remember now. Nurse Lettie discussed it with me. So did the social worker in the hospital."

"And?" Rose didn't want to push, but she knew her mother had to decide whether to be hospitalized if she had another emergency, or to begin hospice care.

"I'll get to it, I promise." Her mother's eyes clouded over. Rose didn't think they were tears, more that she'd lost focus. Literally. Staring into nothingness and seeing it.

"Mom," Rose said, her voice low and gentle, "you can change your mind if you've had second thoughts about treatment."

"It's not so much that. I . . . I don't want to be a burden to you and Kirk."

Rose stood and went over to the footstool next to her

mother's chair, taking her hand as she sat. "You will never be a burden, Mom. I'll do my best to take care of you. Nurse Lettie and I will. Kirk will help. You don't need to think about those things. We'll manage."

"Sometimes I can't think about anything else," her mother said, blowing out a long breath. "I think more about you and your brother than I do about dying." Suddenly, the tears came. Rose bit her lip as she handed her mother some tissues. She'd rarely seen her mother cry. Once was when they put down their dog with metastatic cancer, and the other time was the day they buried her father. If her mother cried over her illnesses and the idea of her death, she'd done it out of view of her children, the way women and men of her generation did.

Her mother tried to hide her tears, but Rose squeezed her hand and told her she didn't need to be brave for Rose and Kirk, that she needed to take care of herself first and foremost.

"First and foremost. How formal. You sound like an attorney." Her mom laughed through her tissue, then suddenly looked serious again. "A mother never stops taking care of her children, Rose. I have taken care of you for thirty-nine years, not always on a daily basis, but I've always put you and Kirk first. It's what a mother does. All her life. I can't stop now."

Chapter Twenty-Seven

What a day. First, she made Ellie cry, then her mother.

Her mom slept the rest of the afternoon while Rose fired up her laptop to catch up on emails and texts. She'd almost gone into her father's office and closed the door so she wouldn't wake her mother with pings and voices, but she chose the patio instead. The air was fresher, with fewer triggers.

Her eyes drifted from the two magnolia trees in full bloom to the different flower beds her mother had cultivated with love over the years. Deep maroon Lenten roses were still producing new blossoms; the red roses on her right were close enough to smell their sweetness; and the peony plants, whose soft pink buds expanded every day, were bursting at the seams. Bright zinnia blossoms covered the flower bed on the right. Her mother tended to them so she could put colorful bouquets on the table all summer long. The gardens were beautiful, and as Rose took them in, she realized they all needed tending. She thought about hiring someone—a high school student maybe—to help weed and water the gardens.

She'd check with Aunt Tess or Mrs. Shaw to see if anyone helped them. Then Rose noticed no one had mowed the grass in a while. Yep, she'd need to find help soon.

The phone vibrated on the table.

"Hey, it's Bill. Is this a good time?"

"Sure. What's up?"

"I've been checking into that photo, and I've found some information."

"Okay," Rose said slowly, reacting to something she heard in Bill's voice. Caution? Reluctance? "Do you have time to talk now?"

"No, I don't, and I'd rather do it in person. How about tomorrow morning? Does nine-thirty work for you?" Bill asked.

"That's fine. How about the bakery? I'll buy you a cup of coffee."

"Nah, let's meet at the paper. Then I won't have to carry these photos around."

"Photos. Plural?" She was hoping for a clue to the woman's name. She hadn't expected Bill to come up with additional photos.

"Yes, and I hope it's not more than you want to know. See you in the morning."

The sky wasn't light, and it hadn't been for the last three hours Rose sat staring out the window. She wanted to reach out and pull the sun from behind the horizon to hurry the day along.

She shuffled down the stairs and into the kitchen, relieved her mother wasn't awake. She never could hide her emotions from her mother, and right now they might as well have been silk-screened on her nightshirt. Rose wasn't good at compartmentalizing her brain or her emotions, but she needed to figure it out and put her sick mother in one box and her cheating father in another. When she was with her mom, she needed to be fully present. Her mom deserved nothing less.

Rose poured her coffee and returned to the second floor. Showering was still a challenge, but thanks to Lettie, she had a plastic sleeve to slide over her splint. Unfortunately, it reminded her of a condom, and she couldn't wait to get it back off again. She showered, dried her hair as best she could, and dressed in jeans and a cotton shirt. When she came downstairs, her mother was sitting at the kitchen table drinking a cup of tea.

"Morning, Mom." Rose walked over and kissed her on the top of her head, then sat down across from her. "How'd you sleep?"

"I slept well and feel pretty good this morning. I think our discussion yesterday eased my mind of a few concerns."

"Thanks for opening up about what you're thinking and feeling. It helps." Rose reached over and patted her mother's frail hand.

"What are you up to today?"

"I'm headed to the *Dispatch* to meet with Bill."

"You were there the other day, weren't you? What are you meeting about?"

Rose squirmed in her chair. "Not a formal meeting, more chatting about this and that."

Gladys yipped. Rose twisted at the waist with minimal pain for a change, reached back with her left arm, and opened the sliding door. The dog ran over to her dish and slurped the fresh water in her bowl.

"I'll take Gladys for a walk first. I know she has a lot of energy, and it would be good to stretch her legs."

"Oh, she'd love that. And so would I."

Rose leashed the dog and hustled out the door. She tried to enjoy the solitude of the morning and soak in her surroundings while Gladys sniffed the grass, then left her scent to let other dogs know she'd been there. Rose was back in the house thirty minutes later, then out again within five minutes. It'd be easier to sit on the steps of the newspaper waiting for Bill to arrive than to hang around home and watch the clock.

Rose noticed the window blinds as she and Bill crossed the newsroom toward his office. She'd rarely seen them closed like they were now. He shut the door behind them, led her over to the small round table in front of his bookcases, and pulled out a chair for her. Bill took a few steps over to his desk, picked up a folder, then returned to the table and sat beside her. His hand rested on top of the file folder. She studied his face and, for one of the few times in her life, held her tongue, waiting for Bill to speak.

"I used the photo you gave me and your father's name to search our databases," he explained. "Articles and images. One of the *Dispatch's* articles from the mid-1980s included images from an event in downtown Albany. I accessed the full file of photos—they were stored digitally even back then—and went through them." He opened the folder and pulled out a couple of photos, then closed the folder again.

Rose's nose twitched. Her hands shook. She reached for the photos, but Bill held on to them.

"This photo is similar to the one you gave me." He stared at the photo for a moment, then laid it on the table in front of her. "And here's another from the same event." He laid that one next to the first. "Her name is Keisha Tyler. I thought I'd recognized her when you first gave me the photo, but I wanted to make sure."

"Her initials are KT. Does she have a middle name? One that begins with an N?"

Bill glanced at his notepad. "Norella. How did you know that?"

"The inscriptions in the books where I found the photo were from KNT. TNT might be better initials. Where does she live? How does she know—did she know my dad?"

"I'm getting to that. She's an attorney, originally from Newburgh. Graduated from Albany Law School and joined the bar a few years after your father. She stayed in the Albany area, worked for the Public Defender's office for a while, then joined up with the ACLU, the Capital District chapter." Bill pulled another photo from the folder. "This is her headshot from the ACLU in the mid-'90s."

Rose looked at the image. No question, this was the same woman. She could see why her father was drawn to her warm smile and bright eyes. Rose looked closer and realized the woman's smooth skin was darker in the official photo than in the candid ones. Her hair was also darker. An afro. "Did she ever marry? Have children?"

"She married in 1993, a fellow attorney with the ACLU. They didn't have children."

"Are they still in the Albany area? Is she still alive?"

"Yes. But there's more."

Rose's legs bounced in the chair, the carpet muffling the sound of her sneaker heels pounding the floor. "Is there a reason you're drawing this out?" She saw additional photos in the folder on the table and didn't like the pace of Bill's presentation, which was a bit lawyerly, like laying out a case.

"I'm trying to put the information in context. Okay? Let's go back to the late '80s. A couple of years after the photo you gave me." He pulled another image from the folder. "This was at an ABA event in Buffalo. You'll see your dad and Keisha. It's a tight shot so you don't see his arm around her. What do you see?"

Rose took one look at the photo and knew what he meant. "Tension. They're both tense."

"This may be why." Bill took the last photo out of the

folder and put it on the table in front of her. He added no description; he didn't need to. Standing between her father and Keisha Tyler was a little girl, a toddler, maybe a couple of years old, her black hair tight and curly. She held one of the woman's hands and one of Rose's father's hands. And the girl looked at him with such love, the way Rose had looked at her father in the photos from the family album. Rose slapped her hands to her chest as if to keep her heart from shooting out.

"Are you telling me my father not only had an affair with this woman, he also had a child?"

Chapter Twenty-Eight

Rose couldn't remember leaving the newspaper office or wandering with no destination. Home was not an option, neither was the diner. She couldn't go anywhere except around one block after another. Finally, exhausted, hungry, and thirsty, she marched into the pub and asked Thom for an Amelia Ale as she passed the bar and sank into a chair at a table in the corner.

"Thirsty today?" Thom asked with a broad smile as he put a cardboard coaster on the table with the logo of green pine trees and brown mountains, followed by a pint of heady ale, also embellished with the pub's logo.

Rose gulped down a quarter of the beer before she took a breath. She lifted the glass toward her mouth to take another long drink, but Thom reached out and gently pushed her hand back down.

He leaned in and spoke with tender words. "What's up? Is it your mom? Your arm?"

Rose kept her eyes on her beer and shook her head once.

"Do you want to talk about it?"

"I can't."

He gave her his most charming smile, sat on the chair next to her, and bumped his shoulder against hers. "Once upon a time, you could talk to me about anything and everything. At all hours of the day and night."

His efforts couldn't coax a smile from Rose.

"We were kids. We thought life was complicated. Ha! It wasn't nearly as much as it is now." She tried to raise the glass, but his hand still rested on her arm. She looked at his hand, looked into his eyes, tilted her head, and raised her eyebrows. He let her take a drink.

"If you're going to chug beer, you need some food," Thom said. "You're not driving, are you?"

"I live, like, two blocks away, you know." She needed a napkin to wipe the foam off her mouth, but there wasn't one on the table. She reached over, pulled a few napkins out of the gray metal dispenser, and passed them over her lips.

"I'm making sure. Sometimes you come in after running errands out of town. What do you want to eat?"

She protested, but he shook his head.

"I am not pouring you another beer unless you eat. Second, you look like you need food. What'll it be? And not a salad. You need something hearty."

"You drive a hard bargain. I'll have a grilled chicken sandwich."

"The house favorite? Loaded?"

"Sure, but skip the onion. Now, can I have another beer?" She gave Thom her most charming smile.

"Coming up. But I'm pouring you a short one. Make it last."

Rose stared at the walls, nodding at Thom when he put a fresh beer in front of her and took away her empty mug. He came back again with a tall glass of ice water. She sniffed the savory aromas of her sandwich when he set the plate down several minutes later, along with a fork and knife.

"Eat up. I'll be back in a minute."

She finished her glass of beer first, began taking small bites from the edges of the sandwich, then finally bigger bites. She thought about her mindfulness meditation training and tried to focus on each morsel of food as she ate. It worked for maybe two bites. But nothing stuck for long. Her mind returned to her conversation with Bill. To the new photos. To the little girl in the one photo.

Thom took the seat beside her again.

"Let's see. Where were we? Right, you were going to tell me why you're upset."

"Thom, thanks for taking care of me, but I can't talk about what's going on."

He appealed to her again with the former boyfriend/girlfriend card. "Let's try this. We'll share secrets. I'll tell you something I haven't shared with anyone else, and you share something with me."

She shook her head slowly. No, she didn't want to do this, but he was tenderly persistent, laying his hand on her arm again as he spoke. "I worry about my kids every day. I know that's probably normal, but some days my fears catch my breath, and I can't breathe." His voice cracked. "I'm afraid I can never do enough to protect them from a psychopath with a gun, from sexual predators who're always looking for new targets, from monsters who try to steal their innocence."

"You and Desi must talk about this stuff."

"Oh sure, we talk about parenting and our worries for the kids. But I haven't brought up these deepest fears of mine. She has enough mother anxiety. I don't want to burden her. I try to suck it up and deal with my own stuff. Your turn. And tell me something real that's bugging you right now."

Rose took a sip of water. "I recently learned my father had an affair when Kirk and I were kids."

His head jerked in surprise. "How did you find that out?"

She explained in a few short sentences, watching his eyebrows rise and fall as he listened. "Your turn."

He hesitated. "Something's going on with Paul. I'm afraid he's into drugs again and I don't want to see him locked up. Again." He recalled how an accident several years ago at the garage where Paul worked as a mechanic required surgery, which led to opioids to control the pain, which led to an addiction. "Then he started dealing—not much but enough to get into trouble—to pay for his habit. He says he's clean now. He borrowed some money from me to open a bike repair place with a couple of his buddies a year or so ago. They also bought an old garage in Washington County to store bikes. I worry because sometimes he says he needs more money but won't say for what. Worse than that, I see how much my mother worries about him." He tilted his head and smiled. "Your turn."

Thom's eyes held hers with the intensity of their youth, reminding her of how they'd shared secrets when they were teens, when they felt they understood each other in ways no one else could. He'd never betrayed her trust. Thom may be the only person capable of understanding what she was going through.

"Remember how I used to talk about wanting a baby sister when I was growing up?" He nodded. "I loved Kirk, but he was a boy, older, and we weren't close. I wanted a baby sister to play with, to have as a best friend. My mom told me she and my father couldn't have any more children, that they were lucky to have me because of medical issues." She bit the inside of her lower lip, a habit she'd worked hard to break. Biting her lips, chugging beer, it appeared some old habits were coming back, thanks to the stress. Thom waited for her to speak again.

"Well, it couldn't have been my father with the medical issue, because it seems he not only had an affair with a woman, he also had a daughter. My baby sister."

Thom looked like he was the one who needed a beer. Or something stronger.

"Holy sh—" He slapped his hand over his mouth. "Are you kidding me? No, no, of course you're not. I mean, that's . . ." He quit talking and stared at her. "How did you find out? But I don't need to know. I, oh, Rose. I can't believe this. What are you going to do?"

She finished her glass of water and pushed a deep breath out of her lungs. "The only thing I can do. I'm going to find her."

The silence between them accented the increasing noise around the bar. The lunch crowd streamed in, seeking cool drafts and hot sandwiches.

"I'm sorry to have you tell me something so important and then abandon you," Thom said, looking toward the bar. "Looks like Bob has his hands full. I've got to go. Call me if you need to talk. Anytime, as long as it's not too close to lunch or dinner."

"Could you please bring me another short beer and a check?" she said. "I promise I won't chug it. I need to sit a while longer."

He hesitated.

"It's okay. I'm fine. At least better. Don't worry." Thom was right. They'd shared deep secrets years ago, and she was glad he pushed her to share what was troubling her. It helped, as much as anything could right now.

She finished her beer, paid the tab, and walked outside, blinking at the bright sunshine. A short walk home wasn't enough. Rose strolled to the park at the base of the falls and watched the cascading water until she was ready to deal with life again.

Aunt Tess was in the recliner talking with her mom when Rose stepped through the front door. The three of them chatted for a while about things that didn't mean much.

"Rose, you're awfully quiet," Aunt Tess said. "What did you do today?"

"I walked around town some, stopped by to see Bill at the newspaper and talk shop for a bit. I'm tired, that's all. I'll clean up the kitchen and head upstairs."

Less than thirty minutes later, she sat in bed, leaning against a cushion of pillows, studying the photos from Bill. She knew the woman's name. She would search the internet or return to the library and check the ABA listing to find out where she worked. And then she was going to find her half-sister.

Chapter Twenty-Nine

Rose lay in bed and inhaled the sweet summer air drifting in through the open window. She rolled onto her back, raised her left arm over her head and stretched, doing a one-arm snow angel in the sheets. She threw off the top sheet and rolled onto her left side, stretching and looking out the window. Then she did some slow shoulder stretches with her right arm, lifting it less than two inches. She needed to exercise more and not in the comfort of her bed. Rose went into the bathroom, brushed her teeth, and tiptoed downstairs. Halfway down the stairs she saw the empty recliner and realized her mother must have slept in her bedroom last night.

She made a beeline for the coffeemaker and didn't hear the dog whining. Only after she'd measured the water, poured the ground coffee into the basket, and hit the "on" button was she aware of the dog's soft barks. She was ready for her first trip outside. Rose tiptoed into her mother's bedroom and lifted Gladys off the end of the bed. The dog seemed reluctant to leave, but Rose shushed her by rubbing behind her ears. She opened the sliding glass door and put Gladys outside on the patio. The coffee pot gurgled. Rose grabbed a mug off the lower shelf of a cupboard, sniffed the fresh brew as she poured it, and turned to check on Gladys. Had the dog even gone into the yard to do her business? She was sitting at the door, staring at Rose, and wiggling.

After setting her steaming mug on the kitchen table, Rose opened the door and knelt to greet the dog. But Gladys raced past her and back to her mother's bedroom. Rose followed her and knocked on the open door. When her mother didn't respond, she tiptoed over to the side of the bed where Gladys was on her hind legs, pawing at the sheets. Rose touched her mother's arm.

"Mom?"

Her mother had always been a light sleeper. With the meds and her compromised health, she now slept later into the morning but usually awakened at the sound of Rose's voice or the touch of her hand.

"Mom?" she repeated. She reached out, placed her hand on top of her mother's. It was cold. She squeezed, but her mother didn't respond. "Mom!" Her mother stirred; her eyes opened a little.

"I'm . . . some . . . thing . . . wrong . . ."

Rose's heart pounded likes waves of heavy rain slamming against the sliding glass doors. Rose reached over to the phone on the bedside table and dialed 9-1-1. "I think my mom's had a stroke," she told the woman who answered her call. "Please send an ambulance." She gave her address, hung up, and dialed the diner. Iris picked up after the fifth ring.

"It's Rose Webster," she said. "Please tell my aunt I think my mom had a stroke. An ambulance is on its way to our house." She hung up and turned to her mother. "Mom, stay with me. Can you hear me?" But her mother's eyes were closed, her breathing shallow. "Hurry," she said under her breath to the EMTs. "Hurry the heck up."

Several anxious minutes later, the doorbell rang, followed by pounding on the front door. Rose raced to let the EMTs in. One of the EMTs carried a black bag slung over his shoulder; the other peppered her with questions as they walked quickly toward her mother's bedroom.

"Was your mom alert when you tried to wake her?"

"She said a few words that something was wrong, but that was it. She was hospitalized about a week and a half ago after she fainted and has been diagnosed with stage 3 lung cancer. And she's on medication because she's anemic."

He paused. "Is she being treated for the lung cancer with chemo or radiation?"

"No, she isn't. She hasn't made a decision about treatment."

"Does she have a DNR?"

"No. Like I said, she hasn't made a decision about treatment, so she hasn't signed any documents like a DNR."

One paramedic stepped to her mother's side and tried to communicate with her, but she wasn't responding. He lifted her eyelids and shined the small flashlight he'd pulled out of his pants' side pocket into her eyes. The other EMT dropped his bag onto the floor beside the bed, zipped it open, and pulled out a stethoscope. The two interspersed their questions to her mother with comments to each other about her pulse, her oxygen level.

Rose held Gladys and stroked the soft spot on the top of her nose. Officer Coyne appeared in the doorway.

"Can I help?"

Rose looked from the police officer to the paramedics.

The EMT listening to her mother's heart spoke up. "Her symptoms don't appear to be life-threatening. I want to get her on oxygen and into the ambulance. You and Ed get the stretcher and portable oxygen."

Rose wanted to help, but she was in the way. She stepped

into the kitchen and watched Paramedic Ed and Officer Coyne hurry down the front porch steps. A minute later, they returned with the stretcher. She stepped back and gave them room to roll the gurney down the short hallway. More footsteps pounded up the front steps. Aunt Tess rushed in.

"Rose, honey, what's going on?" She enveloped Rose and Gladys in a hug, then stepped back.

"I couldn't wake her," Rose said, fighting tears and explaining the morning events.

"Do they know how serious it is?"

"I don't know." Rose's voice was sharper than she'd intended.

"Okay, okay," she said, rubbing Rose's shoulder. "Here, let me take Gladys for you. She doesn't weigh a lot, but it's easier to hold her with two arms. Better yet," she said, lifting the dog, "I'm going to take her to Mrs. Shaw's."

She was out the door, and Rose, without the dog to distract her, fixated on what might have happened to her mom. Was it a stroke? A heart attack? Something to do with her anemia? Her mind raced with questions she couldn't answer, and her fears multiplied the longer it took the medical team to get her mom to the hospital. Rose picked up her coffee and took a sip. She took a bigger drink, crossed the kitchen to the coffeepot, and topped off her cup.

Aunt Tess helped herself to the coffee as soon as she returned, pulled out a kitchen chair, and fell into it. "Sit for a minute," she instructed Rose, nodding to the chair across from her.

"Should I ride in the ambulance to the hospital with Mom?" Rose asked, crossing the kitchen. Then she looked down at her clothes. "Whoops. I didn't realize I'm still in my pjs. I've got to change." She swiveled to go upstairs, but Aunt Tess stopped her.

"It can wait, Rose. The EMTs will make sure your mom's

stable before they put her in the ambulance. Once they do, you can run up and change. I'll drive us to the hospital."

Rose nodded, relieved Aunt Tess was there to make decisions. The voices from the bedroom grew louder. The EMTs and Officer Coyne navigated the gurney through the narrow turn from the bedroom into the hallway. Then they were in the kitchen.

"Mom." Rose jumped up. She put her hand on her mother's arm. Her eyes were open, but she didn't speak. "Mom, Aunt Tess and I will see you at the hospital. You're going to be fine." Her voice cracked, and she fought back tears.

"She's stable," the EMT not named Ed said. "Try not to worry." They moved through the rest of the house, down the front steps, and into the back of the ambulance. Rose followed every step of the way. She gulped when the ambulance door closed, her mother inside, and Rose powerless outside. Officer Coyne backed the police car out, then the ambulance backed out and headed for the hospital. Rose rushed inside, taking the stairs two at a time.

Try not to worry? Worry was all she could do. It was her new superpower. What triggered her mom's attack? And did it have anything to do with Rose's dogged determination to reveal the secrets of her father's past?

Chapter Thirty

"I'm afraid I did this to her," Rose said, barely above a whisper.

Aunt Tess gave her a quick look, then returned her eyes to the road. "What do you mean?"

"Asking these questions about my father's past, him apparently having an affair. I think the stress of my persistent digging may have caused a stroke."

"Rose, we don't know if your mom had a stroke or what's going on. Don't blame yourself." She glanced over at Rose again. "Let's talk about this at the hospital. I'm so worried about your mother I can only focus on one thing right now, and that's driving."

The ER nurse at Saratoga Hospital told them Carly Webster was being admitted, but she didn't have a room number. "Maybe you'd like to wait in the cafeteria. It could be a couple of hours before I have more information." The nurse started giving directions, but Rose thanked her and said they knew the way. After loading food onto a couple of plates and taking the tray to a table in the near-empty cafeteria, the two ate without speaking, then pushed their plates aside.

"What makes you think you've contributed to your mother's medical emergency by digging into your father's past?" Aunt Tess asked. "I thought you let that go."

Rose fidgeted with her coffee cup and was slow to look up. "I stopped asking you and Mom questions. I never stopped trying to learn the name of the woman in the photo. And now I know."

"You do? How'd you find out?" Aunt Tess asked.

Rose told Aunt Tess the woman's name, some of what she'd learned without mentioning Bill or the newspaper.

"And there are more photos," Rose said.

"Of your father with the woman?"

Rose paused. She had to tell it all now.

"With the woman and a little girl, who looked at my dad like he was the most important person in the world to her. Like he was her dad. She was standing between them, holding both their hands."

It took a moment to sink in. "Do you think your father and this woman had a child?"

"I don't know for sure, but yes, I believe the girl in that photo is my half-sister." Rose paused, thinking about what else she'd found in the attic. "I guess the condoms didn't work."

"What condoms?" Aunt Tess shrieked, drawing the attention of a couple who had just entered the room.

"The condoms I found in Dad's travel bag." Rose put her empty cup on the tray.

"Good lord. Condoms. This keeps getting worse," Aunt Tess said.

"I don't think there's anything else." Rose's voice was so soft now that Aunt Tess leaned across the table. Rose was exhausted and knew she looked it. "I sure hope Dad didn't have any other secrets because I can't handle any more."

"Are you satisfied?" Aunt Tess snapped. Her aunt leaned

back in her chair. "When you said in the car that you thought you caused your mom's attack, stroke, whatever it is, is that because you told her all of this?"

"I haven't told her yet."

"Well, thank goodness for that. And what do you mean 'yet'?" Aunt Tess had a look on her face Rose had only seen a few times. Like the week before high school graduation when she got drunk and threw up in the parking lot of the ice cream stand. Then threw up again in the car she'd borrowed from her aunt.

"You are not going to tell her." Aunt Tess's voice was firm. It sounded like an order.

"If you were my mom, wouldn't you want to know?"

Aunt Tess looked at a beautiful bed of roses outside the window. The yellow blossoms glowed as the bright morning sun passed through them. Totally opposite the gloom that surrounded the two of them.

"You were a teenager when your Uncle Al and I divorced," Aunt Tess began. "I don't know if your mom told you why, but I'm pretty sure you and I have never discussed it."

The change in topic surprised Rose, but she shook her head and listened.

"He was having an affair. Maybe not his first, but do you know how I found out?"

Rose had no words, shook her head again.

"From my best friend, Colette. One day she took me aside in the teachers' lounge and said she had something to tell me before word spread. Because in Lake Amelia, gossip eventually went from whispers to stares to everyone knowing a dirty little secret. Colette said she wanted to protect me from being ridiculed." Aunt Tess paused to catch her breath, maybe push back the pain.

"She said Al was having an affair. That was it. She wouldn't elaborate, but she wanted me to know. I later learned

Al was seeing Colette's sister. The double hit of her telling me and the other woman being my best friend's sister—not that Colette did anything wrong—well, our friendship suffered. We used to confide in each other about our problems, but we were never close again. It was impossible for me to have serious conversations with her about what was going on in my life, especially when the main topic was the collapse of my marriage because my husband was having an affair."

Aunt Tess leaned across the table again. "Your mother is seriously ill. Critically ill. Are you sure you want to tell her this now? Please think about it. You don't want to alienate your mother on her deathbed, do you?"

Tears filled Rose's eyes. Was Aunt Tess's situation a fair comparison? Would Rose damage her relationship with her mom if she told her about his affair? She didn't see how. But she didn't have a crystal ball to know everything would be fine if she did share the information. She wiped a tear that had fallen onto her cheek. Now she didn't know what to do. If her mother hadn't had an attack, would Rose even be having second thoughts? She couldn't know. She was sure of one thing that she couldn't share with her mom or Aunt Tess. While it pained Rose to learn her father had an affair and a child with another woman, she was also caught up in a wave of excitement.

She finally had a sister.

Chapter Thirty-One

D r. Connor caught up with Rose and Aunt Tess in the hallway.

"Your mother suffered a stroke," Dr. Connor told them. "Our records indicate she has not signed a DNR form or chosen palliative care. I know she's leaning in that direction, but she hasn't signed any of the medical forms releasing her from our hospital's care yet, correct?"

"Yes, that's right." Rose said.

"When I checked on her about an hour ago, she also told me that she doesn't want to go back and forth between home and the hospital again. So, I think she's ready to decide. I told her to hold off. Don't make a decision. Don't sign any papers until morning. She's groggy, but I believe she understood why. Do you?"

Rose and Aunt Tess looked at each other. They looked at the doctor and nodded.

"Okay. I've authorized treating her and admitting her overnight, with a release in the morning. You can visit her now, but please don't stay long. She's had an ordeal and needs to rest. Come back in the morning and take her home."

They thanked the doctor and found her mother's room, but she was sound asleep.

"I want to stay here tonight, Aunt Tess."

"I understand, honey, but she's getting excellent care. You heard Dr. Connor. We should go home. Tomorrow will not be an easy day, and you need a good night's sleep."

Rose's eyes filled with tears as she looked at her aunt. She was acutely aware of the emptiness seeping into her life. She pulled a small notepad out of her handbag and dug a pen out of the inside pocket.

Love you, Mom. See you in the morning. She drew a red heart. She reluctantly followed her aunt out of the room, down the hall, and into the parking lot. The drive back to Lake Amelia was subdued, feelings raw as a summer sunburn.

"Would you like to come in for dinner?" Rose asked when Aunt Tess pulled into the driveway.

"Do you mind if I don't? I need sleep, and I have to be at the diner early tomorrow."

"It's fine. I'm also beat and ready for a quick dinner, then bed."

They hugged each other over the console, and Aunt Tess promised to check in the next day.

Rose trudged up the porch steps. For a moment, she considered retrieving Gladys, but she didn't have energy for the dog. Besides, she would be back at the hospital by nine and unsure how long she'd be there. She went inside and called Mrs. Shaw to give her an update.

"Remember I'm here if you need anything at all," Mrs. Shaw said. "And don't give Gladys a second thought. She's fine."

Rose piled some leftover shrimp pasta onto a plate and placed it in the microwave. She set the timer and stared at the flashing numbers as they counted down to zero. She thought about how helpful Mrs. Shaw had been taking care of Gladys, how she'd come to appreciate Nurse Lettie's assistance, and how she welcomed Thom's support when she was overwhelmed. Their actions reminded Rose that people in a small town pitched in when someone in the community needed support. Would the situation change if she pursued the identities of her father's mistress and his apparent other daughter? Did they live nearby? Did people in town know Keisha or her daughter? Would people be upset if they learned about her father's adulterous past? He'd been a respected member of the community. Her mom still was. Many of his former friends and associates might criticize Rose for dredging up the past and tarnishing his reputation. She'd seen that happen plenty of times when the news media went too far probing someone's past. Was she doing that now?

After rinsing her plate and putting it in the dishwasher, Rose glanced down the hallway at the closed door of her father's office. She wondered whether it held additional clues. With her mother coming home from the hospital tomorrow, this was an ideal time to search.

The surfaces were free from dust, but the air smelled stale. Rose opened the sliding glass door and let in the cool evening air.

The emptiness of the room surrounded her. Bookshelves with no books or framed photos, an executive oak desk with no papers stacked on the right side, and the missing navy cardigan on the easy chair where her father often read. The former office was as sterile as an operating room. Rose's eyes swept the room a full three hundred sixty degrees as she turned. She couldn't imagine anything hidden in here, not even a receipt for a pint of ice cream from Stewart's. Still, she had to look.

She investigated the desk first, pulling out the center drawer, feeling around inside for any papers that might have gotten stuck. Then she opened the three drawers on the right.

One at a time. Top. Middle. Bottom. Nothing. Same thing in the left-side drawers. Top. Nothing. Middle. Nothing. Bottom. Wait. Was that a piece of paper in the crevice between the back and the side? She ran her fingers along the inside of the bottom left drawer and caught a sliver of wood in her index finger. After removing the splinter with her teeth and looking for any others, she got down on her hands and knees and peered under the desk. Was anything taped to the underside? That was the moment she realized she'd been reading too many mysteries.

She pushed herself up off the floor with one arm, checked the bookcases and the rest of the room, but they held no secrets.

Rose crossed the room, closed the door behind her, and traipsed back into the kitchen. She was halfway up the stairs to the second floor when her phone vibrated. She flipped the switch to turn on the volume and answered the call.

"Hi, Rose. How did it go at the hospital?"

"Not great," she told her brother, lowering herself onto the landing. She filled him in and asked if he still thought he could get to Lake Amelia in a couple of days.

"The news here isn't so good either."

Rose's body tensed, and she closed her eyes.

"One juror got food poisoning, possibly from the sandwiches that were sent in for their lunch yesterday. We don't have any alternates left, so the judge delayed the trial for a day, hoping the juror will be well enough to return tomorrow."

"Have you updated the judge about Mom's latest health issue? Surely, he could understand the situation is more serious now."

Rural judges in places like upstate New York often handled cases involving people they knew or people from families they knew. Or had grown up with. Or had shared one too many pitchers of beer at the local bar. Sure, that could happen in a larger urban area, but it was less likely. There were more judges to handle cases in larger communities if a judge felt they should recuse themselves from a case.

Rose loved and respected her father and his profession when she was younger. She'd worked in his law office one summer. He had treated his clients with total respect and compassion while handling their legal issues, whether the person wore a well-tailored suit and carried *The Wall Street Journal,* or shuffled in wearing scuffed shoes and clothes with frayed edges that were one size too big. But the longer she worked as a journalist, the more cynical she became. A day spent in Philadelphia's jury pool, and the comments she'd received from a judge presiding over a murder case, tainted her opinion forever.

She had been sitting in the witness box during voir dire, when defense attorneys, prosecutors, and the judge questioned potential jurors about why they'd face hardship by serving jury duty. The judge had a history of criticizing the media. Rose explained she was a freelance photojournalist and serving on a three-week trial would present a financial hardship.

"Perhaps we can find you some nice little rape trial that won't take long," the judge replied.

Even the attorneys sitting at the tables thirty feet away gasped in surprise. Rose sat up straighter and was on the verge of lashing out at the judge when the defendant's attorney jumped to his feet.

"I move to dismiss this juror, your honor."

She couldn't leave the courtroom fast enough and had considered filing a complaint, but she also recognized how much power he wielded as one of the city's longest-serving judges. She dropped it, but never forgot.

"We had a closed-door meeting with all parties involved including the judge," Kirk said. "He is sympathetic, but he doesn't want a mistrial. We're so close to wrapping up testimony and moving on to final arguments. I feel it in my bones. We have this case won. As much as I want to be there for you and Mom, I can't leave yet." There was a rustling sound on Kirk's end of the phone, and Rose imagined her brother rubbing his hand over his face. Or through his already graying hair. She shouldn't be so hard on him. He was juggling a lot at work and his mother was dying. "Anything else new there?" he asked.

She wasn't going to tell him her latest discoveries about their father's secret past on the phone.

"Nothing that can't wait. I hope your juror recovers soon. Keep me posted." She ended the call and barely made it to bed before she collapsed and fell asleep.

Chapter Thirty-Two

She was obsessed, and she knew it. Like a dog tracking the fresh scent of a rabbit through the woods, or a reporter following lead after lead until she discovered enough facts to tell a story. Rose could not quit. She needed to be at the hospital soon, but her mom was probably coming home today. Rose may not get another chance to search the attic without her mother asking questions. Rose inched her way up the ladder and looked at the boxes with her father's belongings. She thought she'd checked all of them, except for a box on the other side of the attic that was still sealed and contained memorabilia from Rose's childhood.

Her mother had spent many cold winter days organizing large, three-ring-binders for her and Kirk: cards they'd made for their parents, school photos throughout the years, some photos Rose had taken and articles she'd written for the college newspaper. Rose hadn't gone through it in years. She slid the box over to the opening, then went down the stepladder, juggling the box on her left shoulder. She almost fell twice. The second time she caught herself but lost the box. It hit the floor with a thud.

As Rose caught her breath, she looked around her parents' former bedroom. Growing up, she'd rarely come into the room. Even as an adult, she could count on one hand the number of times she'd ventured into their private domain. Something stirred in her brain; their space was off limits. That rule was irrelevant now. This was no time to be subtle.

The closet where she accessed the attic was empty. So was the other closet. She checked the drawers of her father's dresser, the taller, narrower one, then the shorter but wider dresser her mother had used. She found nothing. Her mom used Kirk's dresser in her current bedroom and had cleaned out this dresser. The master bedroom wasn't as sterile as her father's old office, but it didn't hold any secrets either. As she pulled the door closed behind her, her mother's dresser was the last thing she saw. It sparked an idea.

Rose raced downstairs, glanced at the wall clock as she ran through the living room, and stopped at the threshold of her mother's bedroom. Should she invade her mother's privacy?

As she weighed her decision, she recalled a fight she and Kirk had once had. He'd recently gotten his driver's permit, so he was about sixteen; she would have been nine. He'd caught her sitting on the floor in his room, going through a box she'd pulled out of his closet. She'd lifted out a yellow paisley handkerchief, a key chain, and was reaching for what appeared to be letters when he'd discovered her.

"What're you doing in my room?" he'd hollered.

"I was curious what you keep in the box," she said, showing signs of her career in journalism already.

"You could've asked me," Kirk said, his arms bent at the elbows, his hands balled into fists that rested on his hips.

"I did once. You said it was none of my business."

"It's still none of your business. Mom!" he shouted. "Rose's going through my stuff."

Their mother was in the kitchen and stepped up behind Kirk before he finished yelling.

"Rose, we've talked about this before. People have a right to keep their belongings to themselves. Come here."

Rose picked one of Kirk's letters off the floor and put it back in the box.

"Leave them," Kirk said.

She crawled to her feet and slunk toward the door. Kirk stepped aside to let her pass, but her mother would not let her walk away.

"Apologize to your brother."

Eyes downward, she mumbled, "Sorry."

"Say it louder and look at him," her mother said.

Rose raised her eyes to meet Kirk's searing glare. "Sorry," she said and squeezed past them. Kirk slid into his bedroom and slammed the door so hard it shook the wall.

As she recalled, her mother had given her a lecture about not going into other people's rooms and not touching their belongings without asking. Did she understand? Yes, as much as an inquisitive child could.

That inquisitive child, thirty years later, stood on the threshold of the same room, considering whether to step into her mother's bedroom, uninvited, to go through her personal items. Rose considered it a major accomplishment that she'd paused to think about what she wanted to do. She'd have plenty of time to go through everything after her mom passed. Could it wait? She took a step forward. Then another.

"Hello, Rose." Rose spun around and stepped into the kitchen as her aunt came through the living room.

"Aunt Tess, I didn't expect to see you this morning."

"I wanted to stop in to see how you're doing, but I think we should drive to the hospital separately. Danny called our regular backup cook last evening, and he came in this morning to help. Everything is fine at the diner, but I might need to get back there before your mom is ready to come home." She looked at Rose, still in her pjs, her hair pointing in all directions. "Did you just get out of bed?"

"No, I've been slow to get going," Rose said, discreetly taking some deep breaths to calm herself. Aunt Tess would not have been happy to find her going through her mother's stuff. She needed to get a grip and stop obsessing about her father. His mistress. The little girl.

"Well, run upstairs and get dressed."

The drive gave Rose some solitary time to think, which she desperately needed, but reining in her racing thoughts was challenging. She turned on the radio to lose herself in music.

Less than an hour later, Rose poked her head into her mother's hospital room quietly to not wake her, but she was sitting up in bed, sipping juice.

"Good morning!" Rose smiled and walked over to her mom's bedside and planted a kiss on her cheek, feeling the fragile skin beneath her lips, skin as brittle as leaves waiting for the first snowfall to cover them. Aunt Tess followed her into the room.

"How are you doing this morning, Carly?"

"About as well as can be expected," she said in a thin and quavering voice.

"Do you remember what happened yesterday?" Aunt Tess went to the other side of the bed and rubbed her sister's arm.

"The only thing, Rose trying to wake me." She took another small sip of her juice through the straw, then set the plastic cup on the tray.

"Have the doctors seen you this morning?" Rose asked.

Her mother shook her head.

"I'm going to find a nurse and see what they can tell me."

Rose was back in minutes. "Dr. Connor is on the floor making rounds. He'll stop in soon."

The three women chatted about nothing of importance

with her mother mostly listening. Rose wished she knew more about strokes, so she could tell what to look for in her mother's actions, reflexes, speech. Her speech was clipped. What else had changed? Rose realized perhaps she should spend more time understanding her mom's health issues and less time worrying about her father's past. A twinge of sorrow prompted a welling of tears in her eyes as she realized maybe she'd been too focused on the wrong parent these past several days.

"Hello, ladies," Dr. Connor said, striding into the room. "How are you today, Mrs. Webster?" He looked at the information on the small laptop he carried in his hands.

"Not so great," she admitted. "What's the verdict?"

"I can confirm you had a stroke, but there's more going on that could be associated with the anemia, or the lung cancer, or something else. I'm afraid there are multiple factors working against you right now." Aunt Tess stepped aside as the doctor set the laptop on the end of the bed and moved closer to her mother's side.

"I pay attention to my body, Dr. Connor. I know how I feel." She coughed and grimaced as she swallowed. "It's almost like I . . . feel my heart rate slowing . . . the blood isn't moving through me the way it used to." She smiled at him, a tired smile that seemed to take all her energy. "You might think I'm a silly old lady. I think my body's shutting down, telling me I haven't much time."

Rose sniffed and pulled a tissue from her jeans pocket to wipe her runny nose. She didn't dare look at Aunt Tess or she might not be strong enough to hold back the tears.

"You're not a silly old lady. You're very astute. I've admired the way you've handled yourself ever since the day I first met you." He took her hand in both of his. "I agree with your diagnosis."

"Will you let me go home?"

He held her eyes. "I'll do the paperwork immediately." He looked at Rose. "And you need to complete the paperwork we gave you about hospice and email copies to my office as soon as possible. I'll update your mother's file when I get those documents and make sure Dr. Fisk is aware." He took her mother's hand in his, squeezed it, then picked up his laptop off the bed and walked out of the room.

Before any of them could find their voice, a nurse walked in.

"Okay, Carly. Let's get you dressed and checked out." She looked at Rose and Aunt Tess. "I know you've had a visiting nurse helping at home, and you've been in touch with hospice services, correct?" Everyone nodded. "It's time someone visited you and set things up."

Chapter Thirty-Three

The ride from the hospital to Lake Amelia was as silent as the hour before dawn high in the mountains. Rose had been going through the motions ever since the doctor walked out of her mother's room. With Rose at her side, her mother completed the documents confirming she was refusing further medical treatment and entering hospice care. Nurses tucked her mother into Rose's vehicle, Aunt Tess drove off in her car promising to stop by later, and Rose pulled away from the hospital with her mother for the last time.

Rose was left to her own thoughts spinning in dozens of directions—most important were the calls to hospice to have a hospital bed delivered and to schedule hospice nurses and volunteers. Who would take care of the oxygen her mom would soon need? She would ask the hospice people. What about medications? And what did Rose need to know to care for someone who was dying? She wasn't a nurse. She'd gotten a C-plus in her high school health class. It was her lowest grade. Ever. How was she supposed to handle all these new medical tasks? She forced herself to take a deep breath and recalled her first conversation with hospice. They did this all the time. They'd make sure everything was in place for her mother's care. It was Rose's first time, but not hospice's.

She glanced over at the passenger seat. Her mom's chin rested on her chest, lulled to sleep by the gentle motion of the car, the passing view out the window of summer-green trees and open fields, and perhaps the acceptance of what lay ahead. Days ago, Rose had agreed to care for her mom at home, but only now did she realize all that might involve. Yes, she'd known in an intellectual and unemotional way that her mother was dying. But in their home on Cedar Street, sitting by her bed, holding her hand when her mother took her last breath? That was overwhelming.

Rose braked as her car rounded a curve and an SUV pulled out in front of her. It peeled out of the parking lot at the old bar where she'd seen deputies checking out the stolen bikes about a week ago. It took off in the opposite direction, but not before Rose caught a glimpse of its license plate. It was a New York plate, dented like it had been in an accident, and it appeared the first two letters were CG. Dark SUVs might be almost as common as white ones, but she got tingles up her spine. She veered into the parking lot.

She pointed her vehicle toward the back of the building, put it in park, and hopped out, closing the car door quietly so she wouldn't wake her mother. She peered around the corner. Nothing. No bikes behind the bar. Maybe whoever had taken off in the SUV had picked up some stolen bikes? Was it something to mention to Deputy Stover? She climbed back in the car, grateful her mother was napping, and continued toward Lake Amelia.

After walking her mom into the house and settling her into the recliner, Rose brewed a cup of tea. Next, she sat at the kitchen table and answered the calls that had pinged her phone during the drive from Saratoga Springs. Jeremy had texted, telling Rose he was sorry about her mother's latest medical issue and to text him if she needed to talk. She'd get back to him later, but first she addressed the most important communications from the hospice agency, advising her the hospice nurse and volunteer would visit that afternoon. The hospital bed would be delivered the next morning. She was so intent on medical tasks, she'd forgotten about the SUV at the old bar. Rose was about to text Deputy Stover when the doorbell rang. She opened the door and her eyes teared up.

"I had a little free time and thought you could use help." Nurse Lettie smiled, a smile almost no one other than nurses had, of knowing when people whose loved one was dying needed comforting to help ease the pain. Rose fell into Lettie's hug.

"I'm overwhelmed," Rose admitted.

"You can't help but feel a terrifying storm is coming at you, fast and furious. But remember, you have me and a caring group of people from hospice who are going to see you and your mother through this." She looped her arm through Rose's as they walked into the living room.

Her mom greeted Nurse Lettie like an old friend. The two of them chatted for a short time until her mother leaned back in her chair, exhausted. Rose and Nurse Lettie ventured into her mother's bedroom, clearing space from the top of the dresser and bedside table for her medicine and medical supplies.

"Do I need to make room for the hospice bed? What do I do with Mom's bed?"

"The people who deliver the hospital bed will move this bed and whatever other furniture you want to another room, the garage, wherever you prefer," Nurse Lettie said.

"And they'll set up the oxygen as well?"

"Not the same people. The hospice nurse will show you

and your mother how to use it. It's not complicated. I can go over it too if you want."

Rose made lunch for the three of them. Nurse Lettie left an hour later, promising to return the next day.

The doorbell rang soon after Lettie left, and Rose thought the nurse had left her book or something else behind.

"Thom, what a surprise. What are you doing here?"

"That's a fine greeting for an old friend. I came by to say hello to your mom, if you think she's up to seeing me."

"Thomas Patrick O'Sullivan . . . better come in here." Her mother's voice shook, but it was loud enough to carry into the hallway.

The two of them laughed and stepped into a living room Thom once knew almost as well as his own.

"Mrs. Webster, it's nice to see you," Thom said, gently squeezing her outstretched hand and leaning over to kiss her cheek.

"Sweet of you to visit. How are Desi," she paused and coughed, "and your children?"

Thom pulled his phone out of his back pocket and showed her mom the same photos he'd shown Rose the other day. "Ned is taller than his mom already and will tower over me before he graduates from high school in a few years. The girls are thirteen, both into cheerleading, and they're a handful. I'll bet you remember what teenage girls are like." He smiled and winked at Rose.

"Beautiful children," her mom said. "I see their names in the newspaper. Honor society. Sports. Is Ned still playing . . . basketball?" She coughed again and Rose handed her a tissue.

"Yep. He loves it and hopes to earn a scholarship to Syracuse. I encourage him but also temper his enthusiasm. Those scholarships are scarce." He looked at the photo. "Ned's good, but I don't know if he's that good. I hope he's not headed for a disappointment." He set his cell on the floor next to the footstool and sat. Rose dropped onto the other recliner.

"You and Desi set a wonderful example, working hard," her mom said. "Ned will be fine, on the team or not." She took a breath, and they waited as she searched for words. "How is the pub doing?"

Her mom hadn't spoken this much since she'd come home from the hospital. She'd always liked Thom and Rose sensed she was digging deep to find the words and energy to talk with him.

"We keep getting busier," Tom explained. "Some beverage distributors have even picked up Amelia Ale for sales around the state. Pretty soon we might not be able to keep up with demand. That's a good problem to have." He paused. "I'm sorry to hear things are tough for you. Let us know if you need anything. If you have questions Desi could answer, please don't hesitate to call."

"Thanks, Thom. You're sweet." She pointed at Rose. "I think Rose might need your support more than me. I'm counting on everyone to help her. Not much family for her. Friends and neighbors . . . important."

He swallowed hard and nodded.

"How's your brother? Paul ever have a family?"

"Uh, Paul's a bit of a free spirit. He never found the right woman because he was too busy having fun with his pals: fishing, hiking the Adirondacks, although he's lucky he made it home from a couple of those overnight camping adventures."

"He always did like to party," Rose said, remembering how Thom had bailed out his brother a few times.

"You may have seen the police report in the *Dispatch* when police arrested Paul for cocaine possession, Mrs. Webster. He had enough cocaine on him, he's lucky they didn't get him for distribution. He was fortunate the judge went easy on him.

That was several years ago. He's repairing bikes now but . . ." His voice trailed.

"You look worried," Rose said. "What's up? You know you can trust us."

Thom nodded. "Paul asked for a loan the other day. He hasn't asked for money in a while. I wanted to say yes, but I don't know why he needs the money, and he won't say. I'm afraid he's doing drugs again. Not only that," he winced as if punched in the arm, "Deputy Sheriff Stover came by the pub recently and asked me a lot of questions about Paul and his bike-repair business."

"Do you think he's involved in that stolen bike ring the police are investigating?" Rose asked.

"I don't know, and I was afraid to say too much. I like Maxi, but I didn't want to tell her something that would incriminate Paul if he's not doing anything wrong."

"Family loyalty is important. Only up to a point." Her mother forced the words out.

Rose's head quickly turned in her mother's direction.

Thom leaned in and asked, "What do you mean, Mrs. Webster?"

"Human nature to protect loved ones," she said, taking Thom's hand. "I understand not wanting to tell the deputy about suspicions." She squeezed her eyes tight and took another shallow breath. "But if he's in trouble again . . . You can only protect so much." She coughed. "You can't protect people you love from themselves," she said in a halting voice. "Or from making mistakes."

Chapter Thirty-Four

Did her mother really say that about family loyalty? Thom had left soon after that bombshell and her mother's cautious advice to take care of his brother as long as it didn't put him in an awkward or illegal position. Rose waited for the teakettle to boil, unable to think about anything other than what her mom had said about family loyalty, "up to a point." Did that comment have anything to do with her father's affair, maybe his illegitimate child? Possible illegitimate child, she had to keep reminding herself.

She could never hide anything from her mother, who noticed how agitated Rose was as she raced back and forth between the recliner and the kitchen. After a while she all but kicked Rose out of the house.

"Why don't you take Gladys for a walk around the block, then do something for yourself? Go into town. Sit by the lake. Visit the library. There are a couple of hours before dinner. I'll be fine."

Rose didn't challenge her mother. She walked Gladys around the block, once pulling on her leash when the poor pooch was in mid-piddle. She returned Gladys to her mother's lap with a few more rubs behind the dog's ears and set out.

The library was first. She tucked a scrap of paper with the name of Keisha Norella Tyler into the back pocket of her jeans, as if she needed a reminder of the woman's name. Bill had given her the information three days ago, and Rose wanted to resume investigating Keisha Tyler as soon as she could, but, well, Mom first. She'd searched the internet and confirmed Keisha was still with the ACLU in Albany, but only on a part-time basis. Maybe the ABA directory had more information.

Dark clouds thickened overhead, and drizzle began falling soon after Rose left the house. She didn't think to bring an umbrella, but the mist was refreshing, tapping her face with cool drops as she walked the few blocks to the library. She'd intended to head straight for the reference section, but Carter was at the checkout desk and motioned her over with the flick of his fingers.

"Good morning, Rose. I heard you had a bit of a scare with your mom."

She filled him in and accepted his condolences for the difficult time ahead.

"Any progress with your arm and hand? I know it'll take time, but I thought maybe you're feeling stronger."

"I've gotten a few messages from my Philadelphia surgeon and physical therapist reminding me I need to schedule appointments. They've also asked if I've noticed any change since I started doing the exercises on the document they'd emailed me."

"And have you?"

"It'll be easier to tell after I actually start doing the exercises regularly," she said, embarrassment heating her red cheeks. Rather than dwell on her shortcomings, she changed the subject.

"How's Ellie doing?"

"She's had a rough couple of days, and I'm not sure why. She doesn't always share her struggles with me, although she is more open lately. If you have a minute this morning, would you say hello? She was very chatty with me about your last conversation, and that's a stretch for her. To find a new friend."

"Sure, I'll go find her now. Is she in her usual spot?"

"Probably. And thanks, Rose. I know you have your own problems."

"I'm never too busy to chat with someone who needs a pal."

She grabbed *The New Yorker* and *Vanity Fair* off the magazine rack, climbed the stairs, and found the girl in her favorite overstuffed chair.

"Good morning, Ellie. It's nice to see you again."

"Hello, Dictionary Lady." Ellie lowered her book just enough to meet Rose's eyes. Then the book went back up.

"I didn't tell you this the first time we met, but when I was in school, my classmates called me Dictionary Girl."

"Well, your name is Webster," said the voice behind the book.

Rose flopped into the other chair. She set one magazine on the table between them and began leafing through the other one. A sigh drifted over from Ellie's chair. Then another. Then a louder one. Rose didn't react. Ellie gave in.

"Did you ever notice how much noisier it is when people read magazines instead of books?" She dropped her book to her lap and Rose looked for a hint of a smile on Ellie's face. There was none. She was serious. And seriously annoyed with Rose.

"Sorry, Ellie. I can't concentrate on any books right now. Magazine articles are shorter and easier to read." Rose flipped another page of her magazine. And waited.

"How is your mom?"

Rose closed the magazine and put it on the table. "Not so good, I'm afraid. She's very sick, but she's back home so I can be with her anytime I want." Rose hoped it was okay to put it that way since Ellie couldn't be with her mom at all.

"I'm sorry, Dictionary Lady." Ellie's voice was tender as she shot a quick look in Rose's direction.

The girl's kind words, simple, and so heartfelt, took Rose's breath away. The silence sat between them.

"Yeah, I'm sorry too," Rose said, clearing the emotion from her voice. "What's new with you?"

"Daddy and I are talking about getting a dog," Ellie said, a smile spreading across her face. "He says it's a lot of work and I'll have to learn how to care for it. What do you think? You have a dog, don't you? Daddy and I have seen you walking it around town."

"Gladys is my mother's dog," Rose said, suddenly realizing it might be her dog soon. Or up to her to find the dog a new home. She would put off that task as long as possible. "Your Dad's correct," Rose continued. "A dog requires feeding and walking and playtime and you can't take off on vacation without finding someone to care for it. You could take the dog with you on vacation, but that means you can't eat in most restaurants or visit museums and libraries." Rose paused, letting what she said sink in. "What do you think? Are you prepared for taking care of a dog?"

Ellie rubbed her right fingertips across her lips as she considered the question, a habit Rose hadn't noticed before. "We are in the library most days and dogs can't come in here. What would we do with the dog all day?"

"You're asking the right question before you bring a dog home," Rose said. "A dog requires lots of care, but it gives back a lot of love."

"Yes, that's what I'm thinking about," Ellie said, "a little doggie I could love." She lifted her book in front of her eyes again, the conversation over. Rose picked up her magazines and headed downstairs.

She lifted the heavy ABA directory off the shelf and tried not to drop it. It was her second time through the directory so finding the information was easy. Keisha Norella Tyler was still practicing with the ACLU as Rose's internet search had indicated, and she had a private practice with an office in downtown Albany in the same office building. Rose made some notes on her phone and closed the directory. Okay, she found the woman. Now what?

Chapter Thirty-Five

Rose left the library and strolled along Main Street, but the crowd put her off. Too many cars cruised for precious parking spots and too many people jammed the sidewalks looking into storefront windows, not watching where they were going. She turned left down the next street and headed toward the mountains and the comforting sounds of birds. Rose followed Mountainside Street until it curved around back toward the commercial area. She continued straight ahead on a road with fewer homes and bigger yards. The mountain flattened out this far south to a narrow field, the beginning of the valley that held Lake Amelia. A quarter of a mile later, she hesitated at the iron gates. She took some tentative steps, prompted by her feet and perhaps her subconscious mind weighed down by her father's past and her mother's future.

"Might as well." Rose entered the cemetery.

She followed the pockmarked lane between the head-stones, walked some more with her eyes focused straight ahead, then glanced to the right and stepped onto the grass.

Several plots in, she paused in front of a familiar grave marker: Randall Wallace Webster with his dates of birth and death etched in the polished gray granite below his name. The scales of justice were above his name. To the right was her mother's name, Carly Adams Webster, with her date of birth and a space for what came next. Another plot was to the right of theirs with a metal marker in the ground. Rose's final resting place. She'd bought the plot at her mother's urging several years ago. The cemetery's caretaker had notified the Webster family that a member of the community had purchased several plots surrounding theirs. Rose bought the last plot next to her parents. Kirk and Maria had chosen their burial site with Maria's family in Florida.

Rose pulled out several weeds at both ends of the marker, then stepped back and stared at her father's name. Said it out loud. Her hands squeezed her thighs, even her right hand that suddenly found hidden strength. The words rose from her core and flew out of her mouth.

"You son of a bitch! How could you cheat on my mother? How could you bring so much shame to our family?" She dropped to her knees and leaned on her left hand, letting the tears flow and giving her pain a needed outlet. "Not only that, but you may have had another daughter. You knew how much I wanted a sister and you never told me about her. You shit!"

Words she wanted to say but couldn't to her mother, aunt, or brother, she could finally hurl at a slab of cold granite. If he'd been standing before her, she would have lashed out with her fists. Her left hand pounded the ground repeatedly until she realized she couldn't afford to hurt it, so she screamed until she ran out of what to say and her throat was raw.

Her tears slowed and trickled until they stopped. She sat back on her heels and wiped her eyes with her short sleeves, then stared at the headstone. She'd been so lost looking at her parents' names and dates, their wedding date didn't register. But there it was. Her mother had insisted they put it on the gravestone after her father suddenly died. Maybe he'd stopped seeing the woman and resumed his full attention to his wife and children. Rose didn't know if that happened, but her mother obviously knew something about the other woman, and yet they'd stayed married. Perhaps the tension Rose had seen on his face in that photo with the little girl and her mom proved they were ending their relationship.

Her mom had forgiven her father and taken him back. Should Rose forgive him? Could she?

Hell no. She wasn't ready to forgive him for abandoning his family, even if it was only for short periods at a time. He'd been with Keisha Tyler instead of them. She'd have to let that simmer. In the meantime, Keisha worked less than an hour away in downtown Albany. And the little girl—perhaps a few years younger than Rose now—where was she?

Rose paced the cemetery lanes to give her emotions a chance to calm down and her red eyes time to lose their puffiness. She retraced her steps back into town, stayed one block off Main Street and even then, sidewalks were busy. Many stores that couldn't afford the rents on Main found space on side streets, and that's where Rose spotted Deputy Stover talking with Paul O'Sullivan on the sidewalk in front of his storefront. Paul saw Rose first because his eyes were darting all over, trying to look at anything or anyone other than the sheriff's deputy.

"Hi, Rose. How's, um, your mom doing?"

Interesting. That was the first time she could recall him ever asking about her mother or anything happening in her life.

"She's home now and Aunt Tess and I will help take care of her." Rose turned to the deputy and said hello. Stover was all business, and she wasn't happy with Paul. "It looks like I interrupted a conversation. Perhaps I should move along." But she didn't walk away, too intrigued to learn what was going on.

"It's not a conversation," Paul said under his breath. "More like an interrogation."

"Not an interrogation, Mr. O'Sullivan. I'm asking you to confirm where you get your bike parts, and where you obtained the bicycle you're working on now."

"A man wearing biking clothes and a bright red helmet dropped it off half an hour ago," Paul explained. "He said his name is Frank, that he rode over some broken glass near the park and got a flat tire, but he didn't have the equipment to fix it. He left it with me, while he and his buddy went for a protein shake around the corner."

"Did Frank show you any ID or give you a credit card with a deposit before he left his expensive bike with you?"

"No, Deputy, he did not." Paul tried to hide a smile. "He and I agreed a three-thousand-dollar bike was enough of a deposit. Look, do you mind? He'll be back soon, and the bike isn't fixed yet."

Deputy Stover waved her arm, dismissing Paul, but she watched him walk back into the garage. Another man inside the small store talked to Paul, motioning to the bike. Paul said something to the guy—someone Rose couldn't remember seeing before—and he disappeared through a door in the back. Paul went to work plugging the punctures in the tire and the inner tube.

"Are you looking for a lesson on how to repair a bike tire?" Deputy Stover asked Rose.

"I was passing by when Paul asked about my mom. I wasn't interfering."

"Right, your mom," the deputy said, lowering her voice. "How is she?"

"Running out of time," Rose said softly as the two watched Paul.

The glue to seal the holes apparently dried instantly. Paul walked over to the bike stand and placed the tire onto the frame, checking the cables and spinning the wheel to make sure the connections were secure. Last, he took the bike off the stand and bounced it on the floor. Satisfied, he leaned it against the wall. He wiped his hands with a brown rag, tossed it onto a counter, and wrote up the bill.

"Do you think Paul is involved in the stolen bikes?" Rose asked, turning her full attention to the deputy.

"I don't know, but I'm going to stick around until his customer returns. I'd appreciate it if you would be on your way now."

"Sure, no problem," Rose said. "Oh, wait. I forgot I have something to tell you. When I drove home from the hospital with Mom earlier today, a dark SUV pulled out in front of me where that old bar is. You know, the place I met you and the other deputy that one day?"

Deputy Stover didn't take her eyes off Paul. "And?"

"I caught a glimpse of the license plate. A New York plate. I think the first two letters were CG."

That caught the deputy's attention. She pulled out her little notebook. "Yellow or white plate?"

"Excuse me?"

"The color of the plate. Was it yellow or white? New York State has mostly white license plates, some with the word Empire and others with Excelsior. Gold or yellow plates were issued for about ten years. So, was the license plate yellow or white?"

"Yellow," Rose said.

"Thanks for letting me know. Now please move along."

Rose took one last look inside Paul's shop then walked

toward Cedar Street. He didn't have many bikes in it, old or new. How could he maintain such a small repair shop? Was there that much business repairing bikes in Lake Amelia? Rose was asking more questions than she had answers for, which usually led to more investigating.

Chapter Thirty-Six

The white cargo van with "COMMUNITY THOSPICE" printed in light blue on the side pulled into the driveway about a quarter after nine. Rose greeted the man and woman and showed them to her mother's bedroom, explaining that they needed to move the queen-sized bed into the room across the hall and set up the hospice bed in its place. Rose had stripped the bed while her mother ate breakfast, so the hospice people went right to work.

"Do you want us to set up the bed in that other room or stack everything on the floor?" the man asked.

Rose blinked. She hadn't given it much thought. "I guess you should lean the mattress and box spring up against the bookcase, and the headboard as well." Rose had suggested her mom might want to settle on the couch with Gladys in the back of the house with a view of the patio instead of watching the hospice people come and go, but her mom said she preferred her usual spot in her recliner.

Every thump of wood on the floor and grunt of the man and woman moving bed parts from one room to the other echoed throughout the first floor. While her mom flipped through the newspaper for the third or fourth time, Rose paced in the kitchen, trying to tamp down the anxiety that ramped up when she saw the hospice bed. It made the next steps in her mother's journey more real. Inevitable. Unstoppable.

After the hospice people left, a sense of calm slowly returned in the house. Rose checked on her mom. She had drifted off to sleep, Gladys on her lap, the newspaper spread across her legs. The nurse from Community Hospice was arriving in about an hour. Medicare would cover most hospice services, but nurses visits were limited to a few times a week. Her mom had bonded with Nurse Lettie—so had Rose—and they agreed to continue paying to have Lettie augment hospice care.

Rose poked her head into her mother's bedroom and admired the efficiency of the hospice staff. The bed was made, her mother's pillows and a lightweight blanket on top. A spare set of sheets was on the easy chair near the bed. They'd even set up a white hamper in the corner, which would help Rose keep things organized.

Rose sat at the dining room table and logged onto her computer. For the next hour, she researched hospice care and terminal illnesses, strokes, blood clots, and lung cancer, educating herself on what had happened to her mother and what was to come. Rose would take care of her mother's basic needs and the nurses would handle important medical responsibilities.

After Rose and her mother had completed the medical and hospice forms at the hospital, a nurse had spoken with Rose about how often a hospice nurse would visit and what Rose could do to help her mother with one issue, if she was willing to learn.

"What's that?" Rose had asked as they stood in the hallway outside of her mother's room.

"Fluid will build up in your mother's lungs because of the cancer, causing shortness of breath. It's a common issue for lung cancer patients and can be eased by draining the fluid."

Rose stared at the nurse. "Draining the fluid? In her lungs?"

As soon as the nurse started to explain the procedure, Rose paled and leaned against the wall. The nurse braced Rose with one arm, and gently bent her over at the waist.

"Breathe slowly in and out," the nurse said until Rose's breathing was normal, and she could stand again. "We'll keep that task off your list," the nurse had said. "Few people without medical training are comfortable with the process. It's fine. We'll check her lungs every visit and Nurse Lettie can monitor her lungs as well."

Rose searched for articles on how to drain fluid from someone's lungs during home care and was relieved she wouldn't have to do it. She didn't want to be responsible for making a mistake that contributed to her mother's death. Rose turned her head and looked out the sliding glass doors at the bright sunny day that was such a contrast to the sadness weighing on her. She wished Kirk would hurry up and get to Lake Amelia so she didn't feel so alone. Yes, she had hospice and Nurse Lettie, but they weren't family. She could ask Aunt Tess to come by, but Rose didn't want to burden her when her aunt was dealing with her own grief.

She envied people who had large families, with half a dozen siblings, several aunts and uncles on each side. There was always someone to rely on, someone to share the burden. Both of her parents came from small families, and the few cousins who'd grown up in the area went to college and never moved back. When she was about four years old, she'd asked her parents for a bigger family so she'd have more kids to play with. But they said they couldn't have any more children.

And then her father apparently did.

Rose opened a new window in Safari and searched for images of Keisha Norella Tyler. There she was at annual ACLU fundraising events in Albany, with more images from statewide ACLU events. Sometimes Keisha was alone, sometimes with other people, colleagues or friends, but never the girl. If Keisha had such a high profile in the community, why wasn't her daughter in more photos? Was the girl still alive?

Chapter Thirty-Seven

What made journalism a good fit for Rose, especially at the beginning of her career, was that every day brought exciting and challenging new stories. She enjoyed being nimble to pick up and go, searching for the next adventure, for work or pleasure. She'd bounce from one idea to the next, sometimes one location to the next, not to wander but to avoid being restricted. Except when she was on the trail of a story. Then she could dig in until she'd found all the pieces of the puzzle and learned the truth. Until the truth became more difficult to discover. Until too many people didn't respect the truth and replaced it with rumor and innuendos, lies and blatant falsehoods. When it got to that point, she'd put down her digital tape recorder and notepad and turned her photography hobby into a new career.

It was a sideways move, because she'd always taken photos on big stories, but the newspaper's editors rarely used them. They said they had to use the photos taken by the guys on staff. And it was mostly still a network of guys, nice enough but too often condescending—until she'd broken through with The Shot That Nobody Else Had: a young girl holding her father's hand as he bled to death from a gunman's bullet. Now she was one of the best freelance photojournalists in the Mid-Atlantic and Northeast.

Her thoughts ground to a halt. *Was* one of the best freelance photojournalists, she reminded herself. By the time her battered arm healed, the contacts who'd always called her first might have gotten used to calling someone else. She felt her career slipping away, then felt guilty worrying about her career when her mother was also slipping away.

When Rose realized how often hospice nurses and volunteers, and Nurse Lettie, would visit her mom, Rose was relieved. As much as she loved her mother and wanted to help her, Rose could not sit around all day. Physically could not sit around all day. And she couldn't stop thinking about the dark SUV that had pulled out in front of her at the old bar.

The hospice nurse arrived at ten and Rose made sure everyone had everything they needed, including a fresh pot of tea. The nurse had several tasks to accomplish today, including checking the liquid in her mother's lungs. The volunteer was also stopping by in the morning. Rose figured it was a good time to get out of the house. After making sure her mom was set, Rose scurried out the front door, hopped into her vehicle, and drove the now familiar road toward Saratoga Hospital. A quick check of the old bar parking lot turned up nothing. Back in the vehicle, she continued toward Saratoga Springs. At the next county road—she was grateful she had GPS because there were a lot of them—she took a right.

She was hunting. Thinking about people stealing bikes and looking for clues. She took one county road north for a while, then another one east, then back south. The cops suspected the bike thieves had at least one chop shop where they broke down bikes for parts. Deputy Stover told Rose that law enforcement had checked several likely buildings, including some where high school kids sometimes gathered in the parking lot or behind the building to smoke dope and drink beer. Cops were interested in the bike thefts, but with the increase in illegal drug trafficking, bikes were lower on the priority list.

At one point, she found herself on a road with no yellow or white lines and pitted with ruts. It didn't even appear on her digital map on the dashboard, which showed her driving through a green field. *What am I doing on this fool's chase?* She bounced along, hoping this didn't lead to a dead end, and was about to give up, when a black truck rounded a curve, speeding toward her like he owned the road. Her vehicle hugged the right shoulder. The truck barely slowed as the driver, a cap pulled low over his eyes, flew past her. She got a glimpse of the vehicle in her rearview mirror. It wasn't a pickup truck as she'd first thought but a dark SUV. Was it Paul's SUV? She couldn't tell much more because it kicked up too much dust. Should she turn around and follow it?

Rose slowed and rounded the curve the SUV had just driven, looking for a place to turn around and inhaling deeply to catch her breath. What was she doing driving in the middle of nowhere trying to find a bike chop shop with only one functioning arm to defend herself if she ran into trouble? Despite her doubts, she eased her foot off the brake and crept up the road.

A clearing on the right opened to a small parking lot and ended at a rundown building. It might have once been a gas station because of the two garage doors, but there was no sign of old gas pumps. Or an office. Maybe it was just a garage. Maybe it was where thieves hid or worked on stolen bikes. Had she found the garage Paul bought after Thom had loaned him the money? She'd been driving for a couple of hours, following her nose and the ruts, up one road and down another. But she knew from experience that sometimes all it took to catch a break was persistence. And a little luck. She'd take a little luck any day of the week.

She turned in, parked her vehicle, and got out. Walked alongside the building and peeked around behind it.

Paul O'Sullivan lifted a bicycle out of the back of a navy SUV and set it on the cracked pavement.

"Hey, Paul."

He almost dropped the bike. "Rose, what the hell are you doing here?"

She looked at him, looked at the bike. Another bike rested against the back of the building next to a gray metal door that was propped open.

"I was driving around trying to get my worries off my mind."

"Out here in the middle of nowhere?"

She shrugged. "I kept following whatever road looked most interesting. Then I saw a vehicle drive out of here and I was curious." He couldn't know she hadn't seen the SUV pull out of the lot. He was too busy looking around. Jittery. Like he'd been with Deputy Stover at his shop in Lake Amelia.

"I thought you did your repairs in town."

"This isn't a repair," he said. "I bought this bike online from a guy in Rensselaer County."

Rose stepped closer. "I hope you didn't pay a lot for it. It looks kind of beat up, if you ask me." She smiled. "Not that you did. Ask me."

"I bought it for parts. I'm always on the lookout for bikes I can strip for my repair work."

She scrutinized the building, with cinder blocks crumbling around the corners and rusted pipes sticking out of the wall. "You own this place?"

"I got this old garage about a few months ago where I do repairs for serious bike riders in the area. I can't afford a bigger space in town." He glanced around again.

"Property doesn't come cheap out here either, does it? Unless the property's abandoned or the building is falling down." She smiled her warm, friendly photojournalist's smile, the one she used to wear down people's defenses.

He stuck his hands in his jeans and raised his eyebrows. "You sure are asking a lot of questions."

"Sorry. I don't mean to pry. You know me, always asking questions."

Paul wiped the sweat off his brow with the back of his hand. He didn't disagree. "I've got work to do and you need to leave." He marched toward the back door and stood next to the bike leaning against the building. While his back was turned to her, she quickly pulled out her phone and took a photo of the bike leaning against the wall. She wanted to take a photo of the SUV's license plate, but Paul turned around. She lowered her phone just in time.

"I mean it, Rose, time to leave." He picked up the bike leaning against the building and stood there, waiting until she walked away. Her time was up.

Rose climbed into her vehicle and drove toward Lake Amelia in search of Deputy Stover.

Chapter Thirty-Eight

Rose drove through town twice, but her luck had run out: Deputy Stover was not around. Sure, she could call Maxi and tell her about seeing Paul and the bikes at his garage outside of town. Watching Stover question Paul at his shop must have meant the deputy suspected Paul of stealing bikes, but Rose's stumbling onto his work building outside of town proved nothing. Her suspicions were weak. She didn't want to call Stover again with scant information.

A few more turns of the wheel and she pulled up in front of the *Lake Amelia Dispatch*. Over the years, she'd found it helpful to bounce ideas off Bill, to get his perspective about whether her questions were taking her in the right direction or down a dead end. She walked in the door, said hello to Annie at the front desk, and got permission to wander down the hall into the newsroom.

"Rose, what brings you here today?" Bill asked as she walked over to the printer where he was waiting for copies.

"I stopped in to ask you about something."

He tilted his head and scrutinized her face.

"No, not about that," she smiled. "That's on hold." She almost added *'For now'* but decided the less said about her search into her father's past, the better. Until she had something more substantive to tell him.

"Then what can I help you with?" Bill took the top pages off the printer tray and thumbed through them, likely to make sure he hadn't accidentally picked up someone else's copy. Rose had done that more than once.

"It's about that bike theft ring. Have you heard anything about that bike that may have been stolen at Felton Falls the other night?"

He shook his head, thumbed through a few more pages, and placed a couple of them in the black acrylic tray on the table next to the printer. He took the printouts and tapped them on the table to even the edges, then stapled them together. "Do you have any new information?" he asked over his shoulder.

"Maybe. I don't know. Some suspicions."

Bill straightened up. He leaned against the empty cubicle across from the printer, slid his hand that wasn't holding the printed pages into the front pocket of his khaki slacks, and jingled some coins. "Talk to me."

She told him about stumbling onto Paul and his bike garage, which she suspected was a chop shop.

When she paused, he shrugged his shoulders. "What else?"

"Could it be the same bike or a coincidence?"

"Yes," Bill said. He paused, then smiled. "It's not much to go on, Rose, but you know that, or you wouldn't be here asking for my opinion."

She shrugged. "Yeah, I know. I'm trying to decide whether to tell Deputy Stover." And she told him how she'd seen Stover pepper Paul with questions. "How much trouble did Paul get into before?" She'd looked in the *Dispatch* archives and read about Paul's arrest on drug charges and his time in state prison. A couple of shorter stories mentioned less serious incidents, but Paul had earned his reputation as a trouble-maker. Naturally, the police would want to know if the guy who repaired and sold used bikes in Lake Amelia had any role in obtaining them illegally.

Bill cast a quick glance around the newsroom. "Are you asking about his record?"

"I'm wondering if what happened in his past could influence what he's up to now," Rose said. "And I don't mean drugs. When Thom and I were dating, he often talked about how frustrated his parents were with Paul getting into trouble—petty theft, drunk driving, vandalism."

"Paul O'Sullivan always was a partier. I know he was into drugs, got so hooked he started dealing a little to pay for his habit, and that's when the cops caught him. He was fortunate they didn't nail him for dealing, just possession of a large amount of cocaine. He did his time, then claimed he was done using. Near as I can tell, he still is—drug free, that is. But I'm not so sure he's cleaned up his act as much as some people say. He gets tossed out of bars occasionally for drunkenness, including Thom's. Why don't you ask Thom about Paul?" Bill turned his head as someone called out to him. He looked over and nodded.

"I've got to get back to work. You could mention your suspicions to Deputy Stover but be careful. You don't want to implicate Paul if he's done nothing wrong. The fact that she questioned him earlier might mean she has him in her sights, but tread lightly. And keep me posted."

Rose agreed and walked toward the front of the news-room, thinking about Paul's many brushes with the law. Was he tempting fate with another big mistake?

She glanced over the door leading into the hallway and smiled. The old school-type clock was still there: its round black frame with its white face and black hands ticking off time with the sweep of the red second hand. So many times she'd looked up at that clock, often in fear, wondering if she was going to make deadline. In a nod to the digital age, a rectangular clock was just below it, ticking off the minutes in bright yellow numbers against a black background. She gave the newsroom one last look before passing through the door, remembering all the wonderful memories here, even the stressful ones.

Nurse Lettie's car was in the driveway. Rose had a moment of panic.

"I was in the area and stopped by to say hello," Lettie said when Rose walked into the living room. "I'll be back tomorrow afternoon and can stay through dinner if you'd like. Your Aunt Tess stopped by with a casserole for tonight and other food, which will feed all of us for a few days. The casserole's warming in the oven."

"Thanks so much," Rose said. "What time do you think you'll get here tomorrow?" Rose had hoped to find Deputy Stover at the diner, eating breakfast. Maybe she'd call Stover and see if she wanted to have dinner instead.

"I'm sure I'll be here by two. Call me if you need me sooner," Lettie replied.

Rose went into the living room and sat on the footstool next to her mother's recliner. She reached up and patted Gladys, then rubbed her mother's hand. "How are you doing, Mom? Can I get you anything?"

"I'll be ready to eat dinner early, if you don't mind. Tell me about your afternoon. Did you have a pleasant drive?"

A little more energy drained from her mother's body each day; a few more shadows settled under her rheumy eyes; her voice grew hoarser, and Rose had to lean closer to hear her. Rose hadn't realized how difficult it would be to watch her mother's life slip away. And the most difficult times were ahead.

Rose smiled and told her mom about driving around listening to music on the radio, but that was it. "The hot days of summer haven't quite arrived and all the trees, the hillsides, the fields, are still a bright green," Rose said. "It was beautiful. Are you interested in going for a drive?"

Her mother shook her head. "I am content right here with you and Gladys by my side."

She helped her mom into the kitchen and set the table for dinner. Her mother ate slowly and spoke little. When she finished, she asked Rose if she could sleep in her recliner instead of going into her bedroom.

"Are you sure you don't want me to set up your queen-sized bed in the office?"

"I said I'm not sleeping in that room, Rose."

"Okay. Okay. If you're more comfortable in the recliner, of course you can sleep there."

"It's . . . I'm not ready for the hospice bed," her mother whispered, tears welling in her eyes and catching in her voice.

"I'll make the recliner as comfortable as I can. How about if I put a sheet on it?"

"I'd like that."

Hospice had given them extra padded sheets for the bed and recommended Rose use one on the recliner. She hadn't yet, but she would now. After she put the padded sheet on, she added her mom's favorite sheets and a pillow. She helped her mother get comfortable.

"How does that feel? Do you need any more pillows?"

"It's fine." Her mother smiled, but her next words were stern. "Please don't ask me to sleep in the office again. I've already told you I won't."

"Sorry. I didn't realize it was such a big deal. Are you still angry at Dad?" Rose knew she was treading on dangerous ground, but her mother's sudden sharp tone surprised her. "He stayed with us. We lived together as a family for more than twenty years." Rose's voice cracked. There was so much she didn't know, wanted to know. Perhaps her mother would finally let her in.

"Yes, he stopped traveling so much. We were a family again. But it wasn't that simple." Her mother's fatigue was apparent in her voice. "Some pain in life lingers forever. You must know that by now. Some things that happen . . . between people leave a scar." She coughed and ran her hand across her chest. "I don't want to be in that room and face reminders of what happened." Her mother looked so deep into her eyes that Rose almost couldn't bear it.

"Do you understand what I'm saying, Rose? Some things can never be undone."

Chapter Thirty-Nine

Rose fell asleep in the recliner, listening to her mother's ragged breathing. Tomorrow she'd have hospice or Nurse Lettie set up the oxygen. Her mother had been resisting it, perhaps for the same reason she wasn't ready to sleep in the hospice bed, but from the sounds of her breathing, she shouldn't avoid the oxygen any longer.

Several hours later, Rose awoke with a sore back and pins and needles in her good arm. She couldn't remember the last time she'd fallen asleep in a chair, but she didn't want to do it again. She lifted Gladys off her mother's lap and put her on the patio. The dog scampered to the far corner of the lawn while Rose stretched and loosened the tight muscles in her back. Then she made coffee and emptied the dishwasher. A little yip outside the sliding glass door let Rose know Gladys had finished her business, but Rose didn't want the dog waking her mother. The portable pet gate leaned against the kitchen wall. She put it across the doorway, prepared the dog's food, and filled her water bowl. Then she let her in. The food distracted Gladys for a while, then she sat in front of the gate and whined.

At that moment, her mom appeared, steadied by her cane. "It's okay, Rose. I'm up."

"Can I help you get to the bathroom?" Rose moved the gate out of the way.

"I can go alone. Just keep Gladys from jumping on me, please."

Rose scooped the dog into her left arm. She reached out to take her mother's elbow, forgetting again the limitations in her right arm. It was time to call the doctor in Philadelphia or find someone in the area to determine how well her arm was healing and when to replace the splint with a cast.

After her mom finished getting dressed and nibbling on toast, she returned to her favorite spot on the recliner. Gladys seemed to understand she needed to stay out from underfoot; the dog ran over to the other side of the living room and curled up in her bed.

Rose offered her mother the morning newspaper from Saratoga, but she wasn't interested. She had little interest in the TV as well when Rose turned it on and gave her the clicker. Rose returned to the kitchen and cleaned up the breakfast dishes. It was already after ten. Nurse Lettie was taking care of her mom that afternoon and evening, freeing up Rose for dinner. She hadn't had time to mention Paul's garage and the bikes to Maxi during their brief phone call. She tried to reach Deputy Stover again.

"Hello, Rose. What's up?" Stover answered on the first ring.

No small talk today. Stover must be busy.

"Hi, Deputy Stover. I'm calling to see if Maxi wants to meet at the Brew Pub for an early dinner." Rose had started calling the deputy by her first name when they were chatting as friends and not talking about law enforcement issues like stolen bikes. She'd done it the first time as a bit of a joke, and it stuck.

Stover laughed. "Maxi is on an early shift today, so that actually works. What time?"

"How's four o'clock?"

"Perfect. Maxi will see you then." She laughed again and disconnected the call.

Shoot. She didn't tell Deputy Stover about Paul and the photo she took of the bike. It would have to wait until later.

Rose called her surgeon's office in Philadelphia, explained what was happening with her mother, and asked if they could give her the name of someone in Saratoga Springs or Albany to check on her progress. She mentioned Dr. Levinson, the surgeon who'd helped her with the food tray in the cafeteria and asked the nurse if he'd be an acceptable referral. They promised to contact Levinson's office to send her referrals and information about physical therapy centers where she could continue her rehabilitation.

Lunch was a delicious ham salad sent by Aunt Tess the day before. Rose spread a big spoonful of it on rye bread and added some lettuce. Aunt Tess's ham salad was one of the most popular items on her menu, and Rose and her mother always loved it, but today Rose was the only one who enjoyed it. Her mom ate less than half of her sandwich. Rose worried about her mother's loss of appetite and lack of interest in reading. She mentioned both issues to Nurse Lettie when the two of them had private time later in the afternoon.

"It's a normal part of the process," Lettie said. "She's becoming less interested in worldly things like eating and reading, and more thoughtful about what lies ahead. You could say she's getting closer to having one foot in this life and one foot in the next."

"She may think about what lies ahead, but she's not talking about it," Rose said.

"And she may not. Especially to you."

"Why not? I'm the closest one to her right now," Rose

raised her voice, then dropped it again. "Except for her sister, Aunt Tess. I wonder if Mom's talked with her."

"She may have, considering they're closer in age and Tess may have thought about death herself. With your mother in hospice care, well, it's likely on Tess's mind. Many parents struggle to talk with their children about dying. Don't take it personally."

Lettie's last comment echoed in Rose's head as she walked to Thom's pub. *Don't take it personally? What other way could I take it?* She tried to push it out of her mind.

Rose was halfway through her first beer when Maxi joined her. The server handed them menus and asked Maxi what she wanted to drink.

"You mean you have something other than Amelia Ale?" She laughed. "I'll have my usual pint, please."

Maxi turned to Rose. "It's nice to see you when I'm not working."

"Yeah, about that," Rose began. "Can you put on your work head for a moment?"

Deputy Stover cleared her throat and leaned back in her chair. "What's up?" she asked, arms folded across her chest, chin dipped low, eyes locked on Rose's.

Rose got right to the point. "Do you think it could have been Paul O'Sullivan who put the bike into the SUV at the bottom of Felton Falls the other night?"

Stover waited to speak as Judy set the cold ale on the table. She nodded her thanks and dropped her voice. "Right now, it could have been anyone. Except you. Why do you ask?" Stover picked up the mug and sipped her beer.

She reminded Stover about the SUV that pulled out in front of her near the old bar with the license plate letters CG.

"Right. We checked that. The license plate didn't match up with anyone we've been investigating."

Rose took a sip of beer and explained how she'd been

driving around Washington County, encountered two dark SUVs, then found the garage where Paul was unloading a bike.

"I thought about you and him at his shop and you interrogating him—"

"Questioning, not interrogating."

"And I wondered if Paul is involved with the bike thefts. Look," she said, turning on her cell and finding the photo. "I took a quick shot of the bike leaning against the wall of the garage before Paul told me to move on." She handed over her phone. Deputy Stover looked at it and gave it back to her.

"I can't tell much from that photo."

"But you could show it to the person who reported his bike missing, right?"

Stover studied Rose's face. "Text me the photo and I'll consider it."

"It's a deal," Rose said. "I'm not trying to get anyone in trouble. I can't help but try to put together the pieces of the puzzle."

"Yeah, I get it. Photojournalist hard at work." Maxi paused, looked thoughtful for a moment, then leaned forward and asked to see the photo again.

"What are you thinking?" Rose asked as she slid the phone across the table.

"I want another look." Maxi pinched the photo to enlarge the image and brought the phone closer to her face. After studying the image for another moment, she reached out to hand Rose's phone back to her, but it slipped and dropped onto the table. When Maxi picked it up and looked at the screen again, she froze.

"What's the matter? Did something happen to my phone?"

Maxi's head moved back and forth, back and forth like a pendulum, her eyes never straying from the cellphone.

"What are you doing with a photo of my mom and Mr. Randall?"

Chapter Forty

Rose was stunned into silence. She reached for her phone. Maxi didn't move. Rose stretched her hand out farther and took her phone from Maxi, then placed it on the table. She also stared at the photo. Stared at Maxi. "Your mother? Keisha Norella Tyler is your mother?"

Maxi struggled to find her voice, and when she did, it was crisper than a fall apple. "Yes. How do you know her name? Rose, what the hell is going on?"

Rose massaged the spot between her eyebrows, then pressed hard with her thumb, trying to make sense of what Maxi said. Keisha Tyler. Mr. Randall. Not Mr. Randall. Randall Webster, her father. Her father and Maxi's mother? Keisha Tyler. Rose couldn't stop the names from repeating in her head like a song on an endless loop.

"How do you know my mother's name?" Maxi asked again. "And where did you get this photo?"

"I found it in the attic of my parents' home," Rose said. "In a box of my late father's stuff. In a book inscribed to him by KNT."

Maxi was hesitant with her next question, almost as if she knew what was coming. "And who is your father?"

"Mr. Randall. Webster."

Maxi's eyes darted back and forth as her mind worked to put the pieces together.

"Your mother—" Rose said.

"Your father—" Maxi said at the same time.

"Had an affair," Rose finished the thought.

"You concluded they had an affair based on this one photo?" Maxi poked her hand at Rose's cell phone. "How can you be sure?"

"There was one photo, but I found three books, all apparently inscribed by your mother to my father." She didn't mention the other photos Bill had given her. She'd learned from him how to dispense the information and photos slowly.

"Why do you say *apparently*?"

"Because she only used initials. KNT."

Maxi spotted Judy coming their way. "The hell with dinner. I want to see the books and that photo. Let's go."

"Slow down," Rose said. "I'm hungry and I'm not leaving until I eat. You should eat something too." She ordered a salad as soon as Judy stepped up to their table. Maxi reluctantly murmured that she'd have a burger and, less reluctantly, asked for another round of beer.

"I can't walk into my house with my sick mother in the living room, go upstairs, come back down, and walk out with a bunch of books, without questions," Rose explained. "Besides, the books are in the attic, so I'll have to retrieve them again." Why didn't Rose keep the books in her bedroom? That was poor planning. At least three books were lighter to drag down from the attic than a full box.

"Then when? I'm off tomorrow."

"Okay. I'll collect them tomorrow and meet you here—"

"No, not here," Maxi said. "Besides, I don't want to wait

all day. Let's meet at the diner for breakfast. What time does it open?"

Rose understood Maxi's urgency to find out what was going on, but she had to consider her mother. Who was coming to the house tomorrow morning? The hospice nurse or Nurse Lettie? She struggled to remember who had stopped in today. She was reeling so much from this new information she couldn't even remember what happened before she handed Maxi her phone.

"The diner opens at six, but I can't get there that early," she told Maxi. "I need to make breakfast for Mom and wait for the nurse." She paused, thinking about when she could go back into the attic without raising her mother's suspicions. It would have to be this evening. She could tell her mother she'd found the box with her childhood binder, and she wanted to make sure there was nothing else of hers in the attic. Would her mother question her about that? Doubtful, and it didn't matter. She had to get those books. Maxi was part of this now; Rose had to finish what she started.

"I can meet you at the diner about eight or eight-thirty."

Maxi shook her head. "The place will be packed with tourists by then. I don't want a bunch of people overhearing our conversation." She pulled at the edge of the paper coaster under her mug while she considered the options. "Why don't you come to my place?"

Rose and Maxi found little to say after the shocking revelation, ate quickly, and left the bar with their mugs half full. Her mother stirred from her spot on the recliner long enough for Rose to tell her she was home. On the second floor, Rose picked up the stepladder from behind her bedroom door and walked into the master bedroom closet. She climbed the steps, slid the plywood aside, and found the three books where she'd left them. Back in her bedroom, she set the books on her dresser and looked at the box of stuff she'd retrieved the other day. It was too dusty to put on the bed, and she didn't want to take it into the dining room. She dropped onto the floor and pulled the box in front of her.

She started with the large binder on top, put it on her lap, and flipped through the pages of report cards, crayon drawings, out-of-focus-photos she took of their trip to Disney World when she was eight, and professional-quality images of her trip to Boston during her senior year in high school. One page held her Girl Scout badges from Brownies until Cadets, which is when she left scouting to focus on the photography club and yearbook. The next page of pockets contained different-sized pages with her handwriting, including some poetry and the beginnings of a three-act play about a camping trip to the Adirondacks.

When she turned over the next page, she found her high school graduation program, her name circled in red ink. Beside it, her mother had written, *Love you, Grad!* And in his neat printing, her father had penned, *So proud of my girl! Dad.*

Her eyes filled with tears. He'd wanted her to go to law school and take over his practice after Kirk moved to Florida. During her junior year in high school, she spent the day with him as part of "Take Our Daughters to Work Day." She'd come down to breakfast dressed in casual pants and a loose-fitting, long-sleeved shirt. He sent her back to her room to put on a skirt and blouse. Then they'd driven to the Schenectady County courthouse, where he proudly introduced her to other lawyers.

The spectator gallery in the courtroom where her father's motion was being heard was all but empty. He sat at the attorney's table on the left facing the Judge's bench, and an attorney sat at the table on the right. Rose perched on the bench behind the partition separating the lawyers from the public until her father brought her up to the table with him.

The judge spotted her immediately after surveying his courtroom.

"Mr. Webster," the judge had said. "It seems you have new co-counsel this morning."

Her father stood, his chest swelling with pride. He motioned to Rose to stand beside him.

"Your Honor, this is my daughter, Rose Webster." Her dad couldn't have held back his grin or the excitement in his voice, even if the judge had ordered him to. "She'll be graduating from high school next year."

The judge welcomed her, then got down to business. She considered going to law school to make her father proud, but she'd already told him she wanted more freedom in her career than law books and courthouses allowed.

"But you love firing questions at people," he'd said. "You'd be terrific in court."

"Maybe I can do that in a different career," she'd answered. She was also an excellent writer, so he guided her toward journalism. Among the colleges and universities she and her parents visited was Ithaca College at the southern end of Cayuga Lake in the Finger Lakes. Rose fell in love with the area, with its sweeping vistas of vineyards, hilltop views of the lake, and the ever-inviting state park with Buttermilk Falls. It made sense that a woman who grew up steps from Felton Falls would gravitate toward a community with a similar setting. As far as her education, Rose appreciated she could study journalism and use the state-of-the-art film, photography, and studio equipment. She'd have the best of both worlds.

Rose flipped a few more pages in the binder on her lap, reliving her college years through the photos and letters she'd sent home and her mother had saved. The last pocket contained her gray tassel and the college's baccalaureate graduation program. Again, her mom had circled her name in red.

She also drew a big heart along with the words, *Congratulations, sweetie!*

Her father didn't write on the program but inside the card they'd given her. *You are a talented young woman,* he wrote. *I'm a lucky man to have you for a daughter.*

Sitting on her bedroom floor, seeing her father's handwriting, feeling his love through her memories and his words filled her heart. And humbled her. He'd been generous with his love for her. She couldn't have asked for a better father. She should remember that.

Chapter Forty-One

Rose glanced at the small box on the seat beside her several times during the half-hour drive to Maxi's home northwest of Lake Amelia. The box held the three books inscribed to her father from KNT. Rose had looked at the other photos from Bill and considered including them, but she didn't want to overwhelm Maxi. The additional photos might be too much to absorb along with the books, but Rose's need to know about the little girl in the photo outweighed her inclination to go slow. She put the photos in a manilla envelope and dropped it in the box.

Maxi wasn't kidding when she said her home was in the middle of nowhere in Washington County. Rose finally spotted a dark green mailbox with Stover stenciled in white on the side. She turned into the driveway and pulled up in front of a small cabin with a wide front porch that swept around both sides of the home. Tall pines surrounded the cabin, with dark woods filling in behind them. A chain-link fence jutted out from the cabin about halfway back, extended some twenty feet, then took a right angle toward the woods and disappeared in the trees. Two large dogs, barking and snorting, charged toward her. She was grateful the sturdy fence held them back.

Rose picked up the small box off the seat and stepped out of her SUV as Maxi opened the front door.

"Can I help you with that?" Maxi asked, stepping onto the porch.

"Nope. I've got it."

Rose followed Maxi inside and took a quick glance at her surroundings. "This is a nice place," she said. "I love seeing the woods from every side of the cabin."

"Thanks," Maxi responded, turning toward the living room area with its couches and comfortable chairs. Then she veered left and waved toward the dining room table. "Coffee?"

"Great," Rose said, hoping the conversation would move beyond one-word comments.

Their goodbyes at the restaurant the previous evening had been brief, and the tension between them persisted. Rose knew she'd irritated Maxi by prying into her family, but once Maxi accepted the two of them were probably related—at least that's the way Rose kept thinking—she'd understand Rose's motivation.

She trudged toward the dining room table and put the box down, pulled out a chair, and sat. Her eyes continued to survey the room. The furniture was simple, a lot of knotty pine with cushions in neutral colors of beige and tan, and there wasn't much. A few paintings of the Adirondacks hung on the walls, but no family photos. Didn't most people have a few family photos in their living space? She looked to the other side of the room; no family photos there, either.

Maxi walked up to the table carrying a tray of hot coffee and pastries. "I didn't know if you'd eaten breakfast," she said. "I picked up some muffins and scones."

"My stomach didn't want food earlier this morning," Rose said. "But I'm ready now and these look tasty."

Maxi nodded and sat, took one mug off the tray, and set it in front of her. Then she used a napkin to pick up a muffin and took a bite.

"Did you have any trouble getting the books out of the attic?"

"Mom was sleepy, so it wasn't a problem. Do you want to finish your muffin before I show you what I found?"

"I'm barely stopping myself from grabbing that box and dumping whatever's in it on the table, so, no." Maxi dropped her napkin and muffin on the table and reached toward the box.

Rose pulled it closer to her. These needed to be handed over in a certain order. She lifted the first book out and opened it. "Here's the first book and here's the inscription. *For Randall, with much appreciation for your help at the most important time in my life. KNT.*" Rose closed the book and pushed it across the table.

Maxi hesitated. She shoved her muffin farther out of the way, put her hand on top of the book, and pulled it in front of her. Then she lifted the cover and flipped over a page. Her hands stopped moving. She leaned in to get a closer look, then her body stopped moving. Rose wasn't sure if Maxi was breathing.

"It's your mother's handwriting, isn't it?"

Maxi swallowed and pursed her lips. She nodded. "What's incriminating about this? It's one lawyer thanking another. Show me the others."

Rose removed the other books from the box and put them on the table. Maxi opened their pages one at a time, then exhaled loudly before looking at Rose.

"You found these in the attic of your parents' home? Where were they before then? Do you know?"

"My aunt and I boxed up the books in my father's home office a couple of months after he'd passed and stored them in the attic. I don't know why we included these three books instead of donating them, but we were probably pushing to get everything done."

"You know, these books don't mean my mom had an affair with your father. Was he also a lawyer? She could have been a client. They may have been colleagues, even friends."

"They look like more than colleagues in the photo," Rose said. "The way they're standing so close together and smiling."

"Did you bring the actual photo?"

Rose opened the manilla envelope, removed the top photo, and slid it across the table.

Maxi glanced at it, then flipped it over. "There's nothing written on the back."

Rose shrugged her shoulders. So what if the photo wasn't dated or inscribed? It spoke for itself. Rose thought about one particular photo Bill had given her from his search in the *Dispatch's* archives of her father, Maxi's mother, and a little girl. Rose had to share that one, but only after Maxi saw the other stuff.

Maxi flipped the photo over again, examined the image again, opened each of the books again. She looked up and caught Rose studying her.

"What? Why are you staring at me?"

Rose opened her mouth, but no words came out. She might as well show Maxi the other photo. She didn't know what would happen after that, but she needed to find out. Rose reached back into the envelope, looked at the photo she drew from it, and gave it to Maxi.

"And did this photo also fall out of a book?" Maxi asked without glancing at the image. She sounded like a teacher who wasn't buying the excuse for a student's late homework assignment.

"No. I got it from someone I know at the *Dispatch*. I asked for his help identifying your mother, and he found this photo in the archives."

"You've been going around Lake Amelia asking people about my mother?" Maxi's face turned red, and her voice hardened. "What right do you have?"

"Don't get upset. The guy I asked at the paper is a friend. I've been discreet."

"Hah!" Maxi exclaimed. "You discreet? Rose, you're a photojournalist, a former reporter. Discretion does not come naturally to you."

"That's a cheap shot!" Rose shot to her feet, knocking over her chair. "I was trying to learn the name of the woman who had an affair with my father. Of course, I was discreet. Do you think I want that information whispered between neighbors all over town? Do you think I want to tarnish my father's image, his reputation? Especially when he's not around to defend himself?"

As if someone could defend themselves for having an affair and an illegitimate child.

They stared at each other, waiting.

Maxi shook her head several times. "Sit down, Rose. This is unchartered territory for us both."

Rose righted the chair and sat, but she couldn't keep her hands still. She sipped her coffee. Picked at the scone. Watched Maxi study the photo and waited for her to say something. Anything. When she could no longer stand the silence, Rose asked the question whose answer could change everything between them.

"Is that you between my father and your mother?"

"The way you've been looking at me, it seems you've already decided."

"I think it is you. I don't know."

Maxi touched the photo. She ran her fingers over the image of the three people. Her face softened as she seemed to recall the special moment the photo was taken. Maxi looked up at Rose with tears in her eyes.

"I can't remember where we were, but it was the last time I saw Mr. Randall. My mother never explained why he stopped visiting. Every time I asked, she said he couldn't come anymore and then she'd change the subject." Maxi wiped the tear that had rolled down her cheek. "I can't believe I'm crying over someone I haven't seen in more than thirty years. I was so young, and I never knew him that well."

"But it seems your mother knew him pretty well."

Maxi's head snapped up. She looked at Rose.

"Where was your father?" Rose pushed.

"I don't know. The only parent I've ever known is my mother. I never met my father."

Rose looked at the photo in Maxi's hands. "Are you sure?"

Chapter Forty-Two

"**A**re you seriously asking if your father is my father?"

"Think about it, Maxi. My father and your mother had an affair. Your mother never married your father or told you who he was. It's not far-fetched."

"That's what you think. I think it's a huge leap." Maxi frowned as she put the photos on top of the books and thrust them toward Rose.

But Rose wasn't done.

"What does it say on your birth certificate? What's your father's name?"

Maxi's eyes held Rose's for a moment, then drifted to the woods outside of the tall living room windows. Rose could only imagine the thoughts spinning in Maxi's mind, trying to find a credible place to land. Learning her mother had an affair with Rose's father was enough of a bombshell. It might be unimaginable for Maxi to think "Mr. Randall" could be her father. And although Rose acted like she was calmly handling the whole my-father-your-mother-affair-possible-half-sister thing, Rose's hands were shaking so much she held them under the table so Maxi wouldn't notice.

"The place for the name of my father on my birth certificate is blank." Maxi's voice was as flat as a lake at dawn on a steamy summer day. "I remember the first time I needed my birth certificate," she continued. "It was for my learner's permit. I was excited to take the test and get the permit. Couldn't wait to get behind the wheel. My mom and I stood in line at the DMV. Then she had to use the restroom. She handed me the papers and, with not much else to do, I leafed through them. I'd seen my birth certificate before, but never looked at it line by line. Now I did. And when I saw the blank space where my father's name should be, it hit me. I had no father. It's one thing to have your mother tell you your father is not in her life or yours. It's another to look at a document that makes it seem he doesn't—didn't—exist. My father does not exist."

"Did you ask your mom about it when she returned from the restroom?"

"We were called up to the counter almost immediately, and I didn't pursue it. My mom thought I was quiet because I was nervous, but I couldn't get that blank space out of my mind. I imagined the clerk looking up at me and asking my name. And I'd blurt out, Maxi Tyler Blank."

"How did you get to Maxi Stover? I read a profile piece on your mother—"

"During this discreet investigation of yours?" Maxi interrupted.

"A discreet *internet* search. The article indicated she married another attorney from the ACLU after a long relationship. His name is Luke Zimmer. If your name had been Maxi Tyler or Maxi Zimmer, I would have made a connection sooner."

Maxi shook her head and stared at Rose, apparently not amused by Rose's insistent digging into her family's history. "Mr. Luke wanted to adopt me, but I was seventeen and didn't see the reason. I liked him well enough, but I accepted the way things were."

"So, Maxi Stover . . .?"

"I got married when I was twenty."

"You married a guy named Stover?"

That brought the first laugh of the day and lessened the tension between them. "Rose, I told you I'm gay. I didn't marry a guy."

Rose did some numbers in her head. Maxi was somewhere in her mid to late thirties. She couldn't have married another woman fourteen years ago. "The Supreme Court didn't legalize gay marriage until 2015," she said. "How could you get married?"

"Because Massachusetts legalized gay marriage in 2004. My wife, Izzy Stover—ex-wife, that is—and I met at UMass Amherst where I was studying criminal justice and psychology. When we got married, Izzy asked me if I wanted her to take my name, and I said hell no. I wanted to take *her* name and finally get rid of the blank I'd been carrying around all my life. I changed my legal name to Maxi Tyler Stover."

"Why didn't you drop Stover when you got divorced?"

Maxi sighed and shook her head again, her patience wearing thin. "When Izzy and I split, I kept her name because I'd graduated university as Maxi Tyler Stover and that had been my name for several years. It was my name. I didn't want to go back to Maxi Tyler Blank." Maxi put her hand on top of the books and photographs. "Can we get off this sidetrack now?"

They both silently sipped cold coffee.

"Maybe we should take one of those DNA tests."

"Rose, are you nuts?"

"No, I want to find out if your mother and my father had a daughter. And if it was you. I always wanted a baby sister.

My parents said they couldn't have more children. Maybe you're the younger sister I always wanted."

"Don't go putting that on me. I'm not looking for another family."

Maxi got up from the table and carried the tray of empty coffee cups and pieces of pastry into the kitchen. She rinsed the dishes and slammed them into the dishwasher with such force Rose was surprised broken glass didn't cover the kitchen floor. Why was Maxi so angry? She thought Maxi liked her. She'd asked her out on a date once. If she found her interesting enough to date, why wouldn't she want to get to know her if they were sisters? Maybe Rose was taking this too fast. She never did know how to slow down when in the middle of a search for answers.

"You should ask your mother," Rose said, confident that was the next logical step if DNA testing was off the table.

"I repeat, are you nuts?" Maxi didn't return to her spot at the dining room table. Instead, she leaned on the kitchen counter, facing Rose. "You might as well suggest exhuming the body of your father to test his DNA."

"That's a stupid idea, Maxi. We'd still have to test your DNA."

"It's no more stupid than suggesting I go to my mom after not mentioning my father all these years and say, 'Hey, Mom, is Mr. Randall, the guy who used to come around when I was young, is he my father?'"

"You could tell her I found the photo and explain that I showed it to you because I was trying to learn the name of the woman who had an affair with my father."

"Yes, because law enforcement's job is to help people track down their father's mistresses." Maxi sneered. "And she wouldn't be amused if I ask whether she had an affair with a married man. Nope. Rose, those conversations are not going to happen."

Rose dropped her head and squeezed her eyes to hide the sudden tears. "I'm trying to find answers." Her voice cracked and she put the books in the box and the photos in the envelope. Rose knew this wouldn't be an easy conversation, but she expected more understanding from Maxi. She was in law enforcement, had seen and heard all kinds of situations, was supposed to keep an open mind, and look for facts. "If you asked your mother, we would both know."

Rose picked up the box and her handbag. She practically raced to the front door. Maxi didn't stop her or come out onto the porch to see her off. Rose started her SUV, did a fast turn-around in the driveway, kicking up stones and spinning her wheels. Once she'd driven a couple of miles, and before she got to a major road, she pulled over and held onto the steering wheel so hard her knuckles turned white. Then she released a torrent of tears and pain. Maybe she was trying too hard to connect her father to Maxi, but she knew what she saw in the photos. The little girl had looked at Mr. Randall with love in her eyes. Rose had looked at her father that way. She sat up and wiped her nose with an old piece of tissue she dug out of the cup holder.

Think, Rose, think. Yes, that was it. There was another photo. Rose could see it when she closed her eyes. But she needed to hold the photo in her hand and study it. It could be the proof Maxi couldn't deny.

Chapter Forty-Three

Rose stopped at home and checked on her mom, whose body disappeared under the blankets a little more each day. She fluffed up her pillows and made tea, then threw the ball with Gladys on the patio. The dog deserved more attention, but Rose didn't have much to give at the moment. Its animal instinct was so tuned in to her mother's declining health that Gladys rarely left her side now, tucked in on her lap or between her mother's arm and the side of the recliner. The dog whimpered whenever Rose picked her up and took her for a walk or encouraged her to do her business in the backyard. If Rose needed any more signs her mother's health was failing, Gladys's canary-like instincts would let her know.

Rose took care of her mom, then drove to Saratoga Springs for another session with the physical therapist and a check-in with an orthopedic surgeon. Rose's pushed herself to exercise every day and knew her hand and arm were growing stronger.

"Your range of motion is getting better and so is your

strength," said Debbye, her physical therapist. "You actually moved the needle a fraction on the dynamometer." She and Rose laughed. Two weeks ago in Philadelphia, Rose could barely squeeze the device that measured her strength. When her hand had hit the pavement during the rally, her middle and index fingers had jammed, damaging the nerves. She was fortunate the fingers hadn't broken. Her surgeon put splints on her two fingers when he put the splint on her arm and covered it with gauze. The broken arm and wounded shoulder were limiting enough; Rose complained that the finger splints were too restrictive. She left them on her dresser more often than not, although she remembered to put a mesh sleeve over her fingers to remind her to be careful.

"Keep doing the exercises for your hand. Remember, every other day or three times a week. You don't want to push it. Now, let's check your shoulder."

Rose winced as Debbye's fingers probed her shoulder muscles. Then she took Rose's elbow and raised her arm out in front. Not too bad. Debbye lowered her arm, then lifted it from her side.

"Ouch," Rose said, biting her lip. "That hurts a lot."

"I know," Debbye said, easing Rose's arm back to her side. "Let's do those arm exercises—gently, you don't have to move far or fast—and work on your movement."

Her PT session lasted half an hour. Regaining use of her fingers, arm, and shoulder would take months, not weeks. It would be a tedious process. Rose understood if she wanted to pick up a camera again, she'd have to put in the work. Taking studio headshots for the rest of her career was no more an option than Santa photos at the mall.

She stopped at the X-ray department on her way to the surgeon's office, then took a seat in his waiting room. How many people had sat in these chairs, waiting for a verdict from the doctor about the extent of their injuries? The surgeon in Philadelphia told her she was lucky the damage hadn't been worse. She'd been too consumed with pain and fear at the time to appreciate what he was saying. Now, walking around the hospital and sitting among other people with broken bones and shattered lives gave her perspective. Yes, she was fortunate.

Then her thoughts returned to the conversation with Maxi and the uncomfortable ending. She checked her phone to see whether Maxi had texted. Nothing. Rather than dwell on the situation between them, she scrolled her phone for the latest news and checked her social media apps for updates from friends and colleagues.

"Rose, the doctor will see you now."

She followed the nurse into an examination room. The nurse took her blood pressure, checked her oxygen level, and left her to wait. Finally, the surgeon walked in.

"Hello again, Rose." Dr. Levinson scrolled through the information on his laptop, asking her to confirm allergies to medications. He tapped the screen a few more times and walked over to Rose sitting on the examination table.

"You sustained damage from your fingers to your shoulder," Dr. Levinson said. "I've reviewed the initial X-rays taken after the accident two weeks ago. The broken bones in your arm will heal easier than your shoulder or your hand. See here?" Dr. Levinson gestured to the image. "The breaks were clean, and the bones are still where your surgeon set them. While you won't heal as quickly as a child, you're young enough and healthy. The bones should mend in four to six weeks."

"I'm happy to hear that," she said.

"I always try to start with the good news," he smiled, then turned serious. "Nerve damage is different. You may have noticed some tingling. The hand will take time. And the shoulder, those muscle strains especially, will require many weeks of therapy." He looked at her again. "Does all of this make sense?

"Yes. I asked a lot of questions of the surgeon who put my arm back together and the PT person I met in Philadelphia. They had the same assessment. I'm glad to hear you agree."

"The key is to let your arm heal. I understand you're a professional photographer and I'm sure you're itching to pick up your camera." He smiled at her. "Don't rush it, Rose. Keep doing the exercises and work with the PT staff. If you try to do too much too soon, you'll only set your recovery back. And I know you don't want to do that." He placed his arm on the splint. "Now that the swelling has gone down, it's time to replace this splint."

An hour later, Rose left Saratoga Hospital with instructions on how to care for her fiberglass cast. Focusing on her injuries had kept thoughts of Maxi at bay, but with nothing else to occupy her mind on the ride home, she couldn't help but replay their conversation in her head. Should she check in with Maxi or wait for her to make contact?

Her thoughts were interrupted by the Stewart's sign up ahead. She'd forgotten her refillable water bottle and needed a drink. Several cars were in the parking lot with two trucks at the gas pumps. She pulled into a space next to a white pickup truck. Inside, she opened the glass door to the cooler and pulled out a bottled water. When she turned toward the front of the store, she saw the guy who'd been in Paul's Lake Amelia bike shop when Deputy Stover had questioned Paul the other day. He sat in one of the booths, across from another guy who looked familiar. Their voices didn't carry far enough for her to hear.

Rose took a few steps into an aisle behind a display case, hopefully out of their line of vision but close enough to watch them. Who was the other guy? She squinted as if that would help. And then it struck her. It was the sheriff's deputy who'd been so brusque when she'd seen him and Deputy Stover at the old bar where they'd found stolen bikes. Edwards. That was it. Deputy Edwards. Was he friends with the guy from Paul's shop?

An arm slid across the Formica table toward the deputy, who stretched his arm out. Their hands touched, and as the first guy's hand opened, Rose saw the money. The deputy covered the wad of bills quickly and pulled his hand back. The guy who'd been in Paul's shop stood and walked out. The deputy's head swiveled as if to check whether anyone had spotted them. Rose bent down, knelt on the floor, and pretended to search the energy bars on the lowest shelf until the deputy walked out the door. Then she snuck a look outside. At the blue SUV driving away. With a New York license plate beginning with the letters CG.

Wasn't that the same vehicle that had pulled out of the parking lot in front of her at that old bar?

Was the deputy involved in the bike theft ring with Paul's friend? Was Paul involved or was Stover just looking for information when she questioned Thom in the pub and Paul at his shop? Was the handoff of money something totally different?

She needed to let Deputy Stover know what she'd seen. She paid for her water, made sure the dark SUV had left the lot, and climbed into her vehicle. Before she started the engine, she texted Maxi that she might have information about the bike theft ring. She waited a couple of minutes, but Maxi didn't respond. After another minute she got back on the road.

She was probably a mile outside of town when her phone vibrated. She'd left it on the front passenger seat. Was Maxi finally getting back to her? She didn't connect her phone to the console, finding it too distracting when text messages or incoming calls pinged. But now she wished she could see who texted. She leaned over to pick up her phone and glanced down. The tires bounced on the rough shoulder pavement. A horn blared. Her head shot up in time to straighten the wheel and get back on the road. She forced herself to focus on driving until she was back in town, then pulled over and picked up her phone. Tapped the screen. It was Kirk. He was flying into Albany the next day.

Chapter Forty-Four

Rose was running out of time. Kirk didn't like her poking into the past, and with him in the house as of tomorrow, she'd have fewer opportunities to snoop. She'd been in Lake Amelia for two weeks now, splitting her time taking care of her mother and looking into her father's relationships.

She greeted the hospice volunteer sitting on the love seat, knitting what appeared to be a baby sweater. Connie, an older woman with shoulder-length black hair streaked with gray, was a volunteer, not a nurse, who promised to visit almost every day to read the newspaper articles out loud, or watch TV, or sit in the garden with her mother. Whatever her mother wanted. Her first visit with her mom seemed to be going well.

Rose turned toward her mother. The oxygen machine at the side of her recliner emitted a constant humming noise, like the sound of a neighbor's leaf blower a couple of houses over. Rose stepped close to her mother before speaking, so she didn't have to raise her voice.

"Hey, Mom, how are you feeling?"

Her mother looked up suddenly and Rose realized she hadn't heard her come in. Rose took her hand and gave it a gentle squeeze. Most days Rose held her glance as long as she could, knowing the day was coming when she wouldn't be able to see her mother's face again. Other days, it was painfully difficult to see the change in her mother's appearance. Rose ran her tongue over her lower lip and pushed the building moisture out of her eyes. Her mother handled her failing health with such courage and grace, Rose was determined to do the same.

"Oh, hi. How were your appointments?"

"Look, I have a cast." She held out her arm for inspection and relayed the surgeon's assessment of her broken bones and pulled muscles. "And I actually showed some strength in my right hand during my physical therapy session."

The joy in Rose's voice brought a smile to her mother's face.

"Glad . . . making progress. When can you resume photography?"

Rose couldn't keep the disappointment out of her voice. "Yeah, it'll be a while. But my PT gave me exercises to build my strength and mobility. I'm optimistic. Can I get you anything?"

Her mother shook her head.

"Connie? Would you like a cup of tea?"

"No, thank you, though. I'll pack up my knitting and be on my way." Connie put her yarn, instruction sheet, and pink baby sweater project in her reusable grocery bag and stood. "Should I check with you in the morning about whether to drop by tomorrow, Carly?"

"My son is coming late afternoon."

"Oh, Kirk texted you as well, Mom?"

She nodded, then continued answering Connie in the clipped wording that had marked her speech since the stroke.

"Not sure when Nurse Lettie coming . . ." she paused to take a breath, "But a visit, in morning, would be good."

"Then I shall see you about nine." Connie let herself out and Rose sat on the footstool.

"Kirk texted me while I was driving back from the hospital," Rose said. "He didn't say what happened with his court case, but we'll find out soon because he's flying into Albany mid-afternoon. I get the impression he's coming alone."

"He told me the boys have commitments to their sports teams for the next week. They'll come later with Maria." Her mother reached out and took a sip of water from the glass on the table. Rose watched to make sure she had no trouble setting the glass back down. Nurse Lettie had mentioned her mother set the glass on the edge of the table once and it fell, spilling water on the rug. It wasn't a big deal, but her mother was upset that she'd misjudged, that she'd made a mess Lettie had had to clean up.

"I know you'd love to see the boys," Rose said, "although I'm not sure where we'd put everyone."

"You and Kirk will figure it out when the time comes."

When the time comes. When they came for a visit, or when they came to attend her mother's funeral? Rose shook her head to push the thoughts away.

"Tess also texted. She's coming with dinner." Her mother looked at the small white clock on the table beside her. "In about half an hour."

"She's spoiling us, and I'm good with that," Rose said. Then she realized she wouldn't be able to look through the albums for the photo of her with her father when Aunt Tess was in the house. She thought Rose had dropped her investigation about her father's mistress, and she didn't know about the little girl. Not yet.

"I'm going to look through the photo albums, Mom. Do you want to join me?"

"I'd rather nap."

"I'll take them into the other room, so I don't disturb you."

"Don't worry," her mom said, the corners of her mouth turning up slightly. "A marching band could come through here. I wouldn't notice."

Rose smiled and walked over to the bookshelves on the other side of the room. She pulled the albums off the shelf one at a time and cradled them in her arm. "I'll go into the dining room all the same so I can sit at the table." Her mother was already dropping off. Rose had the albums and the place to herself for at least half an hour.

Her mother had organized childhood photos of her and Kirk into two separate albums. That was different, wasn't it? Wouldn't most people fill one album, then begin another? Kirk was an only child for seven years. That might explain her mother's system, which reinforced the age difference between Rose and Kirk. She was eleven when Kirk left for college.

She turned the pages of "her" album through the infant and toddler years, looking for the photo of when she was about five. As she recalled, the image was of her and her father in the backyard. He'd been sitting on the wide cedar bench. She was at his side, looking up at him. That's the one that reminded her so much of the photo of her father, Keisha, and Maxi. Rose wouldn't think of her as "the little girl" in the photo anymore. The little girl was Maxi.

Rose went through the album twice, surprised she couldn't find the image she recalled. She raised her glass of wine and leaned back in her chair, enjoying a cool sip of rosé, the perfect wine for summer. Some families had an enormous number of photos of their children growing up, but kept them digitally. All the Webster family photos were in the two albums her mom organized. Was there another one? She didn't recall seeing any more in the bookcase or in the attic.

The album with Kirk's photos was in front of her. Might as well look at those. She skipped through his early years and turned the pages slower when Kirk looked to be about twelve. A few more pages. He'd shot up a lot in his teenage years, the same height as their father by the time he was sixteen. She was frustrated. Where was that photo? She thought she'd even seen it while looking at the albums with her mom the other day. She sighed and flipped over another page.

And there it was.

She'd been so focused on looking for an image with her and her father, she'd forgotten Kirk was in the photo. No wonder. Kirk had stood off to the side and behind the bench. He was in his early teenage years. Rose remembered he scowled a lot and kept his distance from his parents. She focused on her and her father, and the look of love on her face as she stared at him.

The photo of her father and Maxi was upstairs in her bedroom, but she didn't need to compare them side by side to see similarities between the two girls. The same oval face. The same smile. The same hazel eyes. Even the same way they tilted their head. Rose took a bigger sip of wine. They had different mothers, but at that young age, they both looked so much like her—their—father.

Chapter Forty-Five

Rose set the kitchen table while Aunt Tess helped her mother to the bathroom. They paused when they came into the kitchen.

"If you don't mind, I'd like to eat on a tray table . . . living room."

"Sure, Mom," Rose said, picking up the plate she'd set on the table. "I'll get the tray tables. Aunt Tess, will you be comfortable in the other recliner? I'll slide the side chair into the room more so we can all chat together."

"That works," Aunt Tess said, matching the slow steps her mother took down the short hallway. Rose watched them turn left, and the door closed. She didn't want to measure her mother's declining health every day, but she couldn't help but notice she was walking more deliberately and leaned more on the person at her side. In another day or so, Rose might not be able to support her with one arm. Thankfully, Kirk would be here soon.

Aunt Tess returned to the kitchen after getting her mom settled back into the recliner. "Do you have some wine for me?"

"Of course." Rose opened the top cupboard and pulled out a glass while Aunt Tess reached into the refrigerator. "Thanks for making dinner again, Aunt Tess. It's one less thing I have to deal with."

"It's no extra work, sweetie." She took the glass, filled it halfway, then topped off Rose's glass. As she stepped closer to Rose, she dropped her voice. "Your mother's so unsteady on her feet now."

Rose nodded. "I didn't expect her to go downhill so quickly." She put a small mound of spaghetti on a plate, then topped it with sauce and a large meatball. Given her awkwardness using her left hand, she wasn't surprised she'd left a puddle of sauce on the counter. Aunt Tess had offered to help dish out dinner, but Rose brushed her off saying she needed the practice.

Aunt Tess picked up silverware, a napkin, then the plate, and disappeared into the living room.

Rose made up two more plates, skipping the meatball on hers. She delivered one to Aunt Tess, returned to the kitchen, and got her plate. The process was tedious, but nobody complained it was taking too long.

Her mother struggled with the food. She wrapped the pasta around her fork and spoon, but as she raised her arm toward her mouth, most of the pasta fell back onto her plate.

"Maybe pasta wasn't such a great idea," Aunt Tess said. "Do you want me to cut that into smaller pieces for you, Carly?"

"Soon I'll be eating mashed potatoes . . . applesauce," her mother said with a hint of a smile. "Could you cut the meatball into pieces?"

"Sorry, I should have thought of that." Aunt Tess pushed her tray table aside and cut the meatball and pasta into bite-sized pieces. "There you go."

Rose watched her mom while she waged her own battle

with the pasta. Her left hand was not adept at eating or brushing her teeth. She hadn't eaten spaghetti since the accident and didn't realize how difficult it would be. After a bit, she swirled some pasta around her fork and got it into her mouth, smiling as she chewed.

Aunt Tess asked for an update on her injuries and Rose spent a few minutes explaining what the surgeon and PT specialist told her. The two of them chatted with glances toward her mother, but she didn't join the conversation. Before long, and with most of her dinner still on her plate, her mom put down her fork and wiped her mouth with her napkin.

"Was dinner okay, Carly?"

"Fine. I'm just not hungry."

"Would you like a piece of toast or some tea?" Rose asked.

"Tea would be nice. Decaf."

"Eat your dinner, Rose. I'll make it." Aunt Tess picked up her mother's plate and was back in a few minutes with tea, which she set on the tray table. "I didn't bring any dessert. I hope you aren't disappointed."

"No need for dessert. I'm fortunate to have a loving sister. Superb cook." She paused to steady her breath. "Sorry I didn't eat more."

"No worries, Carly." Aunt Tess chatted with her mom for a few minutes about how tourist business had increased at the diner and the latest news around town. Before long, her mother's eyelids flickered closed. Aunt Tess put the still-full cup of tea on the table beside the recliner and folded the tray table. Her mother never flinched. Rose followed her aunt into the kitchen and poured more wine. Aunt Tess walked toward the couch in the back of the room but paused when she saw the photo albums on the dining room table.

"Are you working on a photo board for your mom?" she asked, opening an album and thumbing through the pages.

"Um, yeah." Whew, thank goodness she'd put the photo of her father, Keisha, and Maxi upstairs. That would have been difficult to explain. Sooner or later, Rose would have to tell Aunt Tess that Maxi was not just the deputy sheriff who ate at her diner. She was also her niece. Or was she? Maxi was her father's daughter, not her mother's, so technically, she wasn't related to Aunt Tess at all. But the news would still affect her aunt.

"I'm glad you dropped that search you were so intent on," Aunt Tess said, closing the albums and taking a seat on the couch. "Look at your mother. I don't think she can handle the stress of dredging up the past again."

"Again?" Rose's eyes grew wide. "Are you referring to when I asked her about the woman in the photo with Dad a week ago?" Her aunt sipped her wine and didn't respond, staring into the fireplace. She set her glass on the coffee table and turned to Rose.

"You weren't the first person to ask your mom about whether your father was unfaithful. A few years ago, Kirk came for an overnight stay while he was in New York City on business. After he left, your mother told me they had a terrible fight. Kirk had told her how he'd twice seen your father with another woman." She raised her chin and inhaled. "Your mom said Kirk was so angry at your father for cheating on her. When your mom tried to defend your father, Kirk became even angrier. They were not on good terms when he left."

"I know Kirk has a lot of anger toward Dad, and he told me he saw a woman with Dad when he was on a school trip to Albany. But Mom and Kirk have had a lot of conversations since then."

"I'm sure, in time, they got past the argument. I know Kirk loved your mom very much. I mean, loves your mom very much." Aunt Tess's eyes filled with tears, and she reached for a tissue. She shook her head and dried her tears. "Your mother was so hurt when Kirk said he hated your father. She told him your parents had worked hard to heal their marriage. Your father stopped seeing the other woman. It's not like your mother ever forgot what he did, but she forgave him."

"Not everyone finds it so easy to forgive," Rose whispered.

Aunt Tess agreed. "Forgiving is one thing. Reliving it is another. I haven't seen your mother cry often, but that day telling me about her fight with Kirk, she sobbed uncontrollably. She'd forgiven your father, but the memory of what he did left a scar. Kirk's anger ripped that scar open." She paused. "I could see the pain building in your mother when you started asking questions. That's why I've pushed you to let it go." Aunt Tess took Rose's hand. "For your mother's sake."

Chapter Forty-Six

hy hadn't Maxi responded to the text about the dark SUV's license plate? Rose also wanted to tell her about the wad of cash that passed between the two men at Stewart's, one of them a deputy sheriff, but she was not going to text her the info. There was no way to know who might see it. Maxi must be too busy to call, but Rose felt she was holding a hot potato with no one to pass it to.

Rose walked into the only place that could take her mind off everything else: the library. She was so focused on walking up the stairs to the old Victorian house, she hardly noticed the creaking door as she stepped inside. A wave of calmness washed over her. The library was silent enough to hear the proverbial pin drop. Whenever she walked among the stacks and opened their books, her mind wandered into thrilling adventures in outer space, on a deserted island, or in political turmoil in Washington. Only fiction in that last category. She needed that distraction now, because her mind couldn't escape the scary scenarios of her mother's passing or Maxi's lack of contact. She needed something to loosen her clenched fists and lower her elevated blood pressure.

Carter hung up the phone when she walked over. After they greeted each other, she updated him on her mom and her arm.

"I may be able to take some interior and exterior photos of the library in a couple of weeks," she said. "Nothing too strenuous, but I'm getting stronger."

"Terrific," Carter said. "I'd better contact our cleaning company and get them in here. They come once a week to spruce up the place, but if we're going to take photos, we need a more thorough cleaning. And I need to call the kid who mows the lawn. I'll take care of those."

"I can work around their schedules."

"Thanks for your flexibility. I'll let you know. Can I help you find anything today?"

"You sure can," she said, a broad smile filling her face. "I finished the books I took out several days ago and need another book to lose myself in. Maybe sci-fi, maybe a political thriller. Nothing where a woman is in danger or the victim of a crime. And no beach reads."

Carter looked at her, scrunched his mouth, and closed his right eye as he concentrated. He snapped his fingers, catching Rose off guard again. "I have the perfect book. Follow me." He led her to the "New Release" section and tapped his chin with his fingers as his eyes flew over the titles. "Ah, here." He lifted a book off the shelf. "I read this last week. Since you like political thrillers, you'll love this."

She thanked him and took the book, no need to read the blurb or skim the pages. His advice was enough. "Is Ellie upstairs?"

He nodded.

Rose found Ellie in her usual spot and said hello as she walked to the other chair.

"Mind if I sit and read?"

Ellie lowered her book and shook her head.

"How are you today?" Rose dropped into the chair and set her book on her lap.

"I'm having a sad day, Dictionary Lady."

Rose tilted her head. "A sad day? Why?"

"Daddy said there's too much going on right now to get a puppy. He said maybe later. I thought summer would be okay because school's out, but he said no." She sighed. "That's why I'm sad."

"I'm sorry you're disappointed, Ellie. I know you like the idea of having a little doggie to love."

Ellie closed her book but kept it in her hands. "Do you ever have sad days?"

Rose inclined her head a little. "I'm having a lot of them."

Ellie studied Rose. "Because of your mom?"

Rose nodded.

"I'm sorry she's so sick."

"Me too, Ellie. Me too."

"Is it hard to be with her when she's so sick?"

Rose shook her head. "This might not make sense to you, but even though my mom's ill and I hate to see her that way, I'm glad I can spend the time with her."

"I wish I could've spent more time with my mommy before she died."

Rose closed her eyes. Despite her own pain, she felt Ellie's sadness settle over the room. Neither made a move to open their books.

"What happens when we die?"

A shot of pain pierced Rose's chest and she opened her eyes. She didn't expect to have a conversation about death and dying with an eight-year-old girl, especially one who'd lost her mother in the past several months. Rose had heard ministers talk about how difficult it was to console people who'd lost a loved one suddenly. And ministers had training. Rose struggled to find the appropriate words.

It took so long, Ellie said, "I'm sorry. I shouldn't have asked." Her eyes searched Rose's for forgiveness.

"It's okay. You're curious. I understand. I may not be the best person to ask. People have different thoughts about what happens when we die."

"You mean like going to heaven?"

"Yes, exactly," Rose said, relieved. She wasn't prepared to talk about heaven and hell, sinners and non-sinners, Jesus or no Jesus. Rose wasn't sure about her own beliefs.

Ellie didn't move. She had an inquisitive look on her face, like she wanted to ask another question. But she shook her head once, then pulled her book up close to her face. "I think I'll read, if that's okay with you?"

Rose agreed. She opened her book, concentrating on the plot about a violent political upheaval in Washington that was so close to reality she checked the cover to confirm it was fiction. Almost ten minutes later, when Rose looked up from her book, Ellie's chair was empty. That was different. Ellie had never left first before.

Brianna was at the checkout desk when Rose returned to the first floor.

"Have you seen Ellie?"

"She looked serious when she came downstairs. She's in Carter's office."

"Ellie asked me about dying and heaven, and I didn't know what to say. Conversations about the topic are difficult enough among adults. I hope I didn't upset her."

"She didn't look upset," Brianna said. "She told her father she had a question and asked if they could talk in private."

Rose thanked Brianna, checked out her book, and took her time walking down the library steps.

She arrived at the diner between the breakfast and lunch

crowds, took her usual spot on a stool at the counter, and picked up a menu. Iris finished pouring coffee for someone at the other end of the counter and raised the pot in Rose's direction. She shook her head. A couple of minutes later, Iris came over with her pad.

"What can I get you?"

"I'd like a grilled cheese with tomato on sourdough, please."

"Got it. What're you drinking today if not coffee?"

Rose thought. "How about a chocolate milkshake? Can you make it malted?"

"You bet I can."

Rose looked around. While not as peaceful as the library, the lack of noise appealed to her. She thought more about her conversation with Ellie. Carter had said she'd been reading above her grade level almost since the day she first picked up a book. She was smart and inquisitive. A great combination.

Aunt Tess came out of the kitchen carrying two plates holding sandwiches and tantalizing French fries and headed for the booths. The door opened and Maxi walked in. Rather Deputy Sheriff Maxi Stover. She was in uniform. Rose held her breath, hoping Maxi would join her at the counter. Maxi hesitated, looked toward the booths in the back of the diner. Then she shuffled over next to Rose.

"Hi," Rose practically whispered with a sideways glance. "I thought you were going to sit in a booth and avoid me. Did you get my text about the license plate letters?"

"I don't want to avoid you, Rose, and yes, I did get your text. I was off work, so I passed it along."

"The thing is, I think the guy driving it was Deputy Edwards. And I think the guy in Paul's bike shop the other day gave him a wad of cash. But not out in the open. They were trying to hide it."

That got her attention.

"Do you know for sure it was Edwards?"

"He looked different because he wasn't in uniform, and he wore a cap. But I caught a glimpse of his eyes. They were cold as steel in the mountains in January. He didn't like me when we met, and I saw that same surly look in his eyes when he turned toward me. I quickly ducked behind the protein bars."

"Okay. I'll call the sheriff and mention that. As to our personal situation," Maxi said, "I'm overwhelmed and need time to process all this information. The way you pepper me with questions, it's impossible to think around you."

"I promise, no questions right now."

Iris placed a tall soda fountain glass in front of Rose, the outside already sweating from the ice cream inside. Rose unwrapped the paper straw and took a hungry sip.

"A chocolate milkshake?" Maxi smiled. "What happened to your healthy vegetarian diet?"

"Chocolate's good for stress, you know." Rose sucked on the straw again and wiped the foam off her cheek with her napkin.

Iris walked over with the coffeepot and turned Maxi's cup over. "Wait," Maxi said, eyeing Rose's milkshake. "That looks good. I'll have one of those."

"Another chocolate malted milkshake coming up," Iris said, walking away and shaking her head.

Aunt Tess came through the kitchen door again, this time with a single plate of food balanced in her right hand. Her eyes took in the milkshake in front of Rose. After she delivered the dish of food, she stood across the counter from them.

"Rose, I haven't seen you with a chocolate milkshake since you were ten."

At that moment, Iris came alongside and set a milkshake in front of Maxi. Iris, Rose, and Maxi laughed at the look of disbelief on Aunt Tess's face.

"You too? Is this national milkshake day or something?"

Her eyes went back and forth between Rose and Maxi while the two of them sipped their dinks and smiled.

"Tess, order up," Iris shouted from the other end of the counter.

Aunt Tess turned and walked toward the kitchen. "There's something going on with the two of you. I can't put my finger on it, but I'll figure it out."

Rose and Maxi drank their milkshakes and talked about safe topics like what it would take for Maxi's Mets to defeat Rose's Phillies in the upcoming three-game series. They parted with a smile, and Maxi promised to be in touch.

Chapter Forty-Seven

Nurse Lettie took the blood pressure cuff off her mom's right arm when Rose walked into the living room. Rose was out of breath from a fast walk home, thinking more about her conversation with Ellie than what was up with Maxi, more about her mother's future than her father's past.

"What have you been up to?" her mother asked.

Rose told her about her stops in the library and the diner. Nurse Lettie listened as she tucked the blood pressure cuff into her bag, then sat on the love seat.

"Your face is flushed and lined with tension. What's wrong?" Her mother's voice was stronger than it'd been in a while as she peppered Rose with questions.

Rose hesitated.

"Don't stop talking with me now," her mother added.

"But I know you don't want to talk about this . . . dying."

Her mom reached out her hand and pulled Rose toward her. "Come. Sit." She motioned to the footstool. "Let's talk."

Rose shuffled forward and sat. She told her mother about her conversation with Ellie. "I'm not deeply religious, you know. I have my beliefs, but they don't fit into traditional church rules. When Ellie asked me what happens when we die, I stumbled and asked if she meant do we go to heaven. That seemed to satisfy her. But, you know, it got me thinking and wondering about you."

"I'm quite sure I'm going to heaven, not the other place." Her mother smiled.

Rose laughed. "Yep, I know that's where you're headed."

"I'll text you when I get there." Her mother winced as she searched for a breath and pushed out more words. "Maybe I'll dim the lights. So you know I made it."

Rose's eyes filled with tears. "I'm going to miss you, more than you think."

Her mother pulled a tissue from the box on the table next to her recliner, gave it to Rose, then took another one, and dabbed her eyes. "I'm going to miss you, too."

The tears Rose had been holding back so she wouldn't upset her mother flowed freely, her heart broken wide open. They both cried until Nurse Lettie came over with steaming cups of tea.

"You two have begun an important conversation," Lettie said, placing her hand on Rose's shoulder. "I'll head home."

"Lettie, bless you," her mother said. "Thanks."

"You're welcome. I'll see you in a day or two. I'll call or text first." Lettie collected her bag from the love seat and let herself out.

Rose and her mother talked and cried for several minutes, emptied the box of tissues, and started another one. Rose blew her nose one last time, her eyes red, but her pain eased.

"Thanks, Mom," she whispered.

"It helped me too. Don't be too sad for too long. I'll see you again one day."

Rose's red eyes swelled. "Geez, I finally calmed down.

Don't get me started again." She laughed and stood. "I'm going to the bathroom. You need anything?"

Her mother shook her head the slightest bit.

"Okay, I'll be right back."

Rose emptied the small wastebasket next to her mother's chair into the trash can under the kitchen sink, then went into the bathroom and washed her face. Who was that woman staring back at her? She'd never seen such dark circles under her eyes, or lines at the corners of her eyes. Her hair was a mess. How long had it been since she'd showered? Even following Lettie's directions, wrapping her cast in plastic was a hassle, so she'd been taking more sponge baths than showers. But she needed more than a quick wash. When she stepped back into the living room, her mother was asleep, her face lovely and peaceful. Rose watched her until tears threatened again. Then she climbed the stairs and headed for the bathroom.

Rose's phone pinged. Kirk was at BWI airport, having a bite to eat, waiting for his flight to Albany. He texted that he'd land about 3:30 without delays. That meant he should be in his rental car and driving to Lake Amelia by 4:00. She'd better think about dinner. Kirk was more of a meat eater and her mother wasn't eating much. How best to feed them both? Rose walked into the kitchen and opened the freezer. She lifted a package from the top shelf and set it on the counter. According to Aunt Tess's distinct handwriting, the package contained pulled pork. Two baking potatoes were in the bin by the pantry. She and her mom could split one. A check of the produce drawer turned up a head of broccoli and iceberg lettuce. That would do it for food. What about drinks?

She'd stopped at the liquor store the other day for wine, including a couple of bottles of pinot noir, Kirk's favorite. It would pair with the pork. A half-full bottle of single malt scotch was in the liquor cabinet. Another of Kirk's favorite drinks. Should she invite Aunt Tess? Normally, she wouldn't think twice. But it might be nice with just the three of them, especially since Kirk hadn't seen how quickly their mother was declining.

Her mom was awake when she peered around the corner.

"Hey, there. Did you have a good nap?"

"No such thing as a bad nap."

"Dad used to say that, but I don't remember him napping much," Rose said.

"He didn't until he turned sixty. He'd nap before dinner." Her mother glanced at a family photo on the bookcase. "Maybe his heart was failing sooner than we knew, slowing him down."

Rose walked over to the bookcase and picked up the photo her mother had been looking at. It showed the four of them one summer when they'd rented a house in the Outer Banks. They all glowed with suntans and smiles.

"He looked healthy all his life," Rose said, studying the image. "That's why it was such a surprise when he passed suddenly."

Her mother looked sad and distracted as she took the photo from Rose. "That reminds me."

"Reminds you of what?" Rose asked.

"Call Richard Klein's office. Make an appointment while Kirk's here."

"Who's Richard Klein?" Rose replaced the photo on the bookcase and sat in the other recliner, turned her body toward her mother.

"Your father's estate attorney. He updated my will with provisions your father had stipulated."

"What provisions? What were they about?"

"I don't know. Your father told Richard what he wanted."

Rose leaned forward in her chair. "Seriously, Mom, you signed your will without reading every word?"

Her mother held up her hand, palm out. "It was your father's wish. That's all I needed to know." She reached out to her table, pulled out the drawer, and sorted through a few notes with a trembling hand. She handed a piece of paper to Rose.

Rose picked up her cell phone, took the note from her mother, and strolled into the kitchen. Her mother had done legal paperwork for her father for years. She knew better than most people that you always read legal documents before you signed them. Signing papers because her husband had told her to didn't seem like something her mother would do. Rose punched the numbers on her phone's screen with more force than necessary.

Five minutes later, she returned to the living room. "Klein's out of town, but Kirk and I have an appointment the day after next."

"Good. What's for dinner?"

She told her mother what she'd planned, then thought she'd best check and make sure the pulled pork was thawing. And she'd better put the potatoes in the oven. Kirk could pull into the driveway within the hour. He wouldn't have advised his mother to sign a will she hadn't read. What was in it?

Chapter Forty-Eight

Rose popped the cork and left the wine on the kitchen island to breathe. After putting the potatoes in the oven at four hundred degrees, she cleared papers and books from the dining room table, took her laptop up to her bedroom, and moved her mother's papers to one of the side tables next to the couch in front of the fireplace in the great room. She fussed with setting the table, her eyes glancing at the clock occasionally, tracking Kirk's travel. It was almost five when a car pulled into the driveway. A door slammed. Rose hurried to the front door and opened it as her brother strolled up the brick walkway.

"Hello, Sis." He wrapped her loosely in his arms, mindful of her cast, and she smelled his lightly scented orange aftershave. After almost thirty years, he was Mr. Florida from his orange blossom aftershave to his bright red sports convertible, garage kept, of course. Rose and Kirk hadn't seen each other in at least two years. Their busy lives hadn't intersected even around the holidays in Lake Amelia. Kirk's high school-aged boys kept him and Maria busy.

"It's so good to see you. Mom's been looking forward to

your visit." She rested her left arm on his shoulder and stepped back. "Looks like that trial took a lot out of you."

"Yes, but we won, and that's what matters."

"I'll bet you're happy it's over."

Kirk nodded and looked at Rose. "How is she?"

Rose patted his shoulder. "She gets weaker every day. I'm glad you made it before . . ." Her words hung in the air.

"Me too. Let's go inside."

Gladys perked up when she saw they had a visitor, but even though she wagged her tail and wiggled her little body with excitement, she stayed put on the recliner.

"Hi, Mom." Kirk leaned over and kissed her on the cheek. "You look good."

Her mom brightened. "You were always sweet-talking me, usually when you were in trouble."

They all laughed, but the levity didn't last long.

"You're not doing so well, are you?" Kirk took Rose's usual spot on the footstool and gave their mom his complete attention.

The catch in Kirk's voice made Rose's heart ache. It was one thing to hear your mother was gravely ill and quite another to see it with your own eyes.

"It seems my journey is nearing an end."

Rose gave the two of them time to chat alone. "I'm going to put Gladys out," Rose said, walking over to her mother's chair. "She hasn't left your lap in a while." The dog resisted, but Rose had become skilled at lifting her with one arm. She snuggled the dog as she walked away. Soft voices drifted into the kitchen while she stood at the sliding glass door and watched Gladys take care of business. The savory aroma of pulled pork warming in the oven reminded Rose she hadn't eaten in hours. The baking potatoes should be close to done and those earthy scents added to the homey smells of dinner.

Gladys yipped and jumped up on the other side of the

glass door. Kirk and her mom laughed when the dog ran in. Rose imagined Gladys pawing Kirk's legs to get back on her mother's lap.

Rose stirred the pork, squeezed the potatoes to make sure they were soft enough, then put the bottle of wine on the table. Soon she'd turn on the burner where the saucepan held half an inch of water and a cut-up head of broccoli. Dinner would be ready soon. Kind of early for Rose and probably Kirk. She didn't want to interrupt her mother and Kirk. She stood, admiring the way her parents had expanded the kitchen and dining room area and the way it led seamlessly to the couch in front of the fireplace. Rose was growing more comfortable in this cozy space.

Kirk called out from the living room. "Should I help Mom to the table or not yet?"

Rose returned to the living room rather than shout. "Dinner will be ready in about ten minutes. Do you need anything, Mom?"

She shook her head.

Rose looked at her brother and realized he might want to freshen up.

"Kirk, do you want to bring in your luggage or use the bathroom before dinner? I put a second set of clean towels in the downstairs bathroom. I wasn't sure where you wanted to sleep, so I didn't know whether I should put towels there or in the second-floor bath."

"Thanks, Rose. I would like to clean up before dinner. Downstairs is fine, for now. We can figure out the rest later." He kissed his mother's hand and stood, stretched his back, and rolled his neck. Rose heard the soft cracks of his neck loosening up. When he walked toward the bathroom, she went into the kitchen and put the salad on the table. A few minutes later, they all sat down to eat.

Kirk updated the academic accomplishments of his sons.

Carlos was heading into his senior year in high school, and José was two years behind. They were like night and day, Kirk explained. "Carlos can write computer code faster than he comes running to the dinner table. He always has a device in his hands and wants to work with one of the big companies designing code, then maybe teach. José couldn't be more different. He's got his mother's artistic sense. He's more likely to have a drawing pad and pencil in his hands, or a camera. Rose, I think José has your eye for photo composition. He's not sure how his talents translate into a job, but he's going into his sophomore year, so he has time."

"I love the pride in your voice when you talk about your sons," their mom said.

"I know you haven't seen them in a couple of years, Mom. I'm sorry we don't get here more often."

"You all have busy lives." She looked from Kirk to Rose, then glanced down at her plate. "I've had enough. Could you help me back into the living room?"

"Sure thing." Kirk jumped up and helped her into the recliner. He walked into the kitchen a few minutes later.

"She said she was going to nap," Kirk told Rose when he rejoined her at the table. He put his napkin back on his lap and filled his fork with more pork and potato. "Mom told me we have an appointment with an estate attorney. What's that about? I revised her will after Dad passed. There was nothing complicated about it."

Rose sipped her wine and told him their mother had pushed for the meeting. "I asked her why now, but she wouldn't elaborate. Gave me a piece of paper and told me to call." She stared at her brother. "Do you think it has anything to do with Dad's mistress?"

"You think he wanted to leave her something? Wouldn't he have done that in his own will? That doesn't make sense." He finished swallowing, then put his fork on the plate.

They were both silent, maybe waiting each other out. The wine bottle was empty. Rose considered opening another one, but her brother wasn't a big drinker and she'd had enough for the night. Any more wine and she'd have trouble sleeping. And that reminded her.

"Where do you want to sleep?"

"I know Mom usually sleeps in my old room. She told me she'd had my bed taken to the town dump when she moved downstairs years ago."

"The hospice bed is in Mom's room now," Rose said.

"The hospice bed? I didn't realize they'd already delivered it."

Rose got up from the table. "She hasn't slept in it yet. Come on."

Kirk looked into the room and stepped back. "Where's her bed?"

Rose opened the door across the hall. "We can set it up if you want to sleep in here."

He barely glanced in the other room. "I'd rather not. What's upstairs in the master?"

"A couple of dressers. No bed."

He considered his options, quickly discarding the less appealing one. "Can you help me move the mattress upstairs?"

She pointed to her right arm and raised her eyebrows.

"Right. Okay. I'll sleep on this mattress on the floor in his old office tonight. Tomorrow, I'll call Aunt Tess and see if she can help me find someone to move the mattress and frame upstairs."

"He's gone, Kirk. It's just a room."

"It's not just a room, Rose. It's his old office. And it contains some unpleasant memories I'd rather not sleep with tonight." He walked toward the kitchen. "I'll get my stuff out of the car."

Rose stared after Kirk. The two of them, her brother and

her mother, holding so much anger inside and letting it eat away at them. Rose was angry at her father too, but it wouldn't stop her from sleeping in here, would it? The books from KNT came off the shelves right over there. It'd been over a decade, but she could visualize books filling the bookcase. She shivered and goosebumps popped up on her arms. Then again, perhaps she wouldn't want to spend the night with unpleasant reminders, either. She decided to cut her brother some slack and went to find sheets for the queen-sized bed.

Chapter Forty-Nine

Another sleepless night for Rose. She had stared at the walls, the ceiling, her phone, thinking about whether Maxi would contact her soon. When she wasn't thinking about Maxi, she was preoccupied over a meeting she dreaded, but couldn't wait to happen, so she could stop dreading it. Morning couldn't come fast enough.

She refilled Kirk's coffee mug, then set a plate with a piece of toast on the table in front of her mother.

"Are any nurses coming today?"

"The hospice nurse will visit this morning," Rose answered her mother as she sat back down. "And the hospice volunteer offered to come later in the morning so she won't be here at the same time as the nurse."

Her mother nodded and nibbled on her toast. "Is the *Saratogian* on the porch yet?"

Kirk got to his feet. "I'll check." He was back in a minute, unfolding the daily newspaper and reading the headlines. "They arrested a cop—a sheriff's deputy from Washington County—and three other guys for running a bike-theft ring. It's the front-page story. Do you know about this?"

"Arrests? A deputy sheriff?" *It couldn't be Maxi.* She reached for the newspaper, but Kirk kept reading as he walked over to his chair and sat.

"One of the people they arrested is Paul O'Sullivan. O'Sullivan sounds familiar. Is he the brother of your high school boyfriend?"

"Oh, dear," her mother said. "Thom must be upset."

Rose reached for the paper again, wanting to read the news for herself. "Could I please see the paper, Kirk? I'll give it right back." He handed it to her.

"Could you read it out loud or tell me what it says?" her mother asked.

She scanned the article. "According to the paper, investigators arrested Paul O'Sullivan and two other men from Washington County last night and charged them with stealing bikes and reselling them or stripping them for parts. They picked up Paul at his garage outside of town. At least cops didn't arrest him at his storefront off Main Street. It would have been so embarrassing for Thom and the O'Sullivan family if cops had made a scene downtown." She read the next section out loud. "'Also arrested in connection with the theft of the bikes was Washington County Deputy Sheriff Chad Edwards.' It doesn't say more about his role. Arraignment is scheduled for this morning."

"Where?" Kirk asked.

"The Washington County courthouse in Fort Edward." Rose looked at the clock on the stove. "It's in two hours. Do you want to go? The hospice nurse will be here with Mom."

Kirk stopped sipping his coffee and tilted his head, looking at her with questions in his eyes. He took the newspaper from her. "Why would I or we go?" he asked.

"To support Thom and his family. I can go alone."

"I'll think about it." He finished his coffee, stood, and put his mug in the sink. "I'm going to get those towels you left for me."

"Don't you have physical therapy today?" her mother asked Rose as Kirk retrieved his towels from the bathroom and climbed the stairs to the second floor.

"It's okay. I can reschedule."

"Take those therapy sessions seriously, Rose. You need the use of your hand." She tried to push back from the table and coughed several times. "Can you help me up?"

For a moment, Rose thought her mom was trying to make a point about Rose's lingering injuries, but she wasn't. She needed to use the bathroom. Rose used her left arm to help lift her mother and watched her shuffle down the hall, one hand on the wall as she went. Then Rose sat and reread the entire article. Was Maxi involved in the arrests? Probably. No wonder she'd been too busy to reach out to Rose. Maybe Maxi was waiting until she talked with her mother. Rose knew she'd have to let Maxi take the next step, no matter how difficult it was to wait. Waiting was like gardening. Not one of Rose's strengths.

As soon as the hospice nurse settled into the living room with their mother, Rose and Kirk left for the courthouse. They sat behind Thom and his parents. It wasn't the first time the three O'Sullivans had been to court for Paul, and Rose thought it likely didn't get any easier. Or less embarrassing. The charges were severe. A felony, grand larceny, stealing property valued up to twenty-five thousand dollars, according to the clerk who read the charges aloud. Cops had found several expensive bikes in the garage and two more at the shop in Lake Amelia. Paul was a repeat offender. Bail was set at fifty thousand dollars. The two other guys arrested with Paul faced the same charges, but their bail was only ten thousand dollars because they had no prior record.

Rose glanced across the aisle and spotted Deputy Sheriff Stover sitting in the second row behind the prosecutor's table. She and two other deputies leaned toward one another and whispered until the judge admonished them.

The silence in the courtroom was broken when Deputy Sheriff Chad Edwards was brought in and told to take the last seat at the table with the three other accused men.

The judge banged the gavel.

"Deputy Edwards, please rise along with your public defender." The judge waited until they were on their feet.

"Deputy Edwards, you are charged with aiding and abetting those defendants accused of stealing bikes throughout several counties, including the county you took an oath of office to serve. Not only are you charged with committing a crime, if guilty, you have broken the public trust." The judge stared at the deputy. "How do you plead?"

Deputy Edwards's head dropped to his chest. "Not guilty, Your Honor."

People in the aisle behind Rose whispered, "What did he say?"

She turned around. Not guilty, she mouthed.

The judge set bail for Edwards and adjourned proceedings.

Rose and Kirk left the courtroom and waited in the hallway. Thom and his parents were stone-faced as they walked through the heavy wood doors and greeted them.

"I'm so sorry, Thom, Mr. and Mrs. O'Sullivan," Rose said. "I think it's wonderful that you're here for Paul, but it must not be easy."

Thom reached out and hugged her. "It was a surprise to see you in court. Thanks for coming. We appreciate the support."

"You think after your children go out into the world you can let them go, let them make their own way, make their own mistakes. And learn how to fix them," Mrs. O'Sullivan said.

"Unfortunately, that's not the case with Paul," Mr. O'Sullivan added. "So here we are again to bail him out, only this time, the stakes are higher. Felony charges."

"The truth is, we're all imperfect," Thom said, then he turned to Rose. "We're all frail human beings. Life demands a lot of us, tempts us, pushes us, and we all err. Like your mom said the other day, Rose, 'You can't protect people you love from themselves. Or from making their own mistakes.' I would add that the most important thing we can learn is forgiveness." He looked at his parents. "I appreciate how much you understand that," Thom said. "You're always here for Paul and me. When family veers off the tracks, you help them out."

"We taught you well," Mrs. O'Sullivan said, putting her arm around Thom.

"Yes, you did. You taught me you don't walk away from family." Thom turned to Kirk. "It's good to see you, Kirk, although not under these circumstances." He reached out to shake his hand. "You must be in town to visit your mom. I stopped by the other day. I hope things work out as best they can."

"For you and your family, as well," Kirk said.

The courtroom's double doors opened again, and Deputy Stover walked out with the two other deputies she'd been talking with in the courtroom. She looked at their group, nodded to Thom. When her eyes met Rose's, Maxi pinched her lips together, gave the briefest smile, then walked down the hallway.

Rose wanted to introduce Kirk and Maxi, but it couldn't be a worse time. Maybe it would be better to tell him about her first.

"Do you still have business with the court?" Kirk asked Thom and his parents. They nodded. He took Rose's arm and said, "Come on. Let's let them finish what they need to do."

Thom gave Rose a long hug. "Think about what I said," he whispered.

Rose and Kirk had a short walk to the car parked the next street over. He slid into the driver's seat and watched Rose stretch to pull her seatbelt across her lap and snap it in.

"Need help?"

"Nope, I've got it, thanks. Takes a little longer. Umph," she groaned, then smiled when the buckle clicked. Rose stared out the window, enjoying the view, especially when the road came close to the Hudson River. But she also thought about what Thom had said. About the importance of understanding when people err and forgiving them. She shifted in her seat to look at her brother.

"Keisha Norella Tyler."

He shot her a glance. "Is that name supposed to mean something to me?"

"It's the woman Dad had the affair with. She's an attorney in the Albany area."

"Did she tell you they had an affair?"

"I haven't spoken to her. I don't need to. You can tell how close they were from looking at the photo. I'll show it to you when we get home, and you can confirm it's the woman you saw on the street with Dad when you were in Albany."

"You don't have to show it to me, and don't let Mom see it." His booming voice bounced off the windshield. "It was long ago, Rose. I couldn't see her that well. I couldn't recognize her if I wanted to." He turned on his right blinker and veered onto another county road.

She cleared her voice. "It isn't just the woman. There's someone else you should know about—"

"Rose, listen to me. I. Don't. Care. And you'll only upset

Mom if you bring it up. Nothing good can come from what you're doing."

They rode the rest of the way back to Lake Amelia in silence.

Chapter Fifty

"Rose, we need to talk."

It was the middle of the afternoon. She and her brother had finished a late lunch and were staying out of the living room while their mother slept. Rose worked on her laptop at the dining room table. Kirk sat at the end of the couch in front of the fireplace.

"That's what I was trying to do on the drive home." She spoke without looking at him.

"Let's go out on the patio where Mom can't hear us if she wakes up." Kirk slid his computer off his lap and onto the coffee table. "I'm going to grab an iced tea out of the fridge. Do you want one?"

"No thanks. I'm still full." She waited for Kirk to get his drink, then followed him outside. Four chairs sat at the square table with the glass top. Rose pushed one of them back from the table and sat. Kirk took the chair opposite.

"Look, without Dad confirming it, I'm pretty sure he had an affair. When I came home a few years ago, Mom and I got into a fight." Kirk told Rose the same story Aunt Tess had shared. "I chastised myself for upsetting her that day. When we spoke on the phone a month later, I apologized and promised to never bring it up again. Mom doesn't need to hear you dredging up the past."

Rose opened her mouth, but Kirk held up his hand to cut her off.

"Let me finish. I was a teenager when I figured out Dad was probably cheating on Mom. You remember how crazy teenagers are: moody, overly dramatic, vulnerable, raging hormones? Well, maybe you don't, but I see it in my sons and am reminded of my own teenage angst. I didn't know if it was common for married couples to have extra-marital relationships. I couldn't ask Mom and Dad, and I was afraid to ask any of my friends. I didn't want Mom and Dad to look bad. You know how rumors spread around Lake Amelia. Anyway, I was unsure what to make of it.

"It wasn't until my second year in college that I talked to someone. A therapist."

"You saw a therapist? That's a surprise."

"Yeah, I know. I took a psychology class and we studied the long-lasting effects of trauma on children. I'd read enough to know that seeing Dad with that woman and hearing his phone call traumatized me, worried that our family would break apart. I worked with a therapist for about a year and took another psychology class to understand the dynamics of relationships. I'd developed a close group of friends. Finally, I got up the nerve to ask if any of their parents had an affair. Two of the guys' parents had divorced after one parent had cheated. I understood what happened with Mom and Dad wasn't unique. I normalized it, but I never respected Dad as much as I once did."

Rose wiped a tear from her cheek and shook her head. There'd been so much more hurt between her father and Kirk than she'd ever realized.

Kirk took the cap off the iced tea and took a drink. He set

the bottle back on the table, reconsidered, picked it up, and sipped again. Then he continued.

"It wasn't easy for me to commit to a relationship. A few times I thought I'd found the woman I wanted to marry, but I worried what would happen if I lost interest in her. I didn't want to do to my wife what Dad did to Mom. In my late twenties, working for my first law firm in Florida, I began seeing a therapist again. When I found Maria and fell in love, I asked her to go to couple's therapy."

"You weren't fighting or having any issues?"

He laughed and shook his head. "We'd been dating for less than a month, but I knew I wanted to marry her. I told her about Dad's past and why I wanted to see a therapist. She didn't flinch, said she'd fallen for me too. We went several times. After the first session, we stayed up for hours talking about what we wanted in a relationship, in life. That was the night I proposed. Maria and I learned how to communicate, and I healed from my fear of commitment."

He looked at Rose like he was trying to figure out what she thought. "I didn't mean to make a speech, but there you have it."

She filled her lungs with air and pushed it out between tense lips. "You weren't the only one afraid of commitment because of Dad," she said softly. She slid her chair closer to the table and told Kirk about the angry conversation their mom had with their dad on the phone when Rose broke her ankle, how their mom never intended to raise children alone. "I was Daddy's Little Girl, but he left me, left all three of us physically for short periods of time, but probably emotionally for months, maybe years. As I look back on it I realize I probably felt the tension. I must have been unsure of what would happen to our family. Maybe he wanted to keep seeing the woman. And I could tell how much he'd hurt Mom." She scratched the skin under her cast and looked into the yard, at the delicate spikes of flowers blooming on the lavender, and the gentle breeze causing the large bed of black-eyed Susans to sway from side to side. Having this conversation with Kirk was a relief. She was finally shedding the weight of fear and trauma.

"I wanted to establish my career before getting into a serious relationship, so I was in my early thirties when I began dealing with commitment issues. One guy I dated traveled a fair amount. When he was on the road, I worried he was with another woman. When he broke up with me, he said I was too clingy. Ha. I never thought I was clingy, but when I considered how I'd been with him, I had to admit he was right. The trauma of our parents led to the trauma in my life, and my hesitancy around commitment. But, as with you, there's more.

"One day, I found the man of my dreams. It sounds hokey, I know." She laughed. "He was smart, funny, good-looking, attentive, had an interesting job. And he was married. I didn't know what to do. I connected with this guy on such a deep level, couldn't stop thinking about him, wanted to be with him in the worst way. But I worried about getting involved with a married man. I didn't want to bring shame to my family. To my mom and dad." She laughed again, only this time there was no joy in her face. "Nothing ever happened between us. I broke it off before it went too far. You and Mom kept asking why I pushed so hard to find out about Dad's relationship with the woman. Dad was my idol. I learned a lot about life from him, treating people right, making smart decisions. And there he was, making a stupid decision that could shame our family. I couldn't let it go. How could I be so strong and Daddy so weak?"

"What would Dad say if he knew how his actions affected us?" Kirk looked away, but not before Rose saw the glistening in his eyes.

They both stared into the distance until Rose cleared her

throat. "I don't know why he started seeing Keisha or how long it lasted, but I think he would be sad if he realized how much that hurt us, don't you?" Rose looked at Kirk to see if he agreed, but his jaw muscles were tight, his lips pressed close together. She wanted to bring up Maxi, wanted to tell him the rest of what happened between her father and Keisha Tyler. But she didn't want to ruin this moment. They were closer than they'd been in years. There would be time for more conversations.

Chapter Fifty-One

ose's cell pinged. The sun was still low in the sky. Who'd be texting this early? She reached over and lifted her phone off the bedside table.

Can you talk this morning?

She fell back onto her pillows and shook her head a few times to wake up. Then she tapped out her response with one finger.

Not in person. Lots happening with Kirk in town. Meeting with lawyer 10:30. Phone call?

Rose watched the pulsing dots and waited for Maxi. Had she spoken with her mother? Did she learn who her father was?

Phone not my first choice but OK. Call me 8:15.

Rose nodded, then remembered to send Maxi a thumbs up. Where should she take the call? The patio was out. What if Kirk wandered over? She couldn't take the call upstairs in her bedroom because he could hear her across the hall if he came upstairs. The best option was to find a bench at Falls Park or the southern end of Lake Amelia. She wiggled out of bed.

Rose came downstairs forty minutes later. She'd have the routine of showering with a cast covered in plastic perfected by the time they removed it. And she still hadn't found a technique of blowing her hair dry with one functioning hand and one almost useless one. Then she reminded herself to relax. She looked fine. Unless Maxi wanted to FaceTime. Rose looked in the mirror at the bottom of the stairs and fluffed her hair and shrugged her shoulders. This was as good as it got.

Her mom was in the recliner, and Rose smelled fresh coffee coming from the kitchen. Kirk had already brewed the coffee. *Isn't it nice to have someone else in the house?*

"Good morning," she said, heading straight for the coffeepot.

Her brother was at the kitchen table, eyes glued to his laptop. He acknowledged her greeting with a wave of his hand. "I've been looking into this attorney we're meeting with this morning. I don't recall Dad mentioning Klein's name. Why didn't he use the attorney who wrote his will, who'd handled all the family's legal concerns for decades?"

"I guess we'll learn more later." Rose's thoughts centered more on her call with Maxi than on the meeting with the attorney. She took a yogurt out of the fridge, scooped it into a bowl, added slices of banana, then topped it with sunflower seeds. After getting a spoon from the drawer, she took her coffee and dish over to the kitchen table and sat across from Kirk. "Did you learn anything interesting?"

"Only that Klein specializes in drawing up complex wills and his legal documents are rarely challenged in court." He looked at Rose's bowl. "Are there more yogurts?" After Rose nodded, Kirk glanced back at his computer. "Dad's regular attorney, Walt Sherman, is more of a meat-and-potatoes kind of lawyer, handles a lot of general issues, few complicated ones. As far as I know, Dad and Mom didn't have a complicated estate. I'm not sure why they'd need an expert in protecting wills from probate."

"Like I said," Rose mumbled through a mouthful of yogurt, "we'll learn soon enough."

"I prefer going into a meeting prepared," Kirk said, rising from the table and making a breakfast like hers. "I guess we should leave for the meeting by nine-thirty. Does that work for you?"

"Yes, I'll be back by then."

"Back? Where are you going?"

"I need to stretch my legs, and I might as well take Gladys. She could use some exercise." She finished eating, rinsed her bowl, and left it in the sink. Then she grabbed Gladys's halter and leash on her way into the living room.

"Hi, Mom. I'm taking Gladys for a walk. Kirk's in the kitchen."

Her mother's eyes squeezed open and she nodded. Then she dropped off to sleep again.

Rose patted her pocket three times before she left the house to make sure she had her phone. She walked to the south end of the lake and had to catch her breath before she called Maxi.

"It's almost eight-thirty," Maxi said, without greeting Rose first.

"Sorry. Getting ready is no small feat." Rose lifted Gladys onto her lap. "I want to know how you're doing with what I told you, but first, I was shocked to read about Deputy Edwards' arrest. How long did you know he was involved?"

"You know I can't talk about that, Rose. It's an ongoing case."

"I remember how crisp he was with me that day when I saw you and him at that old bar. I wonder if he already knew the bikes were there."

"Rose . . ."

"Okay, okay. But one day you need to explain how you guys solved the case and what went down with Edwards." Rose cleared her throat and continued in a gentler tone. "Did you speak with your mother?"

"Mom and I met for lunch yesterday in Clifton Park at a restaurant with plenty of space between tables. It was convenient since I couldn't get to Albany, and she couldn't make it up to Washington County."

Rose wrapped her arms around Gladys and rested her chin on the dog's head. Softly, Rose said, "Don't keep me in suspense, Maxi. Tell me what she said."

"Your father and my father are one and the same."

"Wow." The word shot out of Rose's mouth, parting the hair on Gladys's head. "You really are my baby sister."

"Rose, since we're both in our thirties, could you delete the baby and call me your sister? No one's called me baby-anything in a long time."

"Fair enough," Rose said. "How did she sound when she told you? Was she surprised you brought it up after all these years?"

"She looked, I don't know, maybe relieved, like she could finally unload this burden she'd been carrying."

"Did she tell you how she met my father, how their relationship started?"

"No, Rose, and I decided not to pry. She was very matter-of-fact about the whole thing. She had a relationship with Mr. Randall, knowing he was married. They'd connect at conferences or when he was on the road for a case. One day, they agreed to stop seeing each other."

"What about—?"

"Don't rush me, Rose. I'm telling you as best I can." Maxi sipped a drink. Rose gave her time to swallow and tell the story her way.

"Mom said she found out she was pregnant after she'd

stopped seeing Mr. Randall. She considered having an abortion, but she dismissed the idea quickly because she wanted to have the baby. Mom had a decent job and didn't need anything from him. She didn't tell him and avoided conferences because she didn't want to run into him. Then he saw us at a political protest in Albany."

Rose gasped. "Was that the photo I showed you?"

"No. Mom says I was only two years old when we ran into him." Maxi paused.

Rose raised her chin and stared at the blue waters of Lake Amelia. Wow, her father didn't know he'd gotten Maxi's mom pregnant. When did he find out Maxi was his daughter? She wanted to ask but bit her lip.

"Mom said it was awkward for several minutes, that your father stared at me, then looked at her. He glanced at her ring finger. No wedding band. He asked Mom to introduce me. I don't remember any of it, but she told me that's what happened."

"But the photo I have with the three of you," Rose blurted. "You were older than two, right? But you said your mom and my father didn't resume their relationship. I don't understand. Did you accidentally run into each other again?" Rose struggled to imagine the sequence of events, wished she could draw a timeline on a sheet of paper. Then again, how much did the details matter? She finally had her answer. Maxi was her half-sister. Rose decided the half thing didn't matter. Maxi was her sister.

"Mom said Mr. Randall, your father, my father," Maxi stumbled, trying to find the way best to refer to him. "Um, when he realized I was his daughter, he struggled with not being able to see me. She relented, allowed him to see me twice a year. Until that photo. An attorney they both knew saw them and said hello.

"'Whose sweet little girl is this?' the man asked them. Mom said his eyes shot back and forth like he was trying to make a point. Like he couldn't tell the woman with the afro and the little girl with the afro were together and the tall white guy didn't fit in?" Maxi was thoughtful. "Couldn't fit in. Mom said Mr. Randall looked at me with so much love in his eyes, she couldn't afford to have us seen with him again. That's the day they broke it off for good."

"And she never saw my father again?"

Maxi hesitated. "Not exactly. She attended his funeral."

"Seriously? Your mom was at my dad's funeral? Where were you?"

"You said it was what, about twelve years ago he passed? I was in Northampton."

Rose glanced at her watch. She and Kirk had to be on the road in about fifteen minutes. Gladys licked her hand as she picked up the dog, put her on the ground, and began walking toward home.

"Maxi, thank you for talking with your mom and telling me. I'm sure it wasn't easy. Are you glad you asked her?"

"Am I glad she told me about my father? It's too soon to say. I'm sorry I never got to know him better. I'm sorry my mom and I never had an actual family with the three of us. In some ways, it was easier to leave the blank after my name. But I'm not a Webster. I'm still a Tyler, always will be."

Before they disconnected the call, Rose asked Maxi to meet her at Thom's for dinner.

"I'm not sure what the rest of the day holds. I'm in a bit of shock and still working this out," Maxi said.

"Look, I understand. It's a lot to take in. Maybe it would help to keep talking about it."

"I don't know, Rose. I need to see how the day unfolds. Plus, the sheriff wants a debrief about the bike-theft arrests."

"I'm not sure how my day's going to go either with this attorney meeting. Kirk thinks it's odd that Dad hired an expert in probate for mom's will. Dad must have known something might be a problem. I guess I'll find out soon. I'll call you later, okay?"

Crickets. Maxi had already disconnected the call.

Chapter Fifty-Two

"All due respect, Mr. Klein. That can't be right," Kirk said. "Why should we divide my parents' estate three ways? There's only me and Rose. Did he want part of the estate to go to a charity?"

Kirk and Rose sat with Richard Klein at a round table in his office. She was glad he didn't ask them to sit across his ornate desk, so tidy it looked like the cleaning crew had just left. Legal tomes filled the bookcases, along with a few family photos. Rose spotted framed photos on the wall of Klein with New York's two US senators and one with the current governor. This guy was a few legal levels above her father's modest former law practice.

"I'm going to explain further," Klein said, his hands folded on top of the papers in front of him. "And I'm giving you the details in the order your mother and father instructed. Your father was very particular about how he wanted this information revealed. That's why I'm taking the unusual step of giving you some details about your mother's will before she passes."

"It's Mom's will but Dad's instructions? That's unusual." Kirk leaned forward and rested his elbows on the table.

Rose was also stunned at Klein's opening remarks, but at least she had an idea who might receive the other third.

"I won't go through the financial details of the stock accounts, bank accounts, and contents of the safety deposit box at Adirondack Trust, except to point out there is a list of items in your materials and your mother left some of her jewelry to her sister, Theresa Adams. You will receive this information after your mother's death. She asked me to meet with you while she's still alive because she knew you'd have questions."

He cleared his throat and slid the top paper over. Then he referred to the document in front of him. "Rose, I understand your name is now on your mother's checking account, and Kirk, you have power of attorney. You'll easily have access to everything after she passes." Mr. Klein glanced at his papers again.

Rose sat in her chair, feet planted firmly on the plush navy carpeting, and waited for the attorney to tell them more. Kirk fidgeted in his chair like a toddler. He probably preferred to be the person in charge.

Klein cleared his throat. "I'm now going to read from the last will and testament of Carly Adams Webster.

"All else from my family's estate, the house at 25 Cedar Street, all stocks and savings, and items in the safe deposit bank at Adirondack Trust, except those designated for Theresa Adams, shall be divided as instructed by my late husband, Randall Wallace Webster: one third to our son Kirk Carlisle Webster of Miami, Florida; one third to our daughter, Rose Caroline Webster of Flourtown, Pennsylvania; and one third to Randall Webster's daughter, Maxine Tyler Stover, of Washington County, New York."

"What? Who?" Kirk stopped fidgeting and sat up straight "Who the hell is Maxine ? It says she's Dad's daughter?"

Rose turned to her brother. "I tried to tell you."

"When?" His head snapped from Klein to Rose.

"In the car on the way back from Paul O'Sullivan's arraignment. Another time I mentioned Keisha Tyler and was about to tell you about Maxi. Both times you cut me off and told me to leave the past alone. Well, here's the past. Dad had a daughter with his mistress."

"That can't be right," Kirk said, looking at Rose. "Dad would have told me if he wanted this woman sharing in the family estate. Mom would have told me when I drafted her will." He struggled to keep his composure. "Wait," he shot a look at Klein. "You amended Mother's will after I drafted it."

"Yes, at your father's request."

"When did my father make that request?"

"About twenty years ago when he updated his will."

Kirk stood. "I need a minute. Where's the men's room?"

Klein gave him directions and Kirk hustled out of the lawyer's office.

"You knew?" Klein asked. "How did you find out about Maxine?"

Rose told him how the photo in the attic led to her discovery of her half-sister. "Dad hadn't included Maxi in his will, so I didn't think she would be mentioned in Mom's will." But Klein hadn't drafted her father's will. The regular family attorney had. Their father must have enlisted Klein years ago —decades ago—to make sure Maxi was named in her mother's will. Her head spun. This was a lot to figure out for someone who wasn't a lawyer. But then she did understand one thing. "Dad hired you in case Kirk and I try to challenge the will."

"He wanted to ensure his instructions were carried out. I gave him my word I would do that. In court if necessary."

"Did he leave you a retainer in case we took legal action?"

"Perhaps we should wait for your brother before discussing this any further." He glanced down and crossed his hands over the papers.

They sat in silence for several minutes until Kirk returned. A new crease dominated her brother's forehead. Rose debated whether he was more offended as an attorney or a son.

"Is there anything else, Mr. Klein?" Kirk asked, not returning to his chair at the table.

"I am to arrange a meeting with the two of you and Maxine at your convenience. We can do that now or after your mother's passing."

Kirk shook his head. "Rose and I need to talk before anything else happens." He motioned to Rose and the two of them left Klein's office.

"You should have warned me before this bombshell hit," Kirk said, tapping the ignition and glancing into the rear-view mirror, then at the camera view on the dashboard.

"Next time I insist I have something important to tell you, maybe you'll listen and stop shutting me down." Rose glanced out the window. "I didn't know Dad was going to include Maxi in the will."

"You keep calling her Maxi like you know her."

"I do. She's the deputy sheriff we saw in the hallway at the arraignment the other day."

Kirk shook his head several times. "Boy, do I have questions for Mom." He put the car in gear and headed for Lake Amelia.

Rose walked into the house first. Nurse Lettie greeted her, then cleared a plate and empty glass from her mother's tray table. As soon as the front door closed and Kirk was in the living room, their mother spoke.

"Lettie, I need to discuss something with Kirk and Rose." She coughed hard a couple of times, wiped her mouth with a tissue, and dropped it into the small wastebasket beside her recliner. "Will I see you tomorrow?"

"Of course, Carly. I'll put these in the kitchen, collect my stuff, and be on my way."

Rose took the recliner and Kirk strode toward the blue love seat, fluffing one of the throw pillows before he sat.

"I'm sure you're upset," their mother said right after Nurse Lettie left. "Tell me what happened with Klein, then I need to tell you something."

"There's more?" Rose blurted, but her mother nodded at Kirk to begin.

Kirk gave her a quick but thorough recap of their meeting with Klein. "When did you learn Father had this illegitimate daughter?"

Rose shot him a look but didn't speak.

"Your father and I had our ups and downs. At our lowest point, he began seeing an attorney. In Albany. When I found out, he apologized and said he ended the relationship." She paused, her voice scratchy and weak, and took a sip of water. "They started seeing each other again a few years later. I told him he had to choose. Her or us."

She turned to Rose and gestured toward her bedroom. "There's an envelope. Top left drawer of the dresser."

Rose was back in a minute and gave the envelope to her mother, who opened it and pulled out a few sheets of lined, yellow paper in their father's handwriting.

"There's more, but, Kirk, can you read this part out loud?" Her finger pointed to a paragraph. Kirk rose from the love seat and drew a chair closer to their mother and Rose.

He read as if he were under oath, careful with each word.

I want to apologize again for not staying true to our vows. I carry this guilt and shame every day and appreciate your love all the more for forgiving me. It wasn't easy accepting I had a child with this woman, the third child you and I tried so desperately to have. You need to tell Kirk and Rose they have a sister. I have not given the child one dollar of support at her mother's insistence, but when we both pass, Carly, I know deep in my heart that this child should share in the distribution of our savings and assets.

She looked at Kirk and Rose. "He'd retained Richard Klein to draft language to include in my will. He figured he would likely die first."

"You forgave him everything?" Rose stared at her mother.

"I loved your father, and I wanted to keep our family whole." Her voice cracked, and she reached for a tissue. "Your father invested well. There's plenty for all three of you."

"He asked you to include this Maxine, and you simply signed the papers?" Kirk's voice went from soft to near shout. "And this doesn't bother you?" Kirk said.

"He made most of the money," she said weakly. "How could I say no?"

Kirk may have had more questions, but he was too agitated to ask them. "I'm going for a walk." He left the house. His car started and backed out of the driveway.

"I guess he's going for a drive instead," Rose said.

"You're not surprised. Did you find out about his other daughter?"

Rose pressed her lips together and felt her eyes well up. "Yes, I learned about the other woman and the girl. Well, the girl's a woman now."

"Have you met her?"

Rose nodded and leaned closer to hear her mother over the ever-present oxygen machine. The conversation had sapped her mother's energy, drained the color from her face.

"Is she a good person?" her mother asked, her eyes boring into Rose's.

"Yes, Mom, she is."

"I hoped she would be." With that, her mother drifted off to sleep.

Chapter Fifty-Three

A unt Tess was on her way with dinner and a request. Rose met her at the door.

"Come into the kitchen, will you? I need a favor."

"Sure. Whatever you need."

Aunt Tess put the bags of food on the counter and pulled Rose to her.

"What is it? What's wrong?" Rose hoped there wasn't more news. There'd already been enough for one day.

"Could I have some alone time with your mom, just the two of us for dinner?"

"Of course." Rose wrapped her good arm around her aunt's trembling body. "I should have made time for you two sooner."

"We've had time these past few weeks, but I think . . . she may be getting close." Rose held her and stroked her back. Aunt Tess wiped her eyes as she looked around. "Where's Kirk?"

"He went for a drive and maybe a walk. I'm sure he's

telling Maria about our meeting with the lawyer. Did Mom tell you everything?"

"Without knowing what 'everything' means, I don't have a clue why you met with the lawyer. And that's not why I want some time with your mom. I'd like to share a few memories, maybe apologize for a couple of things that are nobody else's business."

"Got it," Rose said. "I'll head to Thom's for dinner and text Kirk to meet me there." Rose wanted to persuade Maxi to join them, but after their last phone call, Rose wasn't sure Maxi was ready. Or Kirk. "Give me a minute to freshen up and I'll be on my way."

"Thank you, Rose. I love you."

"Love you too."

She was antsy, but it was too early for Thom's, although a cold beer sounded good. She texted Maxi and asked to meet up with her. After several minutes, during which Rose wondered if Maxi was busy or not responding, Maxi finally texted she'd join Rose at four. Kirk responded to Rose's text that he had to eat somewhere, so he'd meet her about 4:30. She hadn't told Kirk that Maxi would be there. *Is this a smart idea? Hard to know, but it's easier to apologize than to ask permission and have him not show up.*

Rose had at least half an hour to kill. A walk would be nice. She headed for the south end of Lake Amelia, realized it would be crowded with visitors, and spun around, hoping for some space at the foot of Felton Falls.

Young families had set up for a day at the park, spreading out blankets and anchoring them with coolers, chairs, and sneakers. Bright tablecloths, small coolers, bags of paper plates, and plastic silverware covered various picnic tables. Some families sat at tables eating, with fathers stoking charcoal in the grill. Rose smiled at the children running in circles and hollering at the top of their lungs. It wasn't the calm spot she'd sought.

She hiked a short way up the left side of the falls and found a bench under the trees with a soothing view. She stared at the water tumbling over the slate and river rock formations and breathed in the calming aromas of crisp pine and damp earth. Then she closed her eyes and took several slow, deep breaths. After a few minutes of meditative breathing, the stress lifted from her shoulders and the next breath she inhaled traveled to her toes. She flexed her ankles and lifted her heels off the ground, feeling the lightness of her body. Rose absorbed the sounds and sensations of the falls, of the birds singing in the treetops, the chipmunks and squirrels scampering in the woods behind her. The squeal of a toddler broke through the silence, but it was less grating on Rose's nerves now than it was fifteen minutes ago. She lifted herself up and walked back down the path to where her sister was waiting.

Maxi sat at a table in the back, a full mug of ale in front of her.

"I'm glad you could make it," Rose said.

Maxi gave her a tight smile. "How did it go with the lawyer?"

Klein had instructed Kirk and Rose to keep their conversation about her mother's will in strict confidence, but he said they could tell Maxi their father confirmed he was her dad.

"Kirk was shocked to learn about you. He disappeared in his car a few hours ago, I think to process the latest info and call his wife. I asked him to join us so he could meet you." Rose looked over at the bar where Thom was pouring drafts and motioned to him. He nodded, poured another beer, and sent it over with the waitress.

"Are you two eating today?" Judy asked.

"We will, but we're hoping my brother joins us, so we'll wait to order."

"Sounds good. I'll keep an eye on you."

Both of Maxi's hands wrapped tight around her beer mug like she was afraid it would escape. She'd barely glanced at Rose since she'd sat down.

"How are you doing?"

Maxi half laughed. "How am I doing? I spent most of this morning traipsing through the woods with the dogs, pushing me and them until we could barely walk. Then I took one of the hottest showers I've ever had. The hot water stinging my skin gave the pain a different place to land. Until I turned off the water." She looked at Rose. "I keep feeling slammed against a wall." She took one hand off her beer and started ticking off her points. "First you show me a photo of my mom and your dad; next come the books she inscribed to him; third is the photo of me and my mom with your dad, Mr. Randall; fourth, my mom confirms Mr. Randall was my father; and fifth—I hope there's no more because I'm running out of fingers and the capacity for surprises and we aren't even going to discuss the arrests in the bike theft." Maxi took a deep breath. "And fifth, your father confirmed he's my father twelve years after he died. And you saunter in here and say, 'How are you doing?'"

"I'm sorry, Maxi. I never meant to cause you such pain."

Maxi shook her head, then sipped her beer. "I wish you'd left well enough alone. Wish you'd have let those secrets die in the attic."

"Do you? Aren't you glad to know who your father was? To find out you even knew him, had spent time with him?"

"But I didn't know him as my father, and we didn't live together as a family. You don't understand, Rose. You had a mom, a dad, a brother, an actual family. I never had that."

Rose expected Maxi's pain, but she didn't realize how much anger had been building up with every bit of new information Rose passed along. How would Maxi react to the latest news?

"Maybe I shouldn't have come," Maxi said. "I'm not in a happy place. I'd rather feel better when I meet Kirk."

"Too late," Rose said, looking at the entrance to the pub. "He's here."

Kirk walked across the room and pulled out a chair, but before he sat down, Rose introduced him to Maxi.

"Kirk, this is Dad's other, our, er, Deputy Maxine, I mean. This is Maxi Stover."

Maxi put down her beer and held out her hand. "Nice to meet you. Rose has talked a lot about you."

Kirk fired a look at Rose that said, you set me up. His frown indicated he wasn't ready for this. He reluctantly took her hand and shook it.

Judy popped over to their table and asked Kirk what he was drinking. He shook his head.

"Nothing, thanks."

"Are you sure you don't want a beer or something to eat?" Rose asked. "Aunt Tess wants to have dinner alone with Mom so they can talk."

"She texted me."

"So stick around for a bit," Rose said.

Kirk relented and asked for Johnnie Walker on the rocks. "Blue, if you have it. Black if you don't." Then he sat. Then he stared at Maxi.

"I guess my existence comes as a bit of a shock to you," Maxi said. "Welcome to the club. Your father's role in my life shocked me. Recently, my mother told me she had a relationship with your father, and she got pregnant, even though Mom was on the pill."

So much for the efficacy of the pill and the condoms in Dad's luggage.

"That doesn't make you my sister."

"Kirk! You don't have to treat her like she's on the witness stand. Her mother never asked Dad for anything."

"And I'm not asking you for anything," Maxi said. "Rose and I are friends, and we'll remain friends. If you don't want to know me, that's up to you."

Kirk accepted his scotch from Judy and took a drink. "Look, Maxi, I've got nothing against you. I'm not angry at you. I resent my father, and to be honest, I don't hold your mother in very high regard for getting involved with my dad."

"Even Mom said it wasn't the smartest thing she ever did."

"I have a sister," Kirk said. "It's Rose. I'm not ready to wrap my head around having another sister who doesn't even look like me."

"Is that because of the color of my skin?"

"Not at all. My wife is Latina, and we have two sons. It's got nothing to do with race." He sipped his drink again. "I bear a strong resemblance to my dad. Rose looks like Mom. I don't think you look like either of us."

"You do look like your father," Maxi said softly, nodding her head.

Rose sensed an immediate change in Kirk and Maxi.

"You remember him?"

"I was only five the last time I saw him, but I have a vague recollection. When I looked at the photo Rose showed me of your father with me and my mother, it took my breath away. It's like I was standing next to Mr. Randall all over again."

"Mr. Randall? That's what you called him?"

Maxi dipped her chin once.

Rose had had plenty of time to process the news about her father's affair after tracking down Keisha. Then she learned about Maxi. Her process had been slower, easier. Kirk hadn't had the luxury of time to absorb this news. What Maxi said about him resembling their father appeared to have touched him.

Kirk's and Rose's phones pinged at the same time. Kirk was slow to react. Rose read the text first.

"Something's happened to Mom. We need to get home immediately."

Rose grabbed her purse. Kirk stood and took out his wallet.

"I'll take care of the bill," Maxi said. "Go see what's happening. Text me when you know something."

Chapter Fifty-Four

Aunt Tess and Nurse Lettie hovered over the motionless body. They'd lowered the recliner as far back as it would go, shoved the side table against the wall, and pushed the footstool in front of the love seat. Rose struggled to slow her panicked breathing as she quickly crossed the room.

"Is she . . .?"

"Your mom is still with us," Nurse Lettie said, adjusting the pillows on each side of her mother's head and smoothing the light blanket that covered her from under her chin to her toes. "I don't think she will be much longer."

"What can I do?" Rose asked, laying her hand on her mother's leg and gently stroking it.

"One of you could go into the kitchen and get a small glass of water with a little ice, so I can moisten her lips."

"I'll get it." Kirk hurried into the kitchen. A cupboard door opened and closed with a click and the refrigerator dropped chunks of ice into a glass. The kitchen tap turned on and off.

"Rose, could you get a kitchen chair, maybe two?" Aunt

Tess stood on the other side of her mother from Nurse Lettie, one hand on her mother's shoulder, the other hand rubbing the lower part of her own back.

Kirk handed the glass of ice water to Nurse Lettie, who dipped a foam spoon into the water, then ran it along their mother's cracked lips.

"What happened?" Rose asked her aunt, carrying a kitchen chair into the room.

"She collapsed." Aunt Tess set the chair alongside the recliner and eased into it. "We were chatting, although I was doing most of the talking, and she seemed to be listening. Then she took a shallow breath, put her hand to her chest, and fell forward. Thank goodness Lettie was in the other room and came running when I called."

"She was coughing more often this afternoon, and I found a tissue with blood on it," Nurse Lettie said. "It's possible a blood clot in one of her legs broke free and sped to her lungs." She glanced over at Rose and Kirk. "It happened quickly, and because she's been on a high dose of morphine, she didn't feel any pain. Still doesn't." She pushed back some hair that had fallen on her mother's face and stepped aside as Kirk returned with another kitchen chair.

"One of you sit here." Nurse Lettie took Rose's hand. "Now's the time to say any last words. She may be able to hear you."

Rose turned to her brother. "Kirk, do you want to sit with Mom first? I've had a lot of time with her these past few weeks." Aunt Tess stood, but Rose motioned her back down.

"You two stay put," Kirk said. "I'll slide the footstool over." He sat at the bottom of the recliner and began rubbing his mother's feet.

Rose glanced over at Aunt Tess. "Did you have time to say what you wanted to, or should we give you a moment?"

Aunt Tess nodded, then shook her head. "Yes, we spoke and no, I don't need to say anything else, but thank you."

Rose cleared her throat and picked up her mother's hand, surprised it was so cool. Then she looked at her mom with tears in her eyes. "I love you, Mom."

Kirk sniffed and whispered, "Me too, Mom. I love you."

Rose felt pressure in her hand and looked down. Was her mother squeezing her hand? Could she hear them? She smiled. "It's time for you to go, Mom. I'll see you again one day."

Her mother drew a short, raspy breath and exhaled as her body settled into the recliner and her hand fell limp.

"Aw, Mom." Rose cried and rested her head on her mother's hand.

Aunt Tess looked at her sister with loving eyes and brushed the hair off her face; Kirk kept rubbing her toes, his lips moving, but not speaking loud enough for others to hear.

Rose didn't know how long they all remained at her mother's side, but when Nurse Lettie squeezed her shoulder, she stood, and fell into her embrace. Rose pulled away a few moments later. Kirk had left the living room.

"What do we do now?" Rose asked.

"We need to tell hospice your mother has passed," Nurse Lettie said. "They'll come by, probably tomorrow, to pick up any remaining medications, like the morphine, and they'll arrange a time to pick up the bed, the oxygen, anything else."

"What about the funeral home?"

"That's our second call. They know your mom's been in hospice and she took care of the arrangements, including choosing a casket. The funeral home director will come with the hearse, note the time of death, and begin the process of obtaining a death certificate."

"Can you please call hospice while I check with Kirk?" Rose walked into the kitchen and spotted her brother on the couch in front of the fireplace, his head bowed, his cell pressed tight against his right ear. He was probably talking to Maria. She returned to the living room. Lettie was on the phone.

Gladys lay on her mother's lap, whimpering. Aunt Tess stroked the dog's white fur with one hand, the other hand rested on her mother's silver hair. Rose sat on the footstool, held her mother's feet, and she looked up at the large photo on the wall behind the recliners. She'd taken the photo about six months before her father died, the last photo of all of them together. Kirk and Maria were visiting with the boys. Her father had rented a boat and the seven of them spent the day enjoying Lake Amelia. Kirk and her father did a little fishing while the boys watched, too young to fish, but old enough to ask questions.

Rose thought about how they'd talked and laughed that day, told stories, and played games with the children.

At one point, Carlos punched José in the arm. Hard. The younger boy cried out and ran to his mother.

Kirk knelt and took Carlos by the hand. "What have I told you before? Don't pick fights with your brother," he scolded his son. "We're family, and family always sticks together, even when we disagree. Do you understand?"

Carlos nodded. "Okay, buddy, come here and sit with me."

After they'd returned the boat and were back at the house, Rose set up her camera on the table in the backyard, and took several family photos using the timer. She'd made a print of the best one, and her parents had put it on a shelf in the living room bookcase. About a month after her father passed, her mother asked Rose if she could make a larger print to hang on the wall.

Rose caressed her mother's feet as she studied the photo and recalled the challenges of getting a good image with everyone looking at the camera.

Maria and Kirk were shoulder to shoulder. Her arm was

around Kirk's waist, while he had one hand on each of the boy's shoulders. Kirk was doing his best to stop them from wiggling. Her parents stood at Kirk's side. Rose recalled how she had to keep asking her parents to face forward. They'd look at Kirk and Maria, at the boys, and then at each other with warm smiles. Rose would press the timer button on the camera and hurry over next to Maria. When she reviewed the photos, she'd found only one image of everyone facing the camera. That's the one that was on the bookshelf. The rest of the photos showed her parents either looking at Kirk's family or smiling at each other.

When Rose printed a larger image for the living room wall, she chose one of her parents smiling at each other because their love shone through every pixel. Her mother was disappointed when she realized Rose had chosen a different image, but when Rose explained why, her mother listened, then contemplated the photo.

"We loved each other and our family very much," she'd said.

Rose's eyes watered, and she realized the depth of longing already tearing at her heart. Rose wanted to feel her mother's arms wrapped around her one last time, to see that loving smile meant only for her one last time. But what Rose wanted most of all was to hear her mother's voice telling her she loved her one last time.

Chapter Fifty-Five

urse Lettie hustled everyone onto the patio when the funeral home's black hearse backed into the driveway. She kept the three of them talking to block out the sounds in the living room and to stop their minds from thinking about what was going on. Rose responded to a text from Mrs. Shaw and sent one to Maxi. By the time they sat down to dinner, it was after eight and they'd run out of things to say. And the energy to say them. Aunt Tess and Nurse Lettie offered to help clean up, but Rose nudged them out the door, saying she and Kirk would take care of it in the morning. Then she poured the last of the pinot noir into her wineglass. Kirk added another splash of scotch and a couple of ice cubes to his drink. They flopped onto the couch in front of the fireplace.

"To Mom." Kirk tilted his glass toward Rose.

Rose echoed his words and took a sip. "Are Maria and the boys coming?"

Kirk nodded. "You and I are going to be busy tomorrow finalizing plans for the wake and funeral, so I told her it was fine if they flew in the day after next. I'll pick them up around noon. What time does the wake begin?"

"Four o'clock. They'll have time to come here first and change their clothes. I can't wait to see them."

"I've wanted to hug my wife and boys ever since Mom died." Kirk finished his drink and stood. "I'm beat. I'm going to call Maria again and then crash. You sure you don't want to clean up the kitchen tonight?"

"Nope, I don't," Rose said. "I'll make sure we can get to the coffee machine. Everything else can wait."

Kirk glanced at Gladys, curled up in her bed in front of the sliding glass door. "What about the dog?"

"I'll let her out before I go upstairs," Rose said.

"I didn't mean tonight. What do we do about Gladys? Who's going to care for her?"

"That's too big a question right now." Rose walked over and scooped Gladys into her arm. "I'll put her on the bed with me tonight and close the door so she doesn't search for Mom. Gladys and I could both use the cuddle time."

"I'll check the front door." Kirk set his glass on the kitchen counter and left the room. Rose walked back to the couch and sat with Gladys at her side.

"I don't know which one of us needs the other more, but it's you and me tonight, girlfriend," she whispered.

The next couple of days were a blur. Kirk and Rose emailed the obituary to the newspaper, met with the funeral director, confirmed the minister and organist for the service, and accepted hugs of condolences from neighbors and old friends. Aunt Tess made sure they ate well, and so did other people, dropping off casserole dishes, salads of summer greens and early garden tomatoes, and more trays of fruit than they could eat.

After one delivery, Rose opened the box of pastries before she finished closing the front door. She bit into a blueberry scone as she read the note Bill had sent, signed from the staff at the *Dispatch*: *Rose and family: We're sorry for your loss and are keeping all of you in our prayers.*

A hospice nurse and volunteer stopped by the day after her mom's death to collect the unused morphine and other medications. Rose stripped the padded sheets and blankets off the recliner and washed four loads of laundry. She stacked the hospice linens on top of the hospice bed and put the other linens in the hall closet. Rose even washed the pillows her mother had used and made sure they were dry for Kirk's family.

Maria and the boys arrived with a burst of energy, despite the sadness shared by everyone. It was a comfort to have her, Carlos, and José in the house helping, but also laughing and telling stories.

"Come on, guys," Kirk said. "Let's move the bed from the office back upstairs." It didn't take long. Then, while Rose and Maria made the bed and tidied up the room, Kirk and the boys drove to the sporting goods store on Main Street. They purchased two air mattresses and an air pump. One air mattress was set up in the office and the other in Kirk's old room. Each of the boys had their own space, right across the hall from one another.

Before the doors opened to the public for the wake later that afternoon, Rose and Kirk had a few moments alone with their mother in the funeral home's largest parlor. More than a dozen flower arrangements sat on three-legged easels alongside the casket, and rows of folding chairs stood ready for the mourners. Carlos and José had used the travel time to compile a music video of favorite family photos, which left everyone who viewed it misty-eyed. After three hours of shaking people's hands and sharing their hugs, Rose was ready for home, dinner, and bed, knowing the next day would be more difficult.

Dark, threatening clouds blanketed the sky the morning of the funeral, but by the time the service ended and the procession to the cemetery began, only a few puffy clouds remained. As the Webster family walked up the aisle on their way out of the church, Rose spotted Maxi. She reached for her hand.

"Come to the cemetery with us?"

Maxi hesitated for only a moment and joined Rose.

Family and close friends attended the brief graveside service, but the Websters invited everyone at the church service to their home for lunch. Aunt Tess made sure the buffet on the kitchen counters never ran out of food or drink while Rose and Kirk circulated, thanking people for their support.

"Ellie, thank you for coming today," Rose said, smiling at the girl and shaking her father's hand. "Thanks, Carter, for being here."

"It was Ellie's idea." He smiled at his daughter.

"I'm sorry your mom died," Ellie said in a stronger voice than she usually spoke. But Rose remembered Ellie was a child on the verge of adulthood. She wanted to hug Ellie, but the girl didn't seem like someone who'd welcome a sudden embrace.

"Thank you," Rose said. "I imagine it wasn't easy for you to be at the service when you lost your mother not so long ago. So, I really appreciate your coming today."

Ellie lowered her eyes and nodded several times. "Anytime you want to come to the library and talk to me, that would be okay," she said. "I'm there most days. Mornings are best." Then Ellie reached out and hugged Rose. When she pulled away, she took her father's hand and led him to the front door.

"Hey, are you okay?"

Rose turned to Maxi with tears in her eyes. "Yeah, I'm good. Just had a special moment with Ellie. Have you had something to eat yet?"

"Yes, have you?"

Rose shook her head, glancing around the room.

"Come on. You've been the perfect hostess, but you look like you need food. There aren't any chocolate milkshakes in the kitchen, but there's lots of other good stuff."

Thom reached out for Rose before she made it out of the living room.

"That was a lovely obituary in the *Dispatch*," he said, giving her a hug. "I'm guessing you wrote it?"

"Mom and I did together," Rose said. "Thank you for being here. I haven't seen Desi."

"Last time I saw her, she was chatting with Nurse Lettie in the dining room." He looked at Maxi's retreating figure. "I was surprised to see the deputy sheriff. I didn't realize you two were close."

"You'd be surprised. Well, you will be surprised when everyone finds out."

"Finds out what?"

"I can't—shouldn't—say," Rose whispered. "It'll all come out soon."

"You're being very secretive." Thom took a forkful of potato salad from his plate and raised it to his mouth. "I thought you didn't like secrets."

"This one's okay. Actually, I like this one a lot."

Chapter Fifty-Six

"I don't want to go, and I don't understand why you're insisting." Maxi had her mad face on, and Rose didn't blame her, but she didn't want to explain why Maxi needed to go to Richard Klein's office. She'd find out soon enough. If only she'd stop complaining and get into the car. Kirk and Maria had left ten minutes ago, and Rose didn't want to keep her brother or Klein waiting.

"Fine," Maxi finally said in a huff. "But I'm driving."

"You're so controlling." Rose got into the passenger seat.

"That's because you're so pushy."

"Yeah, like you aren't." Rose clicked her seatbelt and looked at Maxi. She sounded put out, but the corners of her lips turned up. Maxi held back a smile, not for the first time. Sisters. They could be so annoying.

They arrived at the attorney's office as Kirk and Maria approached the front door. Maxi had driven like she owned the roads because she wouldn't get a ticket even if a cop pulled her over. Rose wondered if she would receive the same courtesy after people learned she and Maxi were related.

"Good morning, everyone," Klein said, leading them to

the conference table in his office. After introductions, the four of them sat at the table while Klein picked up three manilla envelopes and some other papers off his desk.

"Coffee? Water?" Klein asked, looking at each of them as they declined. "Then let's get right to business. We are here for the reading of the Last Will and Testament of Carly Adams Webster, widow of Randall Wallace Webster."

Rose tried to focus as Klein read about the bequests he'd told them about, at their previous meeting, to Aunt Tess, Mrs. Shaw, and several community organizations. Maxi sat beside Rose, her body ramrod straight, her eyes on Klein.

"To my grandsons Carlos and José, fifty thousand dollars each for their college education."

"Dios mío!" Maria grabbed Kirk's hand. "That's so generous. I never expected she'd give the boys that kind of money."

Kirk swallowed several times but didn't speak. He braced for the next news.

"To my children, Kirk Carlisle Webster and Rose Caroline Webster, I leave my personal items, jewelry, contents of the house at 25 Cedar Street, and items in my safety deposit box to be divided between them, with the exceptions noted earlier.

"The rest of the financial assets including stock accounts, back accounts, and the property at 25 Cedar Street in Lake Amelia are to be divided as instructed by my late husband, in equal thirds among Kirk Webster, Rose Webster, and Maxine Tyler Stover, the daughter of Randall Wallace Webster."

"What? No," Maxi said. "I don't want anything from him." She looked at Rose and Kirk. "Or from the two of you."

Klein handed a piece of paper to Rose. "Your mother asked to have this letter read. She called me a couple of days ago to say she shared this with you and Kirk, but she thought Maxine might understand more after hearing her father's words."

Maxi flinched.

Rose imagined Maxi wasn't used to anyone being called her father yet. Rose took the paper from Klein and, in a shaky voice, read the words she and Kirk heard a few days ago. Maxi had more confirmation she was Mr. Randall's daughter.

After Rose finished, quietness settled over the room. Klein didn't rush anyone.

Kirk spoke first. "Is there anything else?"

"There is," Klein said, his eyes taking in each of them. "Your mother also wrote a letter and wanted it read. This is a copy. The original is in your mother's dresser at home." He slid a piece of paper across the table to Kirk, whose eyes opened wide with surprise.

"Why me?"

Klein shrugged.

Kirk glanced at the paper in front of him. "Does your offer of water still stand?"

"Of course." Klein rose from his seat and left the office. Kirk stared at the table while everyone else stared at him.

Klein's assistant followed him into the office, carrying a tray with a pitcher of water and several glasses. She set the tray on the table. Klein thanked her and said they could pour their own water. After they'd done that and Kirk had taken a drink, he picked up the paper and read.

My dearest children, I know you're dealing with some surprising information these past couple of weeks. I've had conversations with both of you and shared your father's letter about his daughter, your half-sister, Maxine. Your father loved all three of you, and it was difficult for him to walk away from Maxine and her mother, but he was committed to our family. I hope you realize that. Whatever his indiscretion, he came back to us. But he made it clear that when I followed him to the grave, Maxine would be recognized as his daughter and share in the property and assets we'd built over so many decades. Please don't make a fuss, and, yes, Kirk, I'm talking to you especially. It was, is, the greatest wish of ours that you accept Maxine and not chal-lenge my will, which includes the stipulations of your father.

Kirk paused, looked at Rose, then Maxine, and nodded. Then he continued.

I know your father disappointed you, Kirk. He disappointed me. But we all make mistakes. Please find it in your heart to forgive him. Staying angry with him for the rest of your life will only cause you more pain.

Rose, your determination to find out about your father's affair confused me, but when you learned he had a little girl with the woman, as I was sure you would one day, I knew your father's betrayal would also hurt you. Maxine was the little sister you'd always wanted, the one your father and I couldn't give you. You also need to find it in your heart to forgive your father.

Maxine, you and I met one day. You were about ten years old. Randall and I saw you with your mother in Albany. He didn't introduce us, but in your own way, you did. You beamed and said, "Hello, Mr. Randall." The way he looked at you was the same way he looked at only two other people in his life. Our two children. I knew you were the other daughter he'd wanted, that your mother was the woman he'd loved. Maxine, I realized how difficult it was for him to walk away from you, and your mother. I saw her one more time, at Randall's funeral. Our eyes met, and she gave me a brief nod as she left the church.

Maxi sniffed and reached for a tissue from the box on the table. Kirk smiled at her, not a big smile, but a genuine one.

"There are a couple more lines," Kirk said. *I hope the three of you will get to know each other.* Kirk set the paper down. "It's signed, *I love you two so much. Mom.*"

Chapter Fifty-Seven

Rose wished she had a hidden microphone in Kirk's car to hear what he and Maria were saying. Of course, Kirk had already told Maria about his half-sister during his phone call with her after their first meeting with Klein, but their mother's letter and bequests to the boys were new.

"Come in," Rose said to Maxi when she pulled up in front of the house.

"I'd like to go home and read through these papers," Maxi said, pointing to the manilla envelopes Rose had tucked between her seat and the center console.

"I understand, but you'll have the rest of the day for that. Please come in for a moment."

Maxi acquiesced and followed Rose up the brick walkway and into the house.

Kirk and Maria were walking into the kitchen and greeting the boys.

"How'd it go, Dad?"

Kirk looked at Maxi, then Rose. "Do you want to introduce Maxi?"

"We already met her at the lunch after the funeral, Dad. Don't you remember?" José looked at Maxi, then at his father.

"Yes, well, we told you she's a deputy sheriff in Washington County and a friend of mine," Rose began. "But she's more than my friend. Maxine is your father's and my half-sister."

The boys looked confused. Rose imagined the gears spinning in their heads.

"Come on," Kirk said. "Let's sit down on the couch. Grab a couple of dining room chairs for Rose and Maxine, will you guys?"

Rose was curious to see how her brother handled telling his children about Maxi. She thanked José for the chair and pulled it close to the couch. Maxi sat in a chair beside her.

Kirk looked at Maria, perhaps unsure how to begin.

"They're teenagers who've watched a lot of TV and movies," Maria said. "Just tell them."

He nodded and looked at his two sons, sandwiched between him and Maria. "How about some other news first? Your grandmother left each of you fifty thousand dollars for your college education."

"Wow," Carlos said.

Rose stared at her brother. *That was an interesting approach. Maybe the money would impress them so much the other news might be forgotten.*

"What does that have to do with Maxi?" Carlos asked.

Kirk chuckled. "Nothing, actually. Well, almost nothing." Now the boys were really confused.

"Honestly, Kirk, would you get to the point?" Maria sighed.

Rose was glad Maria spoke up before she did. Her lawyer-brother was supposed to be good at presenting information, but he was failing miserably.

Kirk took a deep breath. "Every marriage has its difficulties, and things sometimes happen between a couple. Your grandparents were very happy, but there was a time when your grandfather . . ."

"Strayed," Rose couldn't wait any longer for Kirk to find the words and finished the sentence. She smiled, seeing a side of her brother—the father—she rarely glimpsed. His softer side was appealing.

"You mean he had an affair?" Carlos asked.

Maria smiled. "I told you they'd get it."

"Yes," Kirk said. "He had an affair with another woman for a few years. He never left your grandmother or Aunt Rose and me, but he saw this woman when he traveled for business. Eventually, he stopped seeing her, and your grandparents stayed together for the rest of their lives."

Carlos looked at Maxi, then at his father. "And?"

Kirk was finding out how grown up his older son was. "And they had a daughter together. Maxine. She's my half-sister."

Both boys turned to Maxi. "Does that mean she's our aunt?" José asked.

"Technically, yes, she's your Aunt Maxi," Kirk said.

"But you don't have to call me aunt," Maxi blurted.

"But you're part of our family now, right?" José smiled at her.

"Yes, she is," Kirk said.

"And grandpa kept this secret about the woman and Maxine?" Carlos asked, looking at Maxi. "That's a long time to keep a secret."

His father agreed.

"Does that mean she's going to live in grandma's house with Aunt Rose?" Carlos asked.

"No," Maxi said quickly. "I have a house half an hour from here with lots of woods and two big dogs."

"Okay. Is there anything else, Dad, or can we play Minecraft?"

"You don't have any other questions?" Kirk looked at his sons.

"Nope." Carlos stood and walked toward the kitchen. "Come on, José."

José stood but didn't walk away yet. "I still love Grandpa," he said, then looked at Maxi. "I hope we get to see you sometimes, Aunt Maxi."

The four adults watched the boys leave and let the silence linger.

"That went well, don't you think?" Kirk finally said.

"Sometimes I wish they didn't know as much as they do," Maria said, "But they're smart kids. I'm not surprised they're taking this in stride."

Maria and the boys returned to Florida the next day. Kirk stayed a couple more days to help Rose go through their mother's belongings and financial papers. Then he packed his bag. Rose walked him out to his car, cradling Gladys in her left arm.

"How long do you plan to stay in Lake Amelia?"

"I don't know. I have a physical therapy appointment tomorrow." A car passing by beeped, and they waved, not sure who it was, but in a small town it was probably someone who'd been to the funeral. "I'm thinking of sticking around for a while," she said as Kirk opened the back door of the rental car and tossed his bag inside.

"You in Lake Amelia?" He smiled at her and squinted. "I'm trying to picture it."

"Yeah, me too. I miss a lot of things about the Philadelphia area, but I haven't been surrounded by this many trees and bunnies and birds in a long time. I like it."

"Well, there's no hurry to sell the house. It's in both our names since Maxi didn't want to add her name to the title and doesn't want any of the proceeds when we sell." He looked at her cast. "If we sell. I know you don't need to find work soon. Mom and Dad made sure of that, but I can't see you hanging around Lake Amelia weeding gardens and making flower arrangements."

She laughed. "Nope. But I'll be here a while. I want to get to know my sister. Now that my wish has been granted, I can't walk away."

"I get that." They crossed behind the car, he opened the driver's door, then turned toward Rose. "He should have used a condom."

"Didn't I tell you? I found some in his travel bag."

He shook his head. "I never knew Dad was so full of secrets. There are one or two more boxes tucked way under the rafters in the back of the attic. Maybe you'll uncover more secrets."

"I sure hope not. I've had enough to last a lifetime."

They hugged with the dog in the middle, and she waved as he drove out of the driveway toward the airport, back to his family. Rose turned and looked at the house, then planted a kiss on Gladys's head.

Life had changed in so many ways over the past three weeks. Her mother was gone and the ache in her heart would take a long time to fade. But she finally had the sister she'd always wanted. She had this little white dog to cuddle and love. And she had this house in Lake Amelia, which she had also come to love. The house and the town. Secrets and all.

Acknowledgments

I am grateful to libraries everywhere, to book readers and bookstores, especially independent bookstores. Without all of you, my author dreams would not have come true. I love your feedback and reviews (keep 'em coming!) and appreciate your suggestions. Some of my favorite days are when the muse is active in my head and the writing flows through me. Other favorite days are when I attend bookstore events or book fairs and talk with readers who've read my books or who buy them with eager anticipation of sitting down and reading my words. It's quite humbling to imagine my books in your homes and on your shelves.

I'll never stop growing as a writer and have many people to thank for helping me learn my craft. That includes my beta readers, Viv Lotz, Leslie Costello, Janet Lippincott, and Stacey Parshall Jensen. Thanks for your feedback, even when it's blunt. It's all good and I need to hear it. I received useful advice from so many skilled writers and editors, among them Mark Spencer, Miranda Darrow, and Nanette Littlestone.

My path to publishing has been paved by many supportive women of the Women Fiction Writers Association (WFWA), the Independent Authors Facebook group of WFWA and the smaller and incredibly helpful Indie Author Support Group. Hearts to all of you for helping me learn the next steps and recover from the wrong ones

I'm a member of Sisters in Crime, national, the New England chapter, and the Mavens of Mayhem, upper Hudson

River chapter. Another big shoutout to the Mystery Writers of America. Great writers, great resources.

Back to some of my best friends—Bookstores. Shoutouts to Northshire Bookstore, Saratoga Springs, NY; booked, Chestnut Hill, PA; Big Blue Marble Bookstore, Mt. Airy, PA; Mysteries on Main, Johnstown, NY; Open Door Bookstore, Schenectady, NY; Book Cabin, Lake George, NY; Book Nook, Round Lake, NY; Bookplate, Chestertown, MD; Pocket Books Shop, Lancaster, PA; MochaLisa, Clifton Park, NY; and Barnes and Noble stores everywhere. I love the big bookstores as well, but the indie bookstores are often an author's connection in the community. We need them all. Please support your local independent bookstore.

To my loving and encouraging friends and family—especially Cindy, Mark, Ben, Will, Diane, and David—my heartfelt thanks for believing in me. Thanks also to my extended family—nieces, nephews, and cousins around the country, maybe other places, who knows?

And as always, thanks to Helen for sharing the journey.

About the Author

 JACQUELINE BOULDEN is the 2023 IPPY (Independent Press) Gold Award Winner for Best Regional Fiction, Mid-Atlantic, for her debut novel, *Her Past Can't Wait*, which was also named the 2023 Global Book Awards Gold winner for Psychological Thriller. Before turning to writing fiction, she won several Emmys for reporting. Jacqueline's TV career took her around the country covering politics in Washington, D.C., NASA and the space shuttle program in Florida (including the Challenger accident) and fighting the wind for control of her hat during live shots in hurricanes and blizzards while working in Orlando and Philadelphia. Jacqueline lives in upstate New York with her spouse and their rescue dog, who's teaching them how to speak Beaglish.

Visit www.jacquelineboulden.com and sign up for her newsletter. Follow her on Facebook (JacquelineBouldenAuthor) and Instagram (@jacqueline.boulden). If you enjoyed *Family Ties Family Lies*, please consider leaving a review. It would mean so much.

9 789898 603843